The last thing Captain Sirena expected to find on a desolate island was...him!

When Carmen Ventura takes up her post as commander of the *Strega*, she becomes the new Captain Sirena, the legendary pirate most people think is just a myth created to scare children. Her first quest is to search for the "treasured chest" hidden by her predecessor. But before she can even begin the hunt, she runs into Marko Lucin, captain of the *Levant* and Carmen's most insane adventure yet.

How can the most beautiful woman he's ever seen be a bloody pirate?

Never one to pass up an adventure, especially where pretty women are concerned, Marko finds his ultimate challenge in Carmen. Not only does he fall for her courage, spunk, and intelligence, but the lady pirate can also help him get what he wants—the famous treasure everyone whispers about. His only problem—how long can he play the charming captain before she discovers his true intentions?

She was ready to walk away and leave him stranded...but the man had a treasure map. What if it was real?

Sirena's mind raced. Even with different colors hoisted, after the last night's raid, she ran the risk that the *Strega*'s sails would be detected as soon as they appeared on the horizon. Her ship could not approach the city's defensive walls. Not until all the rumors settled and no survivors would recognize them. On the other hand, she couldn't pass through the Pila Gates as a lone woman. Last time she had spoken to her brother, he had said he'd be docking in Ragusa's harbor on the second Sunday of August. Still two days away, but she should pay him a visit. Maybe he'd been home and had news.

"I possess a map." The man's voice snapped her out of her planning.

She lowered her sword, and her glance, to his feet and flicked a crab into the sea. "Charts are of no interest to me."

"Ah." He stroked his chin, leaving sooty fingerprints on his blond beard. "But this is not an ordinary map." His grin exposed a row of white teeth, a rarity. "It leads to a treasure."

"Treasure means different things to different people." Something familiar reflected in his eyes. She stepped back. Now, where had she seen him before?

"True," he said, "but I believe this map is real."

The same sparkle flashed in his eyes, reaffirming that flicker of recognition, but she still couldn't place the sense of familiarity. "What makes you so sure?"

"I've had it all my life." He shrugged and gave a shy smile. "Call me a captain, but I've never been able to make any sense of the damn thing."

She was ready to walk away and leave him stranded...but the man had a treasure map. What if it was real?

Sirena's mind raced. Even with different colors hoisted, after the last night's raid, she ran the risk that the *Strega*'s sails would be detected as soon as they appeared on the horizon. Her ship could not approach the city's defensive walls. Not until all the rumors settled and no survivors would recognize them. On the other hand, she couldn't pass through the Pila Gates as a lone woman. Last time she had spoken to her brother, he had said he'd be docking in Ragusa's harbor on the second Sunday of August. Still two days away, but she should pay him a visit. Maybe he'd been home and had news.

"I possess a map." The man's voice snapped her out of her planning.

She lowered her sword, and her glance, to his feet and flicked a crab into the sea. "Charts are of no interest to me."

"Ah." He stroked his chin, leaving sooty fingerprints on his blond beard. "But this is not an ordinary map." His grin exposed a row of white teeth, a rarity. "It leads to a treasure."

"Treasure means different things to different people." Something familiar reflected in his eyes. She stepped back. Now, where had she seen him before?

"True," he said, "but I believe this map is real."

The same sparkle flashed in his eyes, reaffirming that flicker of recognition, but she still couldn't place the sense of familiarity. "What makes you so sure?"

"I've had it all my life." He shrugged and gave a shy smile. "Call me a captain, but I've never been able to make any sense of the damn thing."

Kudos for Treasured Chest

Treasured Chest is captivating and action packed. The scenes were so vivid I felt the ship's deck rolling beneath me while shouting commands to the crew and dreaming of being thoroughly kissed by Captain Marko. *Treasured Chest* is an exciting story, a shelf-keeper. – JJ Keller, best-selling author of *Trade Agreement*

I liked the character development and the plot, and it is obvious that Jelic did her homework as the shipping terms, etc., appear to be very authentic. I didn't once come across something and said, wait a minute this is supposed to be historical—as sometimes happens with historical romances. Treasure Chest is fun and entertaining and the plot has some nice twists and turns. – *Taylor, reviewer*

I found Treasured Chest to be a strong second novel for Zrinka Jelic. While I enjoyed her first book, I think Jelic's writing is much stronger in this second book. The character development is excellent, the dialogue convincing, and the plot intriguing. – *Regan, reviewer*

Treasured

Chest

ZRINKA JELIC

A BLACK OPAL BOOKS PUBLICATION

GENRE: HISTORICAL ROMANCE/ROMANTIC SUSPENSE

TREASURED CHEST
Copyright © 2012 by Zrinka Jelic
Cover Design by Jennifer Gibson
All cover art copyright © 2012
All Rights Reserved
Print ISBN: 978-1-937329-73-0

First Publication: NOVEMBER 2012

Published by Black Opal Books http://www.blackopalbooks.com

Dedication

To my wonderful critique partners as well as editors at Black Opal Books. Your keen eyes and insight were invaluable. And to the talented Jennifer Gibson for beautiful cover.

Chapter 1

A heavy curtain of foul odor emanated from unwashed bodies and hung inside the ship's belly. Sweat glued Carmen's shirtsleeves to her heated skin. Overwhelmed by an unbearable urge to hasten on deck and gulp the crisp night air, she sat up, causing her hammock to sway and the ropes to tighten and creak.

A young girl in the bed next to her sang in a low voice. Recognizing the words of the ballad, Carmen glanced at the thin woman twirling a strand of her unkempt hair around her finger.

> "Our children cry in huger,
> "Duke's men ransack and plunder.
> "The *Strega*'s hoists the colors high,
> "When the cannons start to thunder.
> "It's the brave Captain Sirena, aye.
> "May fear chill your bones, greedy lords,
> "For all of you shall die."

It was a dangerous song to sing anywhere else but onboard the *Strega*, yet after each raid ballads sprang up amongst the people. In the thirty years since the slaying of the noble couple, folks found new heroes. These rhymes merely replaced those that had foretold about the return of the good Marquis.

Carmen lay down and turned to her side. The musty smell of the planks intensified the reek.

The *Strega* was an old, three-masted lateen-rigged xebec. Her name meant the Witch. She thrived when her sails were full, and her bulk rolled on the swells of the open sea. Yet, for the past five days their ship remained hidden by the sun-bleached cliffs of the islet, Jabuka, the most remote piece of barren rock in the Adriatic Sea. Its steep coast was difficult to approach and provided a perfect refuge for a pirate's ship. In the open waters, the desolate volcanic spittle of land stood as a lone guardian and a beacon of hope.

Carmen raked her fingers through her salt stiff curls. Minutes stretched like hours. Tonight the change of the watch couldn't come soon enough. The oppressive heat wasn't the cause of another sleepless night. It was the imminent death of their captain that robbed the crew of peace and rest.

While a few pious women murmured prayers, most sobbed. Would God care to listen to these pirates' humble requests? No. No amount of devout petitioning to God would save the old dame. Left with fatal wounds from the last battle, the captain must see the gates of the abyss standing wide open for her.

Every time Carmen closed her eyes, the smoke and thundering canons, crossed swords, slashing metal, cries, and shouting replayed in her head. Though their last raid had resulted in a bountiful booty, the ambush had been reckless. The Grim Reaper had reduced the crew of the *Strega* by a goodly number. Crushed by grief, not one of the women had mentioned dividing the spoils of plunder.

A heavy hand grabbed Carmen's shoulder. Eight years of hard life as a pirate had conditioned her to reach for the handle of her dagger tied to her thigh.

"It's me."

At the sound of Marta's raspy voice, Carmen pushed the knife back in its sheath.

"The Cap'n wants to see you." The strands of Marta's unkempt hair stood rigid as she jerked her head for Carmen to follow. "Now."

Carmen scrambled out of her hammock and straightened. Her head almost touched the low planks of the ceiling. She pulled out her cutlass in its jeweled scabbard that was tucked through the netting of her hanging bed and secured the sword to her waist. The ship bobbed on gentle swells. The soles of her worn, calf-leather boots clicked on the seasoned wood of the floorboards as Carmen followed the swaying hips of the burly quartermaster, who was clad in a tattered, brown frock.

Carmen's mind worked fast. What could the dying captain want from her? She might be the second officer, but the affairs of the ship were usually kept from her. The dowager ruled with a tough hand. Even during her last moments, she wouldn't go down without causing Carmen more grief.

Zigzagging through the maze of swaying hammocks, the two women stepped onto the deck. Carmen inhaled deeply, filling her lungs with warm air. The cannons had cooled since their last firing and the ringing had ceased in her ears, but the sight of guns brought back the memory of the battle. The pungent smell of hot gunpowder filled her nostrils. She hurried on, catching up with Marta's long strides, then climbed three steps to the gallery deck.

One simply didn't become a pirate out of a burning desire for adventure. A mutual understanding existed among the crew—on board the *Strega*, all were equal. Hard work alone would gain a woman status and respect, not her lineage. Over the years Carmen's scraped knees and calloused palms had hardened, but her work had paid off and by the summer of seventeen ninety-six, she had risen from an ordinary boards-swabber to her current position of second officer. Nevertheless, the old lady wouldn't allow her to forget she had chosen the pirate's life over rotting in the dungeons of Duke Ludovico Manin, the last Doge of the Most Serene Republic of Venice.

The last thing Carmen had expected was for their captain to order them into such a dangerous raid. Living as pirates meant risking death every time they went on a foray, but for the captain to rush into the pillage against her old adversary, Privateer Gaspar, without careful preparation, she must have been after something.

A realization struck Carmen at the top step of the gallery deck. The captain was always known as Sirena, the name she chose as a pirate. Not the name Jesus would call her when she met him. She should find out the captain's Christian name before Marta opened the door.

Marta paused in front of the captain's stateroom and turned to Carmen. "This is it, child."

"Why did she summon me?" An uneasy feeling filled Carmen's chest. This couldn't be good. Stepping behind Marta, she glanced at the sliver of a crescent moon covered with a thin cloud. "Wait." She grabbed Marta's elbow before her weathered hand pushed on the nicked wooden door. "What is Sirena's real name?"

Marta gave her a weary look, then the woman's wrinkled face mellowed. "Child, no man or woman knows it." She pushed the door open and ushered Carmen inside the small cabin. The only source of light came from the flickering flame of the half melted wax candle on the corner stand. "She's here, Cap'n."

The offensive smell of death surrounded Carmen. Covering her mouth and nose with her hand did little to block the rotten odor.

The captain's raspy breathing came from the hammock occupying the middle of the room. "Come closer."

Carmen took a reluctant step forward, her stomach churning.

"Closer." With her hand hung over the side, the captain wiggled her blood stained fingers.

Carmen swallowed hard and cast a wary glance to Marta, standing beside the dying woman's bed.

"She has but minutes left." Marta's encouraging nod eased Carmen's anxiety.

She approached the woman hanging to life by a thread. "I'm here, Captain."

The old woman's trembling fingers wrapped around her hand. "Carmen," she panted, her face contorted in pain. "You've always been brave, loyal, and fair." Sirena coughed and blood dripped from her lips. Carmen had to concentrate on the candle. Seeing her captain struggle valiantly for her last few breaths made Carmen's insides twist. "Lousy qualities for a pirate, but—" Sirena's harsh breaths broke up her words. "You proved yourself in many raids—never lost your head. I know you'll do the right thing by these women—do me proud."

'*Do the right thing by these women*'? Confused by the captain's words, Carmen shook her head. She stared at the dying woman's bandages and, from the dark stains seeping through them, Carmen counted a minimum of four wounds. "What do you want me to do, Captain?"

Sirena gave Carmen's hand a faint squeeze as gurgling settled in her throat. "The *Strega* must have her Captain Sirena."

Stunned, Carmen shook her head in disbelief. As did every other woman on the ship, she too dreamt of becoming captain. But there was a hierarchy and Marta was the next in line for the position. "Me? The captain?" There were but a handful of the original crew still serving on board. Still, why would Sirena choose her? "Everyone thought Marta would—"

Sirena drew a long breath before speaking, the effort showing on her face. "Marta is a quartermaster. She will always be your faithful first officer, but you are the one I want to lead."

Carmen gaped at Marta in wonder, expecting to see animosity on the face of the second oldest crew member. Instead, the woman's face crumpled in grief. "The cap'n is proper in my eyes, child." Apparently, the woman didn't want the responsibility that came with the job of captain. "A ship needs a cap'n that can read and write and say those fancy words, and you're the only one who can."

Marta was right, a ship and the crew would benefit from an educated captain. Carmen turned her head back to Sirena. "You never liked me, Captain."

A coughing fit brought foaming blood to Sirena's mouth. She spat the crimson liquid in the cloth Marta quickly tucked under her chin. "Did I ever like anyone?" Short breaths broke her sarcastic tone and choked her words. "You were a weakling when you first came on board. If I was the toughest on you—it's because—I was preparing you for this. Your knowledge of ships and this sea—had to meet my hard rule. I made you what you are today. Be grateful."

Tears stung Carmen's eyes. The captain words reminded her of the hardships she'd endured to abolish her high-society upbringing. She'd had to toughen up and change or she wouldn't have survived a life at sea. Submitting to the captain's brutal treatments for years, had damn well earned her the right to lead. A brave face replaced her frown. She straightened, not wanting to show her fading captain a moment of weakness. She'd do her proud.

"Carmen," the captain said through the pain. "Captain Sirena—must carry on." Her voice was muffled and weak, but her eyes gleamed. "Don't let her name die."

How many crew women would have waited until the captain took her last breath before taking on the name of the infamous Sirena? Carmen owed her that much courtesy. "Aye, Captain, but you are Sirena till the end."

Sirena turned to Marta, a pained moan escaping her lips. "Leave us."

Marta scurried out of the cabin.

"The first time I saw you," Sirena continued, struggling to keep her eyes open, "I was reminded of my younger days. A long time ago I too loved a man."

A sharp breath dried Carmen's throat. She had learned not to show her sorrows, but somehow the captain had seen right through her hard façade.

Coughing forced the captain to throw her head against the pillow. With her shaky hand, she pulled out a small key from a golden chain around her neck. "Find a cache this will open."

Carmen scanned the cabin's stark interior. Blessed Mary, could this be the treasure-trove the ballads spoke of? "A treasure?"

The captain nodded and closed her eyes. In the dim light of the candle, the hollows of her cheeks appeared deeper.

Carmen's fingers closed around the cast iron key no bigger than her thumb. "Where do I begin to search?"

"Read my journals." The captain's squeezed and tugged at Carmen's hand. "Water."

Carmen reached for the skin of water next to the bed and propped the captain's head against her arm, tilting the bag. Liquid trickled down the old woman's chin as she spat a mouthful of bloodied water. Carmen put the drink away and wiped the spittle with a rag.

"There's something I treasured—all my life, but—I had to hide it from prying eyes." Sirena licked her parched lips. Her wrinkled hand grabbed the fabric of Carmen's chemise. "You must find the chest in a year's time elsewise—" Another fit of coughing overcame her.

Carmen's chest constricted. The captain's hold was strong for someone whose life was draining out. "Elsewise what? What will happen?"

Coughing broke Sirena's words. "Someone dear to me will be in peril. Call Marta back in."

The captain held someone dear? How could that be? The tough old lady had never shown a morsel of emotion. Confused, Carmen went looking for Marta. She found the quartermaster standing a few feet away from the door. "She is asking for you."

Marta darted to the captain's bedside. Carmen closed the door and stepped to the other side of the hammock.

"We may be many things but at the threshold of death, we are all still Christians." The captain's hand, crisscrossed with thick veins, reached for Carmen's. "Let's pray."

Though Carmen hadn't prayed in years, she laced her fingers with the captain's frail ones and bowed her head.

Marta folded her hands across her round abdomen and closed her eyes. *"The Lord is my Shepherd,"* she began.

"I shall not be in want." The captain's whisper was barely audible.

"He makes me to lie down in green pastures." Carmen joined in to hide how much she struggled to keep her lips from quivering. Many of her comrades had fallen by her side, yet the captain being so close to death constricted her chest and brought tears she hadn't shed in years.

"He leads me beside quiet waters, he restores my soul." The captain's voice ceased and Carmen shot a glance at Marta without stopping the prayer.

The captain's hand slipped out of Carmen's as Marta continued. *"He guides me in paths of righteousness for his name's sake. Even though I walk through the valley of the shadow of death I will fear no evil, for you are with me. Your rod and your staff, they comfort me."* Fresh tears slid down Carmen's face. She tried to go on but words choked in her throat.

"...and I will dwell in the house of the Lord forever." Crossing herself, Marta finished the twenty-third psalm. "She is gone, child," she said after a long silence.

"Will you—" Carmen sobbed. "Will you announce it to the crew?"

"Of course, Cap'n. As it is my duty." Marta lowered the lids of the deceased captain's eyes. She then placed a silver coin on each eyelid as the dead Sirena's toll for the trip across the bay. "After we give her body to the sea, we must set sails to meet with our contact."

It took Carmen a moment to realize Marta had addressed her as captain. She had taken over the ship, the crew, and the decisions. She was the new Captain Sirena.

Assembled on the deck, the crew of scrawny, proud women fixed their wide eyes on Marta and Carmen, standing at the top of the stairs of the gallery deck. The former captain's body, sewn into weighted sailcloth, lay on the plank tethered over the side.

Marta nodded to two women, who slowly loosened the ropes till the body of their beloved, but departed, leader stood erect over the calm sea. "Unto God Almighty we commend the soul of our sister departed, and we commit her body to the deep—" Collective wails muffled Marta's prayer while the body plunged into the sea.

A large lump formed in Carmen's throat as Marta stepped forward to make the announcement. All of the crew assumed Marta would take over the captain's post. How would they take this surprise? Exhaling deeply, Carmen tilted her chin toward the starry vault beneath which the *Strega* floated, anchored on still waters.

"Corsairs of *Strega*," Marta continued, her loud voice settling the lament of the women. "Our beloved cap'n is now with her maker. Let the Lord have mercy on her soul. Amen." When she crossed herself, each of the women on board followed suit.

"We are all honored and privileged to have served under her command. With her dying breath, she named Carmen her successor." Marta stepped aside, nudging Carmen to come forward. "Kneel," she ordered.

Carmen got on her knees and scanned the faces in front of her. Their bewilderment showed they also needed time to absorb the change.

Carmen Ventura, Carmen Ventura, she kept repeating her name. From this moment, she would be Carmen no more. With the new name assigned, she feared she'd forget her old one in this merciless world of living on the wrong side of the law. Most of the women had taken on different names to protect their families. And according to the ballads, Captain Sirena was a brave and forever young mermaid. She must not cease to exist.

Marta strapped the deceased captain's sword around Carmen's waist, placed the captain's hat on her head, and draped the nubuck doublet on her shoulders. "Now, rise as Cap'n Sirena." Then she turned to the crew. "Kneel before your Cap'n."

A long moment of absolute silence followed while women exchanged confused looks. Sirena's chest tightened. She should step up to the duty of captain and show no fear or mercy to those who disobeyed, but her own strength deserted her.

"Why her?" The holler came from the rear of the small crowd. Carmen's brows furrowed.

Nods and shouts of agreement with their fellow shipmate stirred a cold pit in Carmen's stomach.

"There are other women for the post." The tall and burly girl at the front raised her hand. "Like you, Marta."

Words abandoned Carmen. She had never thought she'd be chosen as Sirena, yet there she stood facing her crew who expected an explanation.

Marta barged in front of her. "Arrrrgh, that's enough." Her angry growl settled the uproar. "The late cap'n chose Carmen, not me. Or you." She pointed to the woman in front then moved her finger to another. "Or you."

Conditioned to obedience, the women lowered their heads. An excruciating silence fell over the crew.

"No explanation is due to you and none shall be given. Kneel, you rats," Marta ordered again, her voice edged with anger.

One by one, the women slowly lowered to their knees, keeping their heads down. Carmen descended three steps to be leveled with the crew members. She must not forget just hours ago she had been one of them.

"Women of *Strega*," she said then paused. Perplexed faces turned their eyes on her. "You have my solemn vow that the affairs of this ship will not change. The same codes will stand."

Slowly, grins and proud smiles replaced the expressions of scorn on the women's faces. Carmen was sure the crew understood, yet she felt the need to re-announce the first and foremost rule on board.

"But above all no boy or man is to be allowed among us. If any woman is found bringing a man on board and to sea in disguise she shall suffer death." Carmen breathed a sigh of relief with the crew's approving shouts. She just had begun to earn the name of Sirena. "The first light is breaking on the horizon. We will set sail for the mainland to meet with our contact. The spoils of plunder are to be divided. Return to your duties."

"Aye, Cap'n." Without further questions the crew dispersed.

"Some resistance is to be expected." Marta took the helm. "You have to earn their trust."

Carmen sat on the steps, sighing heavily. It would take her some time to get used to the name of the Captain Sirena. She played with the key hung from the chain around her neck. The item that would unlock a mysterious chest she must find. Could she ask Marta for help? The late captain wouldn't have ordered Marta out of the stateroom had she wanted her to know of this secret. No, Carmen would have to find the chest the detailed key slotted into. Whatever the old lady had seen in her to promote her to the rank of captain couldn't have been a mistake. She had taken the post and made a solemn vow to continue the old captain's legacy.

The whizz of ropes hoisting the triangular sails disturbed her from her short, tranquil moment. Marta oversaw the activities and barked the orders at the crew. Yesterday Carmen would have taken her comfortable post of ship's mate. No, she was no longer Carmen. Now she was the legendary Sirena. She had to stop thinking of Carmen if she was to live up to the name.

She tucked the key inside her shirt and returned to her cabin. The stale stench of death still lingered in the air. Sirena plopped on the hammock causing the hanging bed to sway and ropes to creak. How had the old captain kept her quest for this chest hidden from the crew? If the box contained treasures of the faraway places, every member would deserve a piece. Perhaps there would be enough gold to spread among them all and put an end to this miserable existence. Was it too much to ask for a home? Nothing extravagant, a small house surrounded by a garden, with herbs she'd plant and a pier to tie her dinghy. A perfect place for her to grow old.

Sirena smiled at the absurd thought. For a woman in her position, no such place existed, near or far. She sighed with longing. Would she never find a place to start over with the one she held dear?

Chapter 2

A flash of silver lightning illuminated the dark sky, stark against the white crests forming on the waves. Soaked to the bones, partly from the rain but mostly from the spray of the sea, Marko gripped the handle of his sword. His vision hampered by the blinding rain, he slashed with his rapier, searching for his opponent. The wood of his argosy creaked with every swell that rolled under the ship's belly.

Most of his crew of thirty men had died in the ambush, and Marko would welcome death instead of losing his ship and its cargo. Or worse, be sold into slavery on the galleons. The attack had caught him by surprise. He hadn't had a chance to return the map to its hidey hole.

How did Captain Gaspar know where and when to intercept him? Silk might fetch a fine price on the black market, but Gaspar wouldn't be after the lustrous cloth. He must be after the map.

"Damn, where is the salty dog?" Marko spat. Keeping the existence of the mysterious parchment a secret for as long as he could remember had him on the edge. The strands of his drenched hair stuck to his face and neck when he snapped his head in the direction of loud laughter.

Another flash of lightning revealed the blade of the Gaspar's sword in front of Marko's nose. His long black beard flapped in the gale. "Give up, Cap'n. She's lost," he growled, but the rolling thunder threw his words to the winds.

"The *Levant* is not lost as long as I stand." Marko lunged at the stout man. Sparks flew as their blades clashed. It took Marko an immense amount of strength to keep his feet from sliding on the slick wood while preventing his enemy's sword from pinning him to the planks.

"As you see, Cap'n," the black-clad figure said, lunging toward him, "staying alive is tiring. The effort requires all five senses. Allow yerself to be killed, you mangy cockroach."

Gaspar thrust forward. Leaping to the side, Marko avoided the blade that sliced within a hair of his heart.

A splitting timber stopped Captain Gaspar's attack, and Marko relaxed from his *en garde* crouch. With his sword in one hand and his dagger in the other, he whirled in the direction of the screeching sound. High wind pushed the two-masted merchant vessel dangerously close to the cliffs. From his peripheral vision he saw a glint of silver and turned to face Gaspar's blade.

The tip of his weapon pressed on Marko's neck, Gaspar snarled, "Big mistake, Cap'n."

A warm drop of blood trickled down Marko's skin as his adversary nicked him. Gaspar's cold eyes traveled to the sword in Marko's hand. "Drop it."

Marko let his sword slip out of his hand. Another peal of thunder muffled the sound of his rapier as the steel hit the wet deck. The *Levant* heeled over. The ship was taking in water, and fast. Both men grabbed onto the ropes flapping in the wind and struggled to keep their feet in place as the side of the ship rose.

This was it, Marko thought. He'd only been a captain for less than two years and he'd already lost his vessel. With merchant ships a constant target for marauders of all kinds and false promises of protection by privateers, this came as no surprise. Many others with far more experience than him had fallen prey to these villains.

Marko's heart pounded. "If it's gold you're seeking, I'm afraid you wasted your time."

"I'm not after your cargo." The pox marks on Gaspar's face became clearly visible with the flash of another lightning. "Enough talk." He scowled and waved his sword. His thick fingers snatched the dagger from Marko's hand.

"Avast, we found it." The shout of Gaspar's man had both captains turning their heads. A sailor stood on the gallery deck, the door to Marko's cabin wide open. Gale-force winds trashed the map in the man's hand as he held it high over his head.

Marko closed his eyes, expecting to receive the deadly strike from the cold steel of Gaspar's sword. *Well, Mirela, or is it Mirabella—makes no difference—seems you'll be a widow before we wed.* In all his schemes to get out of the arranged marriage, he always planned to stay alive, but his destiny had presented him with a different path.

The crater-faced man raised the weapon over his head. The damasked handle delivered a mind-numbing blow to Marko's temple. His body went limp and darkness enclosed him.

Marko awoke to a stench of human waste that permeated the air. Timbers creaked as the ship rocked. Soggy straw separated him from the rotten planks. Men coughing, praying, and groaning painfully coupled with the clinking of chains filled the dark surroundings.

He touched the welt on his head where the handle of Gaspar's sword had knocked him unconscious. The privateer's captain should have killed him instead of locking him in the brig. The swine most likely rubbed his palms together at the thought of the hundred ducats, at the least, hoping Marko's hide would fetch on the slave's market.

Not on my life.

Shackles around his ankles and wrists rattled as he staggered to his feet. Whoever took his boots and doublet as booty would pay dearly. He wrapped his fingers around the iron bars of a square window on the door of his cell. "Psst," he hissed, squinting to see in the darkness "Anyone here from the *Levant*?"

Marko wiped the sheen of sweat off his forehead and waited on an answer. The hushed sounds in the brig ceased. If any of his men survived and were locked here, no one would want to announce the association. The fact they served under him could work to their disadvantage.

"It's me, the captain." He tried louder this time, anticipating the outcome.

"Silence," the guard's voice thundered, followed by the sound of liquid sloshing in a glass bottle.

Marko sat upright in the corner and buried his head in his hands. Gaspar couldn't read the map. That had to be the reason he kept him alive. He'd be better off dead, though. Getting captured instead of dying with honor destroyed his reputation of a dependable captain.

Muffled sounds of hurried footsteps came from the deck above. They carried down the stairs. A glimmer of sunshine penetrated the dark belly of the brig as the hatch opened. The footfalls stopped in front of his cell. Marko flattened his back against the uneven bumps of the raw wooden wall. Unpolished timber pricked his skin. This hole was obviously not meant for humans.

The keys rattled and the door opened with a clatter.

Gaspar stood at the entrance. The light of an oil lamp in his hand made his sunken eyes appear to sink even deeper in his ghoulish face. "Get on your feet, maggot." He slurred his words together, handing the lamp to the guard behind him.

Despite his pounding heart, Marko remained seated. "Why didn't you kill me?"

"All in good time." Gaspar brandished the sword in Marko's face. "Your head's worth more alive." He frowned, cocking his head. "For now."

Marko's mind raced. Examining Gaspar's face, covered in thick hair, he concluded the captain must have lost his wits. Why the hell would he be worth more to Gaspar alive? There wasn't a ransom posted on him. At least none he knew about. The pug face his father wanted to force him to marry couldn't be with his child. Well on second thought, he guessed that her maid could be.

But who would bother to send a privateer's brigantine after him for impregnating a servant? "Why would I be worth anything to you?"

Surprise flashed in Gaspar's widened eyes. "You don't know?" Astonishment quickly faded from his stare. "Of course you wouldn't."

A lump formed in Marko's throat. What he wouldn't give for a tall goblet of wine? But given his circumstances, plain water would do. No. He forced his thoughts to focus on Gaspar's words. What did this captain know about him?

Gaspar loosened his pressure on the blade. "You see, I'm in possession of a certain letter."

Marko glanced over Gaspar's shoulder, then back at the crazed man in front of him. Confusion quickly replaced

Marko's surprise. He frowned, shrugged, and shook his head. "What letter?"

A wide grin spread on Gaspar's face and he returned his sword to its scabbard. "Your mother's love letter to your father."

Marko's eyes never left Gaspar's face. He held his breath but couldn't suppress his snort. "What use is such a letter to you?"

"It will lead me to your mother."

Chains clinked and pinched his skin as Marko sprang to his feet. "What are you talking about? She passed away years ago." He swallowed trying to steady his voice while a wave of anger washed over him. Gaspar's rotten teeth would meet his knuckles, if only his hands weren't manacled. To take him as a prisoner was bad enough, but he'd be damned if he'd allow this man to belittle his mother. "She was a virtuous woman of noble birth. Unlike you, I at least know who my father is."

Gaspar rolled out a low chuckle. His shaking beard dispersed bits of recently eaten ship biscuits onto the floor.

The grin vanished from Gaspar's face. His hand on the pommel of his sword, he pulled the blade half way out and stepped closer. "Small words from a small man. I've been called worse things."

Frustrated, Marko scanned the walls of the holding brig. The dim light of the oil lamp, in the hand of the guard standing by the door, revealed the etching of the names of previous occupants and lengths of stay in these fine quarters. Gaspar cleared his throat, causing Marko to snap his glance to the stout captain.

Without breaking eye contact, Marko cocked his head. "Let me guess, you can't make sense of the map?"

Gaspar's eyes scrutinized him. He pushed the sword back in his sheath. "Something tells me you can't, either."

Marko's hopes of survival died with Gaspar's guess. But there was one card he had left to play so Gaspar wouldn't keelhaul him. "What is this nonsense about my mother?"

"It is you who is the bastard of the two of us. Right you are, of noble birth she was, but abandoned you all the same she did. She left you to be with her pirate lover. When he got himself killed, she took the helm." Pausing, Gaspar leaned forward. "Your mother is Sirena, the cap'n of the *Strega*."

It took Marko a moment to process Gaspar's words. He burst into laughter. "What? This cannot be."

Of course he'd have to be deaf not to hear the stories. He didn't know what was more farfetched, the infamous Sirena and her ship the *Strega,* or her vast treasure many desired and searched for. He'd known of the folk tales since his childhood— pirates helping the people—and as fine as the sentiment sounded, the stories were nothing but myths to entertain the unwashed masses. None could prove they saw the ship or its crew. Or perhaps, the corsairs left no evidence of their existence behind. Yet, just as Captain Gaspar, people believed it was all real.

"I don't know where you get your information from, Captain. Neither the *Strega* nor this Sirena or her crew of pirate women exists. Never did."

"We'll see about that. First I have to find her. Shouldn't be hard with you as the bait. There's a hefty prize on her head or any of the crewmembers and I intend to collect every coin." He straightened. A sly smile appeared on his lips. "But before I hand her over, she'll squeal out every hiding place of her treasure."

"Where would you look for her?" Finding a ghost ship could take a lifetime and Marko did not plan to stay a prisoner for another day.

Gaspar let out a snide laugh. "All I have to do is spread the word of your capture. She'll crawl out of whatever hell hole she is in and find me in a day. Savvy?"

Marko raised a finger. "If what you said is true and she abandoned me at birth, what makes you think she'd come to my rescue now?"

For a moment Gaspar held his glance and then sneered. "I know her better than you think. She mothered you from afar."

This was too hard to comprehend. Stunned by Gaspar's words, Marko lowered his eyes to his dirty feet. He would be more surprised *if* he believed in the tales of Sirena. "This makes no sense. Why didn't you snatch me when I was but a wee lad? It would've been easier."

Gaspar faced him, raking his fingers through his thick beard. Lowering his hand, he scowled. "I would've. The salty wench of your mother hid you well. A prisoner used the love letter as a plea to bargain for his life. It was worth it. I killed his sorry keesters all the same. With time, the reward on her head grew bigger."

Marko yanked on the irons, causing more pain to his wrists. Damn, he couldn't find a weak link. "How can you be so sure about any of this?"

"I served on the *Strega* when the ship was still known as the *Capella*. A fine ship she was in the Duke's service." Gaspar grunted as if agreeing with his own statement. "The renegade cap'n turned coats and took the vessel with him to fight for his cause." He circled his raised finger. "Take from the rich—spread the spoils among the poor." Shivers prickled along Marko's spine when Gaspar leveled his murderous eyes with his and grumbled, "As if thieves and beggars would protect anyone's hide save their own. The stupid notion got the lubber of your father killed."

With two fingers, Marko rubbed the lump on his temple. His headache seemed to intensify with each minute. Blessed Virgin, the long years at sea for certain drove Captain Gaspar to madness.

"Quite a story you told." Marko lowered his eyes to the filthy floor. "Look, Captain, kill me or let me go. Either way you'll save yourself time, not to mention ridicule."

"Have no intention of doing one or the other. At least not yet. Nor will I be ridiculed." Gaspar pointed at Marko. "Belay that landlubber talk of yours. It won't be long before she comes to your rescue." He was still wagging his finger as he strutted to the door. "All of this will take some time to sit right with you. So I'll be leaving you to it."

The heavy door thudded shut as Gaspar left Marko's cell. Darkness surrounded him in an instant. Keys rattled and footsteps faded on the wooden planks.

Marko dug his fingers in his scalp. Should he believe Gaspar? A distant memory, or could it be a long forgotten dream, surfaced in Marko's mind. He couldn't have been more than a five years of age when a lady in colorful frocks visited him at night. She'd hummed a song until he'd fallen asleep. By the morning he'd woken alone in his room. Next to his bed stood a finely-carved rocking horse. The mysterious map was tucked under the saddle. There had been times he thought he'd seen her face in the crowd, but that was all so long ago.

With a sigh, he reclined on the damp straw and braced his head with his arm. He had to plan his escape and not waste precious time on buried memories and tall tales.

But what if?

Chapter 3

The dark Adriatic glistened in the silver moonlight while the two rowboats bobbed on its swells. Cold winds of *Tramontana* rushed the small and steady waves toward the narrow coast nestled between cliffs.

Through her looking glass, Sirena spotted the torch signal on the hill. "Onward," she ordered, collapsing the telescope.

The women continued rowing. As they approached the pebbled beach, only splashes of oars on the surface were heard. Knowing the hazards of exposure by venturing onto the mainland, many women preferred to stay on the *Strega*. To a few of them, the possibility of seeing their family members after months at sea washed away their fears of capture. They dreaded not just their own seizing, but by the Duke's decree, anyone who associated with pirates faced death.

With the *Strega* securely hidden and guarded by Marta and the remaining crew, Sirena could afford to oversee the task of replenishing their supplies. Clutching the tiller, she steered the boat toward the coastline. The women raised the oars at her order, allowing the skiffs to glide through the water. Pebbles scraped along the bottom planks. Water splashed around Sirena's ankles as she jumped onto the shore. A bustle of activity followed when the crew unloaded the sacks containing the precious portions of their booty to be given up in exchange for food and drinking water.

The shapes of two mules sprang from the darkness. Sirena's heart rejoiced as the cart, and the man holding the reins, came into view in the light of the torches. A small group of people followed the buggy.

"Whoa!" The thick-mustached man pulled on the reins, stopping the mules in front of her. Relief quickly replaced the worry on his face. "The news of a raid gone badly reached us. I came here almost every night for the past week."

"Unfortunate business, I'm afraid, Antun." Unable to utter the words she wanted to give him, she cast him a long glance, hoping he'd understand what she couldn't say.

"We feared for you." He scanned over the busy scene of a small crowd greeting their members then shot a look of surprise to Sirena. "The old captain?"

A stab of sharp pain split her insides. The late captain's dear friend, and their secret contact, Antun had not gotten the answer from Sirena's face. She pressed her lips together and shook her head.

Antun stared at her for a few seconds until his shoulders, clad in a brown jerkin, dropped. "You are wearing her doublet and her hat." He pointed at the hilt of her sword strapped at her old baldric. "You have her cutlass. She handed the *Strega* over to you. You're the new Captain Sirena."

A sharp breath escaped her as she nodded.

"I'm not surprised. You two were so alike." He jerked his head toward the boats. "How did the crew take it?"

Marta had said the same, but the only similarity between her and the late captain was the ability to read and write. "They are adjusting and so am I." The cold and crisp wind wrapped around her. She pulled the nubuck doublet tighter around her shoulders. "Living up to this name and gaining the crew's trust is a big challenge."

"The women will come around." He patted her arm. "And fear not, the people will continue to hide food from the Duke's men to supply you."

"Thank you, Antun. Your support means a lot in these times." She sniffed and turned her head in the direction of the men unloading the sacks of food, barrels of water, and demijohns of wine and olive oil from the cart. Her gaze fell on a slim boy with dark hair and torn clothes. To see him here, helping these men, squeezed her heart. Yes, the years at sea toughened her, but the sight of the child shattered the fortress she built around herself. "Is that Nikola? My, he has grown."

A smile stretched Antun's lips. Twisting, he faced the boy. "Nikola," he called, nudging his head, "come here."

The boy let go of the corner of the bag and climbed onto the cart. "Yes, Papa?"

Antun sat the boy in his lap, turning him to face her. "Remember Carmen? She's the new Captain Sirena."

Nikola's big, warm eyes scanned her from her boots to her head and settled on her face. "Where is the other one?" he asked with the sweet innocence of a young lad.

Tears invaded her eyes with realization the child didn't know her. She swallowed the large lump in her throat and leaned toward the boy in the oversized coat. "She's in Heaven now."

Nikola stared at her for immeasurable amount of time. "I hope she's watching down on us."

Antun patted Nikola's shoulder. "I'm sure she is, son."

Sirena forced a smile to her trembling lips. "You were just a little boy the last time I saw you. But look at you now, how old are you?" *Eight years, six months, two weeks, and four days*—yet she had only been able to give him a year with her.

A proud grin lit his face. "I'm eight and a half." He chewed on his lip and added, "And a bit."

The same smile she'd seen on a different man reopened a slowly-healing wound. She exhaled with a shuddering breath. "Almost a man and looking like your papa more and more."

"For real?" Nikola turned to Antun. "People say we are nothing alike."

She couldn't help but let out a short laugh. "You be good for your mama and papa and listen to them." Reaching into the deep pocket of her doublet, she pulled out a sequin. "Here, buy your heart's desire."

"Wow!" His eyes lit with fire, he took the silver coin in his dirty fingers. Placing the metal in between his little teeth, he bit down hard. A smile stretched his lips and he examined the money, flipping the token from side to side. "I think I'll keep this forever. Wait till I show it to my brothers."

A quiet chuckle escaped her. The boy wouldn't know the real coin from forged, but his actions made him appear sweet. Sirena straightened and ruffled Nikola's dark hair. An unbearable urge to pull the boy in her arms and kiss him filled her, but she planted her feet and pushed the desire down. "Where did you learn to do that?"

"Papa does it all the time." He slipped the coin inside his pocket and shrugged. "And so does Mama."

His words were a slash to her heart. "Now go and help the others."

He nodded and Antun planted him on the sandy ground. The boy skittered off to join the working crowd. Clenching her hands into fists, she pressed her lips tight. This was for the best. The boy would grow up in a family who loved him as one of their own.

Antun's shoulders rose and lowered with his long breath when she turned her gaze to him. "I see your grief, but it would be too dangerous for everyone if he knew."

She choked a whimper and reminded herself once again that she'd left her life behind the day she'd boarded the *Strega*. "It makes the pain worse," she said through her tight throat and forced air to her lungs. "Raise him well. He is all I have left."

"You have nothing to worry about. We love him as one of our own." Though Antun meant the best, his words gave her little comfort. If anyone suspected him of helping pirates, the Duke's men would hang his entire family.

"Cap'n, the swap is done," a melodious voice came from behind her.

She turned to the same young woman who had sang the ballad in the bunk next to hers over a week ago, when she had still been one of them—Carmen the pirate, not Sirena the captain. "Very well. Gather the crew for our return."

"Aye, Cap'n." The girl nodded and left.

Hand near the pommel of her cutlass, Sirena turned back to Antun. Intense pain sliced through her chest. For an instant she relived the moment she had left him behind. Oblivious to her tears, Nikola had slept wrapped in his blanket when Antun had taken the bundle from her arms. "Until the next time."

"One more thing before you set sail." He waved his hand over his shoulder. "There's a girl who wants to come on board."

The *Strega* could always take on another crew member, but Sirena had to be careful who she took on. She too had come onboard through the same man. If this woman came recommended by Antun, he'd checked out her story. She'd most likely gone through quite some ordeal and now her life was in peril. "Bring her forth."

Antun nodded at a scrawny young girl. Gulping, the girl stepped forward. Sirena cringed at the sight of bruises and cuts in various stages of healing on the girl's face. Fear reflected in her sunken eyes, but Sirena also caught a glimpse of determination to survive, to live despite whatever hell she might have gone through. "She's but a child, not more than fifteen years old."

Her wispy dirty blonde hair shook with her head. "Seventeen," the girl blurted.

Sirena narrowed her eyes and inspected the girl, from her worn shoes to the torn neckline of her tattered gray dress. The girl's face showed a hard life, but Sirena believed she lied about her age. "What is your name?"

"Ang—" the girl's voice croaked. She licked her cracked lips, sending a frightened look to Antun. "Angelia," she whispered.

Sirena's heart mellowed—a dangerous emotion for a pirate—so she hardened her expression. "Who did this to you?"

Angelia sniffed and raised her glance. Anguish filled her eyes. Her chin shook. "Gaspar," she managed before letting her head drop. "He held me captive for days. Beat me every day."

A tight knot formed in Sirena's stomach. Many would choose death over being Gaspar's prisoner and living to tell about it. "Did he ravish you?"

Angelia raised her head again, cast Sirena a sideways glance, and shook her head. "He tried, but he couldn't.

Then he got angry, said it was my fault." Fresh tears left streaks on her dirty cheeks.

A shiver shook Sirena. Perhaps there was more to this girl than met the eye. "How did you escape him?"

"When he passed out drunk on top of me, I took the keys and his cash purse." Horror reflected on Angelia's face. "His men are after me for whoring and thieving."

"That's Gaspar, all right." Antun nodded, frowning. "He always keeps tight strings on his purse, but it is his ego that hurts him the most."

Angelia's demeanor didn't sit right with Sirena, but every hopeful recruit chewed their nails. Hell, she'd been no different. Unlike her predecessor, Sirena felt Gaspar was the kind of enemy she would rather not engage. Mostly out of fear he would line up innocent people in front of her cannons. The man switched sides to his advantage. He'd fought with pirates against privateers, and he'd fought and harassed the freebooters on the government commissioned ships. And it seemed the despicable pig still fancied the latter. Perhaps someday she'd find a way to bring him down.

"I heard him talking to someone." Angelia spoke fast, her blood-shot eyes wide. "He's got a ship loaded with gold and very few armed men. I know his heading."

Sirena stared at the girl in suspicion. This might be a trap, but if she'd learned anything from the old captain, it was never to play by the rules. "You do?"

"I—" Angelia turned her head back and forth between Sirena and Antun. "I'll be of help. I can cook and sew, scrub the deck. Just take me on, please. I'll prove myself to you." The pleading in her voice matched her expression.

Pebbles crunched under Sirena's boots as she circled Angelia. "We have a cook and every woman can stich. You'd trade the rest of your life for the prison at sea. The only difference between rotting in dungeons and serving on board is you'll eat three square meals and see the sun every day. The *Strega* and her crew must remain a myth. Therefore you can't change your mind once you join us."

"I'm used to life not pampering me." Angelia's eyes tracked Sirena. "In my eyes, to rot away in the dungeons would be worse."

"If Gaspar's men don't kill you first." Straightening his cap, Antun quirked his eyebrows at Sirena. "What do you say? Would she'd make an acceptable pirate?"

The *Strega*'s crew had thinned in the last raid. Sirena could use another pair of hands, but this girl appeared to be a weakling. And Sirena wouldn't be able to protect her. Tucking her thumb on her baldric, she stopped to face Angelia. "The crew women are hard. They will daunt you if you show the slightest weakness," she said as she continued circling the girl.

"I'm not weak." Angelia raised her voice. "Grew up with four brothers. I know how to fight."

Reminded of her own childhood, Sirena ceased pacing. A smile crept to her lips. Being the youngest of four and the only girl, her brothers had taken on the role of protectors. She glanced at the two rowboats. The seated women held oars, all eyes tuned on her. Angelia's story wasn't much different from any of them. Years ago Carmen too had been a weakling and had stood with trembling knees before the old captain, begging to be taken into the crew of pirates.

"Let's see what you're made of." Sirena tweaked her head toward the shore. "Take to an oar."

Angelia's eyes widened. "Thank you, thank you," she gasped, walking backward.

"Angelia." Sirena's stern call made Angelia halt. "From now on it will be, 'aye, Captain,' to you."

Angelia smiled for the first time, exposing short and uneven teeth. "Aye, Captain." She turned and galloped toward the shore with the enthusiasm of a real pirate then climbed into one of the rowboats.

"You have a good heart, like the departed captain." Antun smiled, twirling the ends of his moustache. "May God be on your side." He whistled and the mules' hoofs pounded the sand.

With heavy steps Sirena returned to the shore and climbed into the rowboat. One by one, the people on the beach disappeared into the darkness. Nikola paused and faced them. She waved to him. He raised his hand and wiggled his fingers. Lowering his arm, he ran after Antun and the group. Only God knew if she'd see his angelic face again in this life.

Twisting, she faced the women, who waited on her command. Her fingers wrapped around the smooth wood of the tiller. "To your oars."

"Row, row, row..." Their steady and low voices kept the rhythm of their swaying bodies while oars stroked the water in perfect unison. The added cargo slowing down their progress against the current, the little skiffs reached the *Strega* in twice the time it had taken to get to the coast.

"See to the provisions." Sirena shouted the order over her shoulder, her boots echoing on the seasoned planks.

Marta ran to open the cargo hold to oversee the unloading. "You heard the Cap'n."

The smell of the low burning oil lamp mixed with the scent of the wood as Sirena entered her cabin. Out of the cold wind, the warmth of the interior enveloped her and she shed her doublet. From the built-in cupboard, she pulled out a map of the Adriatic Sea, encased in ornamental cartouche, and unrolled the chart over the small table. Sailing ships and sea serpents decorated the water while bears and deer dotted the landscapes. Angels held shields, banners, drapes, and swags at the top.

The door to her room opened abruptly, allowing the cold air to rush at her feet. Marta stepped in, breaking Sirena's concentration. "The new girl knows not her place, Cap'n. If she's not in my way, she's in someone else's."

"She must learn the ropes as every new recruit before her did." Dragging her finger on the map, Sirena traced their new heading. "Bring her to me."

A moment later, the frail hem of Angelia's frock and her worn shoes came into Sirena's view. She raised her head from the chart of the geographic area and turned the long sheet around. "Show me where Gaspar's heading."

Angelia's eyes traveled from the map to Sirena. By her baffled expression Sirena expected the next comment. "I can't."

Not unlike other women of lesser means, the girl was illiterate.

"Very well." Sirena sighed, flipping the map back around. "Did he mention any islands?"

"I heard Lastovo. He'll be there in four nights." Angelia's voice trembled. "And he'll have a precious prisoner on board. Someone you'll rush to save and so you'll surrender."

"A *precious* prisoner? Peculiar that." Sirena leaned over the table and examined Angelia's face. The departed Sirena had mentioned she had held someone dear. Could Gaspar be trying to lure the old captain out, not knowing she'd died? What could he know about her that no one else did?

Sirena shook off the notion and focused on the two southern Adriatic islands separated by the wide channel. In an instant, she recognized Gaspar's route. Since ships had become sleeker and more maneuverable, they journeyed through narrow passages. It was no wonder Gaspar hadn't bothered to arm his vessel. He had chosen an old, abandoned watercourse, most likely thinking no one passed through there. Springing to her feet, she knocked the chair on the floorboards as she pointed to a place on the map where the streams comingled.

Angelia's wide eyes met hers and Sirena quickly pulled her finger away from the table.

Sirena nodded toward the door of her cabin where Marta stood. "Go with her. You have three days to learn how to fight."

"Three?" Angelia winced and stepped back. "But Gaspar would be there in four."

Sirena arched an eyebrow. The girl was observant. This could be good or bad. "I said go with Marta."

Angelia raised her fists to her face. "I know how to fight."

Sirena planted her hands on the map and leaned over the table. "Throwing punches won't send our enemy scrambling. You must learn how to thrust the sword into a man's flesh."

"Aye, Captain," Angelia whispered as fear filled her face.

The girl needed some encouragement and a quick pep talk. The pounding of Sirena's fist shook the table and made Angelia flinch. "Pirates are not shy—stand tall and be counted," she growled with a scowl.

Angelia swallowed with effort, took in a long breath, and straightened. "Aye, Captain." Her loud voice surprised even Sirena.

Sirena picked the chair up from the floor and sat down again. "Now go."

Angelia scurried out. One hand on the knob, Marta paused. "Cap'n, she must harden or she'll die." Adjusting her bandana, she left Sirena's cabin.

Sirena leaned back in her chair. Perhaps she was a tad too harsh with the new crew member—but blood and ashes—Angelia would not survive long enough to get a taste of her first battle.

The change of plans would be the ultimate test of Angelia's information. If Gaspar expected the *Strega* to ambush him in four nights, the bilge rat would get the mother of surprises in three.

Chapter 4

Marko pinched his nose, drew another deep breath through his mouth, and held the air for as long as he could. While his eyes had adjusted to the perpetual darkness on his first day, the rancid stench of decomposing waste still had him gagging.

His bottom lip between his teeth, he tapped his fingers along the door frame, feeling for the nails. With the tip of the rusty spoon, he tried to prod the metal spikes out of the hinges. The utensil snapped in half and clinked on the floorboards.

"God damn the carpenters who built this ship." He tossed the spoon's handle aside. The planks were coming apart but the door hinges wouldn't budge. Aggravation set him on edge and he almost forgot about the stale air.

He sat on the musty straw and picked up his dish. Like looters after the battle, cockroaches scurried across the plate when he shoved his hand in the cold mush. Swallowing another gag, he scooped the lump in his fingers and forced the gritty, fish-smelling muck into his mouth. He downed the mush fast with a swig of brackish water. The shorter the time he held a portion inside his mouth, the less he'd have to be subjected to its abominable taste.

Despite his efforts, the bite brought tears to his eyes, but he needed sustenance. No wonder piracy spread like a plague. Under the lash, even loyalty to duke and country eroded.

A heavy fist pounded on the other side of his cell's door. "Your pewter," the guard demanded.

The metal scraped the floor as Marko crawled on his knees and pushed the dish under the door. He clenched his teeth in anticipation of the chunky guard's response. This would be the third tarnished plate he returned without the spoon.

The man groaned and the plate clunked against the door. "Where's your spoon?"

"You didn't give me one. I ate the slop you served with my fingers." Tapping his toes, Marko waited. With any luck this guard was the dumber of the two of them. His captors seemed less frightening than their food.

"My apologies, your majesty," the man sneered. "What's the matter? Our cook's burgoo not good enough for you?" Sounds of his feet dragged on the floorboards. "Ungrateful bastard," he mumbled before pounding on the next door.

A scarce meal a day wouldn't provide Marko with enough strength for an escape. To conserve his energy from lifting the iron chains, he crawled to the outer wall. Hollows in the wood helped him to pull himself to a standing position. Tapping his hands on the plank, he felt for the loose knot in the wood and dug the round cork out. He covered one eye and placed the other over the small gap he'd discovered by accident during the second night of his imprisonment.

The very tip of the bright red sun still cast fiery colors over the sky and the sea. No other ships or land appeared on the horizon. He'd pondered the ways to escape and paid very little heed to Gaspar's story of Sirena. Come to think of it, this was the first time she crossed his mind. A set of pirates for his parents? Now that was just infuriating and disturbing, not to mention unhelpful. He had neither the time nor desire to further reflect on this topic, not when he had to find a way out of this damned place.

Heavy footsteps approached his cell's door and the clinking of iron keys drifted to him.

Marko quickly closed the hole and shoved the broken spoons under the straw in a soggy corner. No one would care to look there.

With the first glimpse at knee high black boots, Marko's heart sank. Gaspar stepped in through the narrow door. The oil lamp in his hand revealed the rest of him as well as the poor condition of the brig.

"Tomorrow at nightfall you'll be dangling, strapped to the main mast, and your mother will have no choice but to surrender. The ship and her crew, too." Gaspar's torso shook with raspy laughter. The mocking amusement filled his voice and heated Marko's face. "What say you? Is it time for merriment?"

Marko swiped his forearm across his sweaty brow. The odor of urine soaked straw filled his nostrils. How would Gaspar lure a mythical creature out of the tales and onto the sea at the precise day and time? "I say you are mad."

Ceasing his chortle, Gaspar glared at him. "Mad say you?" He scowled. "I wouldn't be doubling the rations of rum to all hands if I wasn't sure of my success."

Marko arched an eyebrow. Excellent. His luck had just turned. By nightfall all of them would be passed out drunk. He had to find a way to get out of this hellhole. A set of keys hanging from Gaspar's belt drew his attention. What else would Gaspar be willing to share? Slowly, Marko stood and stared his enemy in the eye. "I'll be dammed if I'll let you succeed."

"Don't be daft, maggot. If you attempt anything, I'll kill you where you stand." Gaspar clutched the handle of his sword. "Standing as a buffer between me and Sirena may just save your scurvy ass."

"What guarantee can you give me?" Anger burned through his veins. With a swift move, Marko stepped behind Gaspar and wrapped the chains around his neck. "Shall we die together?"

The guard standing in the doorway charged forward with his hands on the handle of his cutlass. But the skinny mariner halted when Gaspar put his hands up.

Gaspar lunged backward and forced Marko against the wall. He knocked the wind out of him, then ducked, and slipped out of Marko's hold. Rapier unsheathed, Gaspar pressed the blade against Marko's chest.

"Thousand blunderbusses!" Gaspar spat, shaking in anger. "If I didn't need you for a greater cause, you'll be dangling from the mast right now." He leaned closer. Enough for Marko to get a firm grip on the key ring and a whiff of rum breath. He waited until Gaspar pulled back. The metal ring slid out of the loop on Gaspar's belt, and Marko, in a sleight of hand, had the keys up his sleeve.

Gaspar wiped the spittle off his beard. "Guards," he shouted. His eyes narrowed to thin slits. "It's not too late to have you flogged."

The two guards banged their shoulders in an attempt to pass through the narrow doorway at the same time. "A—aye, Cap'n."

"Tie this dog to the yardarm." Gaspar turned toward the exit. He grabbed the whip handed to him by the guard and said, "By god, it's been a while since I used my cat-o-nine-tails." His loud voice resonated with joy at the upcoming event. "The crew will have a thrill tonight."

Marko's heart pounded. Not from fear. From the possibility the guards would discover the keys he shoved up his sleeve. Twisting, he managed to inch his hand behind his back and slide the ring down his breeches.

He stopped at the watchdogs' stare and gave out an exhausted laugh then scratched his behind. "Terrible itch, mateys."

The two mariners grabbed him by his elbows and shoved him away from the wall.

"Avast, Cap'n." The one with no neck and a belly resembling a cannonball remarked, causing Gaspar to halt by the door. "The poxy lad is so scared, he already filled his breeches."

Marko jabbed his elbow in the guard's abdomen and the man doubled up in pain. "Those are my boots, you scurvy bilge rat."

The commotion wouldn't gain him his knee-high captain's boots back, but the distraction would prevent Gaspar from finding the keys down his pants. His short window of opportunity closed when Gaspar's sword pressed against his chest. Marko panted while the guards held him pinned to the door.

At the sudden rush of pounding footsteps on the deck all of them angled their heads toward the shifting boards overhead. Marko eyed their expressions carefully as the panic seemed to spread above. A whizz of a cannonball reached their ears and the guards eyes widened as they realized they were under attack.

A loud splash indicated the missile had missed the boat by inches. The ship rocked on the waves. Marko grabbed onto the nearest guard to steady himself. His captain's training and years at the sea told him this was not a miss, but a warning shot.

The hatch opened, and an officer scurried down the stairs.

"What in the blazes is going on up there?" Gaspar shouted at a man clad in a white and navy uniform.

"Captain!" The young man swallowed hard. "It's the *Strega* and she's coming at us at full tilt."

Bafflement filled Gaspar's eyes. His ashen face stared at Marko in bewilderment. The pale looking captain cocked his head left then right until finally, he seemed to regain his composure. "Betraying wench," he thundered. "Sirena wasn't supposed to be here yet." Sheathing the blade, he wiped the sweat off his brow and stormed out of the prison toward the stairs leading out. "Smartly," he said, gesturing for guards to follow him. "All hands on deck."

The guards scurried after Gaspar. Marko's cell door stood wide open and left him in a state of surprise at his unexpected freedom. He quickly gathered his wits. First, he had to get out of here alive, then he'd thank whoever had attacked. The officer seemed certain it was Sirena's ship. Maybe the same madness plagued entire crew.

Marko glanced at his fetters. This good luck, however sudden, still was not on his side. The ship was under attack and if it sank with him shackled at his ankles and wrists, he might as well have been tied to an anchor.

Another thunder of cannon fire ripped through the ship and urged him to hurry. Shuffling out of his cell, he saw the hands of imprisoned fellows waving out of every window. He couldn't ignore their cries for help. Shoving the keys into a pair of dirty hands, he said, "Help the others."

Soon the cannon fire ceased, and the shouts and metal clashing above confirmed that hand-to-hand fighting was going on while he still searched for a tool that would free him from the shackles. As men got out of their cells, he shouted, "Anyone from the *Levant?*"

Those who heard and chose to answer shook their heads and carried on ransacking the place for anything that would remove their bonds.

The men halted when a few women in tattered sailors' suits barged down the stairs. "Quick," one woman said as she stepped to him, holding a heavy iron lever. "Not much time."

"Who are you?" he asked while one of them worked fast to remove his restraints.

Through her stringy hair, she cast him a side glance. "We are the corsairs of the *Strega.*"

"Cannot be," he gasped. Could this be a hallucination? No. He wasn't locked up for that long.

"Seeing is believing." Irons clinked as the scrawny woman tossed them aside. "You're free." She moved to the next man.

Massaging his sore wrists, he stood rooted. If the sounds of the raging battle didn't convince him otherwise, he'd have believed this was a dream of a sort. Or worse, he, too, had caught the maddening disease that seemed to spread among Gaspar's crew.

"Sirena will sink this ship." One of the women grabbed his arm. "Get as far away as you can," she shouted over the blast of a blunderbuss, giving him a sharp slap between his shoulders. "And *while* you can, go!"

Sirena? His mother? Had she come to his rescue? Questions swarmed him as he ascended the stairs. *No, no, no, concentrate on survival, then you can think of her.* Besides, there was only one lady he'd honor with that title—the one who'd raised him—regardless of Gaspar's story.

Panic engulfed the upper deck, throwing it into chaos. Those still alive scrambled like minnows. They jumped overboard and swam in all directions. The xebec couldn't be armed with more than twenty-four guns, but the crew of women swarmed the larger and unprepared brigantine. The corsairs employed their usual tactics—they swept alongside Gaspar's ship and boarded her. The fine bulwark running along the sides of the deck were set on fire, illuminating the night sky. Women in rags armed with muskets, spears, and scimitars plundered through what now seemed like an abandoned ship.

Marko raised his head, catching a glimpse of the prow of the attacking ship. The black letters on the weather beaten wood spelled, *Strega. In the name of Jesus.* Marko quickly crossed himself. The tales were true, but what about the rest of Gaspar's story?

Moments later, a few pirates swung overboard and clambered onto the privateer's deck. The surviving sailors dropped their weapons. The fighting was over. Gaspar's ship was lost, but where could the captain be hiding? Typical of Gaspar, the cocky captain wouldn't stand by his men in the battle. Most likely he didn't consider these men his. They had come with the ship, while the owners had commissioned him to take the helm.

Marko crouched behind the tack line. If these women found him on board, they may mistake him for one of Gaspar's men. It was time for him to make a discreet exit. The short sword made a sucking noise as he withdrew the blade from the still warm body of a deceased mariner. He wiped the blood on the ropes of the line the man had been working on. A hilt of a pistol in the dead man's hand drew Marko's attention. Carefully, he prodded the weapon out of the lifeless fingers. The gun was still primed. The poor lubber hadn't got a chance to pull the trigger before death claimed him. The pirates' attack came so fast and vicious, the sailors had but one option—abandon the ship. Marko was about to leave himself when a loud call came.

"Cap'n, we got 'em!"

He returned to his spot behind the barrel and raised his head in the direction of the commotion. Bloodied and bound, Gaspar and his two officers were pushed in front of a small crowd.

"We found 'em in the cockpit." A burly woman placed her foot on Gaspar's behind and shoved him forward.

Joyful shouts and laughter spread among the pirates when the stocky captain took a nosedive in front of a woman in a leather doublet. A red bandana framed her forehead and held the long curls cascading down her shoulders in place. Marko couldn't determine the color of the cold eyes inspecting the captives that knelt in front of her.

Strangely, he wished he was the one of the captured men just to be on his knees in front of this sea goddess. She possessed a beauty he hadn't seen before. God, and only a few of his friends, knew how many women had passed through his arms like water. This mesmerizing captain radiated a lethalness that captured him. Danger shimmered around her like an aura. She would not succumb to his charms as countless others had. He wanted her. The challenge of seducing her tensed his body, and he shuddered as a sensuous shiver shot up his spine.

"I see bravery abandoned you along with your men, or was it you who left your crew?" She spoke with a sarcastic tone, but not a pirate's slang. He understood she was a woman of standing and education. "So you thought you could hide in the dark, stuffy quarters of the midshipmen."

Beauty and brains. Marko couldn't peel his eyes away from the woman her crew addressed as their captain. But could she be Captain Sirena? If she was, she couldn't be his mother. The woman appeared far younger than him. No way could she have a grown son.

Gaspar lowered his head, exposing his thick neck. The opportunity to get rid of the scum bag for good presented itself. Marko took careful aim. One clear shot was all he needed, but he lowered the gun. The cruel captain was now a prisoner of these women and as such, it would be them who determined his fate. Nonetheless, he'd have to get close to the mysterious captain and find out her true identity.

"The two of you are free," she said, nodding toward the officers behind Gaspar.

Gaspar's bully gofers snapped their heads around, scanning the sea surrounding them.

"Where would we go?" one of the men protested with a shrill voice. "It's the middle of the night and there's no land in sight."

"I am sure you can swim like the rest of your crew. Grab a piece of the wood and drift. Keep heading north and you are bound to find land in a day or so." She then turned to Gaspar, narrowed her eyes and said, "So we meet at last." With the sword raised over his head, she delivered a blow to him that would knock any man cold and caused Marko to flinch.

The pirates' leader grimaced over the limp body of Gaspar. For a moment there, Marko thought she'd spit at him. "Lock him in the brig and make sure this ship sinks."

Waving their weapons, the crew cheered then set to work.

There was one more thing for Marko to do before he slipped away from the ship. He sneaked into Gaspar's cabin. His heart dropped to his stomach. At the first glance, it appeared as if the pirates ransacked through the quarters. In two strides, he closed the distance between the door and the square table. A vast numbers of papers covered its surface and after rummaging through the pile, he found what he wanted. An ink drawing of an unnamed island on a thin scrap of leather. He shoved the soft parchment inside his shirt and headed out.

It would be difficult to swim with a sword strapped to his belt and the gun wouldn't be of much use once the matchlock and the powder got wet. He discarded the weapons by throwing them into the sea. Diving in, he swam with effort against the current of the sinking vessel. A barrel drifted by him when he came up for air and he grabbed onto the round cask. The northerly current pushed him in the right direction, as the pirates' commander had said to the two officers. There were plenty of cliffs with deep inlets where she could wait until the Navy had combed the area. Instinct urged him to find the intriguing captain and get answers to his questions. But would she be friend or foe?

Chapter 5

The *Strega*'s cannons had not yet cooled and the smell of burnt powder lingered in the air. Thankfully, the ringing in Sirena's ears had ceased. In recent months it had taken her longer and longer for the sensation to ease after the battle. The day would come when her hearing wouldn't recover at all. This inevitable hearing loss happened to many who were exposed to mortar fire. The urge to find a more serene lifestyle surged even harder through her mind.

The ships tattered sails flapped in the night breeze as the *Strega* glided away from the privateers' two-mast brigantine. Set ablaze, the embers flew high into the darkness, briefly sparking bright as stars. The flames engulfed the upper square canvas on its foremasts. Lines snapped as loud as pistol shots when Gaspar's vessel careened into the depths of the sea.

Waving their weapons over their heads, Sirena's crew cheered when the swirling waters swallowed the burning ship. White foam boiled on the surface. Soon, the sea calmed down and resumed the appearance of spilled paint as far as the eye could see in the moonlit night.

The weather-beaten wood of the *Strega*'s main mast scraped Sirena's palm as she patted the nicked timber. The ever dependent xebec had not disappointed her during the first raid under her command. She'd deployed the old captain's tactics. Fear had spread at the sight of the ghost ship and its crew of mermaids who lured sailors to their death. Most had abandoned their posts and jumped overboard before she had ordered to her ship open fire. The triangular sails hoisted to the head of a low mast gave the *Strega* the advantage of speed and maneuverability over bigger brigantine than the one they'd just sunk. Her ship had caught up with Gaspar's so fast he had no time to prepare for the battle.

She glanced at the sky, getting lost in its vastness. If the old captain was watching her now, she had to be proud. Then again, who was to say the old lady had ascended to heaven? Sirena lowered her gaze to the dark surface of the Adriatic. For all anyone knew, their dear captain's soul might rot in the pits of hell. As perhaps Carmen's would one day.

"To our Cap'n!" her crew toasted, yet again.

Sirena turned to them. Dressed in tattered men's sailor suits, the women raised their bumpers of raided grog. The seasoned hide of her knee length doublet creaked as Sirena honored them with her leather canteen filled with water. Someone had to keep her head on, and Sirena as the captain carried a huge pack of responsibility to these women and her ship. God might have been on their side during this raid, but she still had not gained the crew's complete and utter trust.

She sloshed the liquid into her mouth, washing away the salt and quenching her thirst. "May Venetians keep sending their merchant galleons filled with riches our way."

Nods and deep sighs followed the guzzling of the crew's fiery drinks. "May they, Cap'n."

A scan of the dirty faces confirmed the crew waited on her to decide Gaspar's fate. "Fetch the dog from the brig," she shouted, throwing her fist in the air.

Rising theirs, the crew cheered louder.

"What shall we do with this one?" A raspy voice came from behind Sirena as the crew parted, booing and ridiculing the bound man.

Dried blood spoiled the white of Gaspar's frilly sleeves. Marta kicked his behind, causing his pot belly to jiggle as he staggered and stumbled on his way to the square gallery.

"You pig." The kick of a sailor's worn boot on his fat behind, caused him to lose his footing on the dew-slick deck, but he steadied himself. "Kneel in front of the Cap'n."

A mocking smile spread across his greasy face. "I don't kneel in front of a wench. Where's the old doxy that calls herself a cap'n?"

Sirena ignored his question, struggling to keep her anger from showing on her face. It had to be the flicker of her eyebrows that gave Gaspar an answer.

"Ah, I see. She breathed her last." He pointed his chin at her. "You're the new head skirt."

The sight of the man made Sirena's heart race and churned her stomach. Reminded of Angelia's story, she shuddered. The newest crewmember's cuts and bruises were still very fresh, but they'd mend in time. The emotional scars this man had left her with might never heal.

The metallic sound of a blade unsheathing pierced the dead silence as Marta drew a long sword out of its scabbard. "We'll see about that."

One blunt stroke behind his fat knees brought him straight down. Beads of sweat dotted his wide forehead. A pained expression replaced his mocking grin.

"The rumors are nothing but lies." He spat the words.

Two stairs above, Sirena towered over him. "And what rumors would that be?"

"That the crew of the *Strega* is band of pirates. You're a pack of crazed, loose lipped wenches." His attempt to stand met Sirena's boot pushing on his shoulder. He let out a loud grunt as his knees thumped back to the deck.

Digging her heel deeper into his meaty shoulder, Sirena fixed her eyes on the snorting pig and gave him one of her well-known gazes, serene and prolonged, as eloquent as the words she was about to voice. "Who are you calling turncoats?"

His snort changed to a full coughing fit and ended with a long wheeze. "You shall address me as Cap'n."

"On this ship, I'm the captain. Besides, it's nothing but a title to you." Anger slowly burned its way into her head. "You mangy cockroach," she said in a language he'd understand. "You abandoned your men and left them to our mercy."

Cocking his head, he reminded her of an overfed fowl. "You leave the men's work to men." His last word came out high pitched as Sirena deepened the pressure of her heel on his neck.

With narrowed eyes, she dropped her voice to an ominous one. "Avast. These women cost you your ship, crew, and cargo, which had been stolen from another merchant doubt not. You also lost your honor." She released her hold on him and placed her foot on the beaten wood of the deck. *Honor*, this man knew not the meaning of the word. "And I'll leave it up to the women who conquered the pathetic likes of you to decide your fate."

The women broke into chat. "Walk the plank, walk the plank." Panic flashed in his beady eyes as he turned his head from side to side. "Where are your men? They'll beat this nonsense out of you."

Sirena snorted, unsheathing her cutlass. With the blade pressed to his neck, she struggled not to slice his throat. "It's the likes of you that makes us live as corsairs." Her words came out through gritted teeth.

The women's chant grew louder. "Walk the plank, walk the plank."

"The women have spoken." Although she didn't like the role of executioner, she would prefer to keelhaul the bastard, but the verdict had been drawn. There was a chance he could survive and keeping him alive was like putting a poisonous snake in her sleeping cabin. With a single nod, Sirena signaled Marta and the burly woman yanked him to his feet.

"Damn you all." Fear reflected in his shouts as several women eagerly pushed him toward the plank. Fresh blood poured out of barely closed wound above his eyebrow.

"Pig, rot in hell." Angelia's shriek rose above the women's low chanting. She spat in his face.

Sirena's calf boots pounded on the seasoned wood as she headed to her room. The decision had been made, her part was over. With luck, the dangerous swine would reach hell in time for supper. No doubt the old captain would have killed the pompous gasbag. Would Carmen ever live up to her name? And would she ever stop feeling as if the old woman was watching her every move, questioning her every decision?

When the first light broke the darkness over the horizon, the crew would hoist the merchant flags, cover the name and set sail for the waters of the Republic of Ragusa. Though no one could prove the *Strega* and her crew of women existed, staying out of the sight would be challenging. There were many coves and inlets where they would hide during the day. She may not have the experience of sailing the seven seas, but Sirena knew every port and island of the beloved sea she called home.

The door to her stark cabin opened and closed with a creak she was getting used to. After lighting the oil lamp on the corner stand, she removed her worn buskins and coat, tossed them at the foot of the bunk, and plopped down. Bracing her head with one arm, she picked up a book bound in worn leather. Her eyes perused the passage in the old captain's journal.

"Under the vanishing star
"Where the lion's guards are,
"Deep in the rock, of a hue,
And over waters blue."

Bilge rats, Sirena exhaled in frustration. For the past five days she'd read those words over and over and this riddle was the only clue to where her predecessor could have hidden the item in need of finding. Was it worth her trying to decipher the vague puzzling rhyme? Deep in the rock could mean an underwater cave, but why would there be lions? Unless, the departed captain had meant Mediterranean sea-lions also called Adriana. Their habitat included such places. The clue of blue hue wasn't of any help. This entire sea was blue, this trunk could be anywhere.

"Pah," she shouted, closing the book. Oracles of Apollo from the ancient Greek city of Delhi would have made more sense. She removed her bandana and pulled on a loose end of the string releasing her hair, then turned on her side and extinguished the light.

Covering a yawn, she listened to the merriment on deck. After the well rounded Gaspar had taken his plunge, one of the sisters had brought out an accordion and took the celebration to a whole new height. Hands clapping, feet stomping, the women sang:

"Through pillage and plunder we ransack and loot,

"What anyone calls us we don't give a hoot,

"Raise your flasks and drain them fast,

"Unfurl the sails from the masts..."

Sirena's mind returned to Nikola, growing healthy and calling another woman his mother. The title should have been reserved for her. Unbearable pain pierced her heart and constricted her throat. She wanted to scream. Instead, she buried her face in the crook of her elbow and swallowed the torment, bottling her anger until the next battle.

"Show a leg!"

Sirena woke to Marta's shouting on the deck.

"It is dawn, you scurvy lubbers!" the quartermaster went on, waking the women. Many must have slept wherever they passed out. After the last night's drinking, there'd be the devil to pay today.

The tight ropes of Sirena's hammock creaked as she sat up. One glance out the small window confirmed the ship stood still. Scallywags. Marta knew the heading, why weren't they moving? Sirena scrambled out of the netted bed and shoved her feet into her scarred leather boots.

The light of the sun trying to penetrate through the fog forced her to squint as soon as she stepped on deck.

"All hands to braces!" Marta bellowed then turned to her.

Flat sails answered Sirena's question before she confronted Marta. "Report."

Marta stopped shouting for a brief moment. "Doldrums. Have the whole crew on edge."

A crew member broke to a vulgar tune, encouraging the rest of them to join.

Marta raised both hands. "The sails spilled, Cap'n as soon as the ship sailed between these islands." She joined in the singing.

"Where are we?" Sirena buttoned up her doublet as the chilly air of an early morning sent shivers to her spine.

Marta's grin disappeared and she leaned on the giant helm. "Hard to tell. The fog's thick. I reckon the ship is a dog's tail away from Ragusa."

Pressing the looking glass to her eye, Sirena scanned the surroundings. Green lush islands loomed through the mist. "These are the Elaphiti Islands." Understandable. They had intercepted Gaspar's vessel farther north and now her ship had steered into a windless trap.

"The fog should lift soon and winds will pick up. You'll see. Our sails will be full and the *Strega* will cut through the water like a knife." Marta continued to hum the rest of the song.

A line of smoke raising straight into the gray sky caught Sirena's attention. Peculiar that, if islanders burnt the brush to clear the land, there should be more than one column. This appeared to be single fire meant as a signal. And judging by the thickness of the rising stack, the blaze burned wild.

She lowered the telescope. "Have the anchor lowered."

"You heard the Cap'n. Anchor down!" Marta repeated, barking over the women's singing voices.

The order was passed along the ship to its prow and followed by creaking of the capstan then a loud splash.

Sirena peeked through the telescope again. "Bring the dinghy down."

"Lower the dinghy!" Marta gave Sirena a weary side glance. "Where are we going?"

"You're minding the ship." Sirena tied her hair in a low ponytail. "I'll take six of the best pirates and make a trip to the smoking island."

"Aye, aye." Trustworthy Marta resumed her watch over the deck. Her face was impossible to read, but she never questioned Sirena's decision or the orders. The stout woman had served under the old captain with never as much as raising an eyebrow.

Tied to the *Strega*, the small boat bobbed lazily on the calm water. The crew of women took to the oars, while Sirena held the rudder. Soon the blaze causing the smoke appeared on the beach of an islet. She stood. The telescope allowed her to scan the coastline. A man fed the fire with dry grass and twigs. It was obvious he wanted to attract attention. Judging by his tattered and dingy shirt and breeches, and the untrimmed beard, he was a beached mariner. He'd cause nothing but trouble. She should order the boat to return to the ship and forget him. But, the strong current, coupled with women's fast rowing, caused the dinghy to lose its steerage-way.

"Oars up." Sirena tried to gain control of the small vessel speeding toward the coast by hurling the anchor overboard.

Two of the women jumped out into the waist deep water and pushed on the prow before rocks scraped the bottom.

Sea splashed around Sirena's knees as she disembarked. The man ceased his activity and stood transfixed.

Despite a painful-looking sunburn on his face and neck, he managed a grin. "Oh, thank God, you saw my signal." A hint of fear rushed across his face. Could he be one of Gaspar's men?

She crept closer to him. Her women, armed and ready, followed two paces behind. Soot covered his face, but the deep turquoise of his eyes stood out and locked on her. No human could have eyes blue like his, as if they were made from the very waters they sailed on. Could he be a merman? Even though the tales embellished her and the crew as mermaids, she had heard of real sea creatures capable of growing a pair of legs instead of their fish tail and venturing out onto dry land. In all her twenty nine years she had never seen one, but she feared the tales nonetheless. Those breeds between men and fish possessed powers that could bewitch them all and take their souls to the depths of the sea for all eternity.

"Water," he whispered hoarsely. "Please." The young man raked sooty fingers through his blond curls and stared at them as if they were the mythical water nymphs called *Rusalki.* "Do you understand my tongue?"

He couldn't be a merman. Every tale she had heard depicted the sea creatures as mute. This one spoke, not in pirate's lingo, but as an educated man. Still, she must exercise caution. Her sword slashed the air between them as she pressed the blade to his neck. "Are you a man?"

His eyebrows arched. Tattered lace rolled from his wrists as he threw his hands up. "What in the name of god—"

"Answer!" Sirena barked putting a hint more force to the blade.

Hands above his shoulders shook while his Adam's apple twitched with a hard swallow. "Last time I checked, I was," he said with high pitch voice, but as he continued, he seemed to regain his composure. "And in the presence of beautiful maidens, I am always a gentleman."

Giggles came from the women standing on the shore. Pebbles crunched under Sirena's boots as she stepped behind him, sliding the blade to the back of his neck. Facing her crew gave her the advantage of rear and frontal attack, if need be. A few of the women covered their sheepish grins with their hands and ogled him.

She flashed a look around, half expecting to see his comrades stepping out from the pine trees a few paces from the beach, but no one appeared. This was no man. She had seen the bravest of them shaking in their boots under her cutlass. This one had barely flinched. "Why are you here?"

His shoulders lowered with his exhale. Hands still in the air, he turned to her. His eyes traveled along her blade now pressed to his chest. "My crew abandoned me on this desolate island." But his casual tone didn't match his tensed body. He could be lying.

Hmmm, but she had thought his cockiness had cost him his ship. Unable to stand the intensity of his stare, she lowered her glance to his bare feet on the sun-bleached pebbles. Shiver her timbers, never before had she succumbed under a man's gaze. Even her late husband, god bless his soul, had always said she'd made him work hard for a morsel of her love. With great difficulty, she forced herself to look at the marooned sailor's piercing eyes. "You are seeking safe passage, I presume."

"You presume right." He lowered his hands to his hips. "To Ragusa, if that is your heading."

Her mind raced. Even with different colors hoisted, after the last night's raid, she ran the risk that the *Strega*'s sails would be detected as soon as they appeared on the horizon. Her ship could not approach the city's defensive walls. Not until all the rumors settled and no survivors would recognize them. On the other hand, she couldn't pass through the Pila Gates as a lone woman. Last time she had spoken to Carlo, he had said he'd be docking in Ragusa's harbor on the second Sunday of August. Still two days away, but she should pay her brother a visit. Maybe he'd been home and had news.

Of course, she would have to transform into a polished lady, if she hadn't forgotten the proper upbringing. After eight years living as a ruthless pirate she tended to dismiss the refinement from her mind. Funny that, how had her priorities changed.

"I possess a map." The man's voice snapped her out of her planning.

She lowered her sword, and her glance, to his feet and flicked a crab into the sea. "Charts are of no interest to me."

"Ah." He stroked his chin, leaving sooty fingerprints on his blond beard. "But this is not an ordinary map." His grin exposed a row of white teeth, a rarity. "It leads to a treasure."

"Treasure means different things to different people." Something familiar reflected in his eyes. She stepped back. Now, where had she seen him before?

"True," he said, "but I believe this map is real."

The same sparkle flashed in his eyes, reaffirming that flicker of recognition, but she still couldn't place the sense of familiarity. "What makes you so sure?"

"I've had it all my life." He shrugged and gave a shy smile. "Call me a captain, but I've never been able to make any sense of the damn thing."

With the sword returned to its scabbard, she jerked her head to the women. "Bring him water and extinguish the blaze." She nodded at him. "Let me see the map, Captain."

He reached into his shirt and pulled out a rolled parchment, then handed her the scrap with steady hand and stare.

One of the women brought him a water skin. Taking the container from her hand, he cast her one of his charming smiles and sent the girl off, blushing and giggling. He gulped, liquid trickling down his chin and soaking into his shirt. Judging by what was left of the cloth covering his powerful shoulders, he must have been a captain.

Sirena unrolled the leather scrap and stared at the ink drawing of an island. The map showed no name, in fact there were no words anywhere on the patch and she couldn't figure which way the chart should orient. "It doesn't point to north."

He drew a long breath. "That is why the map is mysterious."

Turning the scrap up-side-down provided no further clues. She rolled the hide and handed the map back to him. "I believe it is false. I know this sea well, but the depiction is most likely someone's imagination. We are returning to our ship. My heading is to Ragusa in two days."

Another grin stretched his lips and narrowed his eyes to blue crescents. "It will be my privilege to be the guest on your ship, Captain…"

She stepped away from him and barked the order. "Back to the boat." He'd find out soon enough, and just what made him presume she'd be the captain?

The fog had cleared by the time they left the smoldering pile. The group climbed into the small craft. Rowing against the current of rolling swells took a lot of effort and the unexpected guest was more than eager to take his place at the oar. Holding onto the rudder, she gawked at him each time he looked away from her. Now it wasn't only his eyes that made her believe he was familiar. It was the way he bit his lower lip and rowed.

As the *Strega* came into view, nestled in the small cove with high rocks, he scrambled to his feet. Craning his neck, he stared. His eyes widened and mouth dropped opened. He turned to her. "Are you the notorious Sirena? She is supposed to be ten feet tall."

"Yes, so I've heard." One hand on the rudder, she cast him a suspicious glance. He didn't react to the discovery of Captain Sirena's existence the way she'd expected. Though she and her pirates were still very much a myth—and she'd prefer the folk tales to remain that way—this man exercised unusual calmness. He must be one of the survivors of the last night's raid. They would talk no doubt. The tales would spring and so would a new ballad or two. Heck, how tall would she get in this song? And then the whole pomp would settle, until the next raid. "Return to rowing."

What should she do with him? The only place men occupied on her ship was the brig, but she couldn't put him in lockup. The other free space would be the cargo hold. Surely the bare planks would be more comfortable than a desolate island and even he could rough it for a couple of days. At least the crew hadn't questioned her about this decision. Yet.

A pirate threw the rope ladder over the starboard. Sirena was the first one to climb up, with their unexpected guest following.

"Cap'n?" Marta's stern look met her on the deck of the *Strega* and filled Sirena with a sense of dread. Even if the quartermaster didn't speak her concern, Sirena felt her disapproval slide over her skin. This must be the first time she saw Marta questioning her superior's decision. "Another prisoner?"

Chapter 6

After days of enduring the splintered wood inside the brig on Gaspar's ship, and sharp rocks on the desolate islet, the sun-warmed deck of the *Strega* soothed Marko's battered soles. The sight of the burly woman, looking down on him from the gallery deck, filled him with a whole new dread. In an instant he recognized her as the one who'd forced Gaspar and his two buffoons to kneel in front of Sirena. The easy way she held the helm showed her experience at sea. She had to be an officer, perhaps a quartermaster.

The tall scowling woman appeared even larger up close. "Is he a prisoner, Cap'n?" She repeated the question in her brusque manner.

"Not a prisoner." Sirena answered after a long sigh, but her shipmate still appeared as if she didn't believe he was only a guest. "I am to meet my youngest brother in two days and need him to get me through the Pila Gate of Ragusa."

"Two days?" With both hands propped on her wide hips, the large female jerked her head toward him. "Long time to keep him around."

Sirena nodded. "It is, but the *Strega* suffered damage in the fight that claimed our..." She paused, her gray eyes slid in his direction, then back to the same woman. "We can use a man's hand."

The ship's officer jerked her head toward him and scanned him as if he was a prisoner. "What to do with him?"

"I don't know." Sirena sounded all but indifferent when she sat at the table, opening the ship's log over the colorful map. "The cargo hold is empty."

At her nonchalant shrug Marko's mouth hung open. "Now wait a second." He stepped hurriedly up to the captain and raised his hands. "I am not cargo. I am—was— the captain of the *Levant*. I sure as hell won't creep into the cargo hold."

Sirena snapped her head up. Those eyes of hers, gray like a reflection of the moon on the calm sea, could freeze a man where he stood. "*Levant,* you said? We caught some news of Gaspar sinking that ship." She straightened. "Were you his prisoner?"

Damn, Gaspar and his men must have bragged about sinking his argosy and the story had spread. No use pretending and carrying on this charade. The girl who'd removed his shackles would recognize him. "Gaspar used the storm as a veil to ambush me. High waves pushed my ship straight to the cliffs. And, yes, he took me as a prisoner. Your women saved me and I am deeply grateful." Arms stretched wide, he spun around to face curious expressions of the gathering crew. With a deep bow, he offered his gratitude and faced the captain again.

"Peculiar that," she crooned with only a slight twitch of her eyebrows, pen poised over the page. She must be used to men bowing to her. "The only prisoners on his ship are his own men who disobeyed him." Slouching over the book in front of her, she continued. *"A precious prisoner."*

He cleared his throat, hoping to drive her attention, but she buried her face in the book. A slow smile crept to his lips. Had she spoken of him as *precious?*

She snapped her head from the page and cocked an eyebrow. "Your gratitude is accepted, now take the cargo hold."

"Don't you have a cabin for me on this ship?" Hands propped on his hips, he studied her, waiting on her answer.

Dark curls met her ample cleavage, clad in a frilly and roomy man's shirt. An intricate small key hung on a long chain, dangled in front of her bosom. A tight black jerkin with golden embroidery and oversized buttons covered her smooth chest. He hadn't caressed a woman's breasts in months, and judging by Sirena's coldness, he wasn't about to anytime soon. What kind of spell gripped him? Since when did one particular woman matter to him? Especially on a ship full of saucy wenches.

With her head bent over the table, Sirena wrote, her quill scratching on the paper. After powdering the ink, she set the leather bound to the side and traced her finger along the detailed markings of the seasoned ox-hide chart. According to Gaspar, the *Strega* had been a military ship before turning colors and would therefore have been equipped with such detailed maps. "You're not in a position to request anything. Marta will show you to—" She paused and one corner of her mouth twitched to a half-smile. "—*your quarters.*"

His muscles tensed as Marta's large palm patted his shoulder. "Take it boy. Or you'll bunk with wenches who had not set their eyes on a man for quite some time, unless they intended to kill him."

Boy? He didn't know if he should take Marta's remark as an insult or a compliment. "The cargo hold is not acceptable."

It had to be his irate tone that caused Sirena to cut him a stern glance. Slamming down a compass, her hands curled into fists, she stepped to him, her nose barely an inch from his. Her cold yet spellbinding eyes locked on him. "Not acceptable, you say? So please, *signore*, enlighten me, what would suit *His Royal Highness?* The captain's suite?"

If it weren't for the anger flashing in her eyes, he'd have reveled in her lavender scent. Holding her challenging stare, he pressed his lips together and gave her a tight smile.

"I thought you'd never offer."

"I didn't offer," she snarled.

But he pretended not to hear her and sauntered past the stunned captain, headed for her cabin. The door shut behind him before Sirena could utter her veto.

Lying on her hammock, he inhaled the faint scent of lavender from Sirena's pillow. Her hard shell had the *Strega*'s crew fooled, but not him. She was a lady. The tough demeanor she put on drove him wild with desire to discover more about her. Beneath her act she harbored an intense passion that needed to be unleashed, the kind that would set his ardor down. She might think he hadn't noticed her studying him in the dinghy. He'd tried to keep his look at the waves swaying the boat, but he felt her gaze on his face each time she fixed those mesmerizing eyes on him.

Sirena couldn't have been a captain for long. The women exchanged puzzled glances with her every order. She should gain their full trust soon or she'd face the prospect of a mutiny. Perhaps if he suggested a friendly fencing competition, the crew of women would cheer for their Captain. Not to mention bring him closer to her.

Fuming with anger Sirena burst in through the door. "What is the meaning of this—*signore*—what is your name?"

He overstated her welcome with his arrogance. Had any of his men acted in such disrespect on his ship, they would have been given the taste of his sword, or flogging at the very least. But he wanted to awaken some emotion in her, even if he'd have to suffer her wrath.

"Marko. Captain in front." With his hands behind his head, he grinned. "You offered me your quarters. And they are—" Tipping his head, he scanned the ceiling planks. "Acceptable."

Thick hands grabbed onto the hanging bunk and she flipped the bed up-side-down. Air was knocked out of his lungs as his body thudded on the floorboards.

Her booted foot pressed on his back stopped his attempt to get on his feet. "Men on this ship stay in the brig, *Captain Marko.* And you are trying your best to earn your place there."

He chuckled softly with her boot still on his back and glanced over his shoulder. Meeting her glare, he stopped. "You wouldn't."

"You don't want to try me."

To his surprise, the pressure of her foot lessened as he continued to chuckle, and she released her hold on him.

"The famous Captain Sirena," he said as he rose from the floor, dusting his hands.

The low ceiling brushed his hair. Her intelligent eyes met his and his amusement ceased as he savored her angelic appearance. Unable to resist the impulse, he reached out to catch a ringlet of her hair between his thumb and forefinger. "The stories of your bravery precede you, but none spoke of your beauty."

"My beauty?" She grimaced and retreated to the open door where she leaned against the solid wood. "Listen, Captain Marko, or whatever you—"

"I love the way your eyes darken to stormy gray when you look at me."

He stepped closer to her. Her words might have said she hadn't had any desire for his flattery, but her parted lips and the soft puff of air that escaped her told him differently. Had his compliment deprived her of words?

"My eyes are not gray. They are...um," she mumbled and dismissed the notion with a wave of her hand, but the blush in her cheeks betrayed her. "Who cares for such nonsense? Besides, I'm sure you flatter all the girls."

Damn. The little captain saw right through him. Yes, he enjoyed quite a reputation among ladies, and many had succumbed to his charms faster than a ship could travel a knot at full tilt. "That is all in the past now. For you, I'm ready to forsake all the others."

Fierce fire flashed in her eyes. "You don't know a thing about me. Listen, I'm here to make you understand. You cannot occupy my quarters."

With one hand placed on the door next to her face, he leaned toward her. "There is no glory in kicking a poor captain out of your cabin, nor is there shame in bunking with me for a night. Or two."

The blush on her cheeks deepened and gave her that irresistible appearance of a yielding maiden. "Who do you take me for, *Captain*? Some saucy wench?"

Stunned by her words, he pulled back. "I hope you are as sharp with a sword as you are with your tongue."

"I can handle a blade just fine." She swiped his arm aside and strutted onto the deck.

He followed her. "Then why don't we settle this with a friendly fencing match?"

At the top of the stairs, she halted and turned to him. "A fencing match?" Her eyes narrowed to thin slits. Propping her hands to her slender hips she drew a long breath, her tanned cleavage, peeked above the delicate fabric of her white shirt.

Rats! A thought of his hands molding her celestial body sent a sharp twinge to his groin. Since the moment he'd seen her, he thought of nothing else. "And to make it fair, I'll even let you use two swords."

"You'll let me?" Her sharp eyes examined his face. "Tell you what, Captain Marko." Exposing her white teeth with her grin, she closed the distance between them in three long strides and unsheathed her cutlass. "I accept your challenge. Draw your weapon." The tip of her sword graced his Adam's apple when she gave him a pitiful smile and purred, "Aw too bad, you are unarmed."

He cast her a sheepish look. How could he challenge her to a duel without his rapier? "I'll have to borrow a sword for this occasion."

"You can have Marta's if you agree to her judging this match."

"Who else?"

The captain's right hand wouldn't be an unbiased referee.

Marta already unsheathed her saber and turned the gold crusted handle to him. "I'm a fair and honest maid, don't you worry overmuch."

The crew gathered quickly and formed a wide circle, taking their seats on the coiled halyards, planks or stairs under the *Strega*'s main mast.

"There's but one rule," Marta grumbled, standing in between him and the woman who turned his mind up-side-down. "Give us one hell of a fight." Taking a long step back, Marta cleared the floor.

His heart pounded. Never before had he fought a pirate or a woman. Sword in each hand, Sirena waited for his first move. Expectation of certain finesse left him when she had not accepted his handshake before the sword fight. Neither had she bowed to him. How foolish of him to hope for the proper etiquette from a corsair. However, that didn't excuse him from neglecting his gentleman's ways. His lips tight, he bowed to her. He swung the blade in front of him, slashing the air. In two swift steps, he closed the distance between them. Sirena crossed her blades over her head and parried his thrust. Her crew cheered.

"I let you have the first one." Stepping back, he assumed the *en garde* crouch waiting on her attack.

"Ha!" She spun on her heel. Her swords slashed inches from his torso, missing the fabric of his already tattered shirt. "You don't have to go easy on me just because I'm a woman."

Marko flexed his neck muscles and staggered backward with her last word. Yes, the magnetic little captain proved in just two moves she could handle the sword. Nonetheless, he'd make the sweetest rebel of the Adriatic Sea dance for this victory.

She seemed tense, but her mocking smile made him wary. The applause broke among their audience. One of them strummed a guitar.

Prancing sideways, Marko and Sirena circled each other. Eyes fixed on him, she swayed her blades. He dodged them, and her swords slammed on the deck's planks. Her short moment of disadvantage gave Marko a chance to strike.

With a flick of his hand, the tip of his sword braced Sirena's wrist. Then he brought the blade right up to her throat. "I'd very much appreciate if you let go of one weapon, *Captain*." He offered her his seductive smile, inclining his head when he made his request.

She winced, releasing her grip of the sword in her left hand. The cutlass thudded on the planks. The crew booed their contempt of his upper hand.

He kicked the weapon aside. "Now the chances are even, I would say." She was a pirate and any good pirate would keep an advantage in reserve until needed.

Sirena's jaw hardened. He made her heat up in anger, all right. Answering her oncoming lateral stroke, he warded off the near slashing of his shoulder. More cheering came from the audience. The guitar kept in rhythm with the fast exchange of sword-strokes. With each of his leaps, she stepped backward blocking his blows. Their weapons crossed in the air. He leaned forward, applying pressure to her blade. Would the pirate captain fight fair until the end? Sweat glistened on her cleavage and clouded his mind. For one brief second, his arm relaxed, his gaze fixed on the key on her heaving chest. Groaning, she pushed back and shoved her foot against his abdomen to kick him away. How could he hope to win when God equipped her with such allure?

Stumbling backward, he lost his balance and went sliding on his behind on the smooth planks. Seeing the opportunity, she raised her hands above her head and charged. He sprung to his feet. She parried. He ducked. A moment of distraction cost her, he took advantage, pressed the tip of his sword to her unguarded flank. She halted and frowned at him before her glance dropped to his blade.

"As it seems, Captain, we'd be sharing the cabin." He panted, gloating.

"Did you forget?" The end of the handle met his forehead delivering a mind-spinning blow before he could straighten. "I'm a pirate."

Pain ripped through his head and traveled to his neck. How could he forget? The same move she'd used on Gaspar. His saber clattered on the planks of the deck and for one long moment all motion stopped. His legs folded underneath him and his body slumped. Darkness surrounded him.

He came to consciousness at the splash of cold water over his head. His head throbbed as if marlinspike, used for separating the strands of rope, raked through his brain. He pressed his palm to his brow.

With her feet wide apart and hands propped on her knees, Marta leaned over him, exposing her blackened teeth with her grin. "He's alive, Cap'n."

"Very well," Sirena's shout came from afar. "He can take the cargo hold."

Spitting the salt water, he took Marta's offered hand and got to his feet.

"If it's any consolation you put up a fair fight." She tapped his shoulder and left.

He flipped his drenched hair off his face, scanning the deck for Sirena. His head still spun from the blow. Standing on the swaying ship made him groggy and he staggered to the side, gripping the ship's railing for support.

"The only time I come near a man is to thrust my blade through him. Did you think I'd let you bunk with me?"

Marko lifted his gaze to the voice dripping with victorious joy. Her feet planted in a wide stance and her hands placed on the banister of the gallery deck, Sirena smirked.

Approaching her, he gave his answer in form of a single nod and a sly grin.

Just as she was about to leave, he wrapped his hand around her wrist. The scratch he'd left on her skin shone a deep scarlet. Giving him an annoyed stare, Sirena tried to wrestle her hand free, but Marko only tightened his hold.

"I need a word with you." He nodded toward her cabin. "In private."

Obviously unhappy about his request, she had no choice but to follow him when he dragged her behind him.

Inside the cabin, Sirena stalked to the opposite side of the room where she leaned against the wall with her arms folded in a defensive manner.

Reminded of Gaspar's shout as he realized Sirena had attacked him a day early than he expected her to, urged Marko to alert her of a possible traitor among her crew. "Can you trust your women?" he asked, closing the door behind him. "I think you may be in danger."

A deep crease appeared on her forehead as her eyebrows drew together. "My women, every single one of them, are ready to lay their very lives for me. How can you accuse them of betrayal? You don't know them like I do."

In one long stride, he closed the distance between them. "You run one tight ship and fight better than many men I know." His finger traced her jaw. "I also know you have enemies." Hands planted on her shoulders, he pulled her closer and dropped his voice to a whisper. "And people are driven by greedy desperation."

Her soft lavender scent enclosed him, tensing him with anticipation when she surrendered to him. His jaw twitched while he struggled not to taste her sun kissed skin, by pressing his lips to her delicate throat.

To his dismay she pushed her elbows to his chest and freed herself from his hold. "As you said, I have a ship to run." She rubbed the side of her neck and opened the door. "There'll be a thing or two a man can do around here. The guns could use a good clean up."

Holding his tongue, he followed her to the deck. He was a captain not a common lubber, but to work up a good sweat would help him to free his mind of the grip she had on him.

Marta strutted up the stairs, biting into an apple. She swiped her forearm across her mouth, mopping trickles of juice. "Cap'n, the valve on the sea-cock is stuck." Bits of chewed fruit spat out of her mouth as she spoke.

"I'll see to it first then take care of guns," he said, searching Sirena's face for approval.

But she kept her eyes on the horizon sprinkled with green islands and nodded. She avoided looking at him. A smug smile stretched his lips.

He helped himself to a piece of fruit from the net hanging on the wall, tossed the apple in the air and caught it behind his back, then bit into the crisp ball. After the slop he'd been forced to down on Gaspar's ship, the sweet taste filled his mouth with pure pleasure. Pirates even ate better than privateers or merchants.

With a twitch of surprise, Marko caught Sirena's whisper when she leaned closer to Marta. "Keep an eye on the crew. We may be harboring a traitor."

"Did he say so?" Marta tilted her chin toward him, her voice laced with ice. She shook her head. "All it took was one man to bring mistrust among us."

Sirena's eyes returned to him. "We can never be too cautious."

Marta sighed. "Aye, Cap'n."

The apple suddenly turning sour in his mouth, Marko scooted down the stairs. It wasn't his intention to bring mistrust among these women. With any luck, Sirena would follow her instincts and be able to find the traitor.

"Captain," Sirena called after him, her voice cool.

He stopped, turning to face her. Hands behind her back and head held low, she gave him a seductive glance from under her lashes.

"Yes, Captain?" Marko took another bite.

She pursed her lips, her shoulders rose as she drew a long breath. "I suppose we can share the cabin."

The half-chewed piece went down hard as he swallowed. "What brought this sudden change of heart?" he said as the acid burned his throat. The realization struck him. They'd share the quarters. Hopefully, she was a deep sleeper, and he'd be able to snoop and find some evidence of his parentage.

"You are right. A captain should not occupy the cargo hold. You can sleep on the floor of my cabin."

"Well, well. I'm glad you accepted my captain's status at last. I'll be pleased to sleep on the planks like any dog."

She glanced left then right, then back at him. "Not a mention of our arrangement to the crew." She nodded fast. "One word and I'll kick you out."

He bowed to her in mock gratitude. "My lips are sealed, my lady."

As it seemed, he too was earning his place on this ship—starting with Marta. He'd need the crew's trust to move freely about. So he'd better make haste if he wanted to find the answers to all his questions before Sirena discarded him—after she used him to pass through the Pila Gates.

Chapter 7

Night breeze flapped the ropes and furled the sales. Propped up with pillows, Sirena sat in her swaying hammock anticipating Marko's return. At the drunken giggling of two females approaching and their staggering steps faltering in front her cabin, Sirena peeked through the tiny window.

"Ladies," Marko slurred, an arm wrapped around each girl. "I must bid you good night."

God's bones, the man was drunk for the second night in the row. What was Marta doing? She knew liquoring up to any degree for no reason was not allowed. Anger burned through Sirena as she lay back on the hammock and turned to her side trying to ignore the scene going on below her window.

Last night, though, he had miraculously sobered up as soon as he had stepped inside her cabin. He had lingered over her while she'd pretended to be fast asleep. Then he'd set to searching her cabin, tip-toeing from one corner to the next. When he'd found the drawers and cabinets locked, he'd finally lain in his blanketed corner. She'd found herself wishing she could snuggle with him. Instead, lulled by the ships gentle rocking and his soft snores, she'd dreamt.

There was no ignoring him tonight. Even drunk, his deep, masculine voice stirred butterflies in her stomach.

"Bunk with us." The girls dropped their voices to an alluring tone. "We promise you, you *will not* be disappointed."

Sirena recognized the owners of the sugar laced voices. The girls had come aboard after they'd worked as whores. Though Sirena had never envied such life, suddenly jealousy ripped her. Those kinds of women knew just how to hook a man and get his undivided attention. Would their guest prove to be a gentleman as he had claimed and decline their invitation? Or take them up on their offers?

"Hmm, I'm sure I wouldn't." Liquid sloshed in the glass bottle and he let out a long sigh. "To my greatest regret, I must turn you down."

"Aw," they crooned.

"But, you said you loved me," a woman screeched.

"He said he loved *me*," the other retorted.

"Ladies, please. You must've heard me wrong."

"Where will you sleep then? With our Captain?" Amazement laced the crew woman's voice and a moment later all three burst into gales of laughter.

"The Queen of Ice?" His drunken roar filled the air. "The thought sends cold shivers through me."

Deep anger simmered in Sirena, and her chest tightened, as she prepared for a crushing of said gent when he entered her cabin. Why had he battled her so ferociously to share her lodging only to spend his nights in arms of the experienced girls? The fault was hers, she realized. She had asked him to keep their little arrangement a secret.

When the two sets of clumsy footsteps and slurred voices faded, the door to her stateroom opened. Sirena peeked through her lashes. Marko stepped inside. Standing tall, he tugged on the end of his tattered shirt. In two quiet steps he closed the distance to the small table where she'd left the old captain's journal opened on the page with the riddle. He raised the low-burning oil lamp. Slouched and frozen, he stared at the words for a long time. His fingers traced the letters over and over.

He extinguished the light and darkness swallowed the cabin. With a loud groan, he lowered onto the floor. "I know you are awake."

In spite of the fact she was still miffed at his conduct and wasn't in a mood to converse with him, she was glad he was aware she only pretended to be asleep.

"I apologize for my hurtful words," he whispered. "But I agreed to keep this agreement between us a secret."

His gentlemanly apology melted her anger, and she sighed. Kicking the covers off, she sat up. Her hammock swayed, and she grabbed hold of the fringe. "You don't need to justify your actions to me. About the riddle—it strikes me that you appear to know its meaning."

The silhouette of his broad shoulders loomed in the darkness when he braced himself on his elbows. "I knew you left the book out on purpose. Seems familiar, but I'm not sure, or perhaps I'm a bit drunker than I thought. Go to sleep, Captain," he said, pulling a shabby blanket over his head. "Tomorrow is the last you'll see of me."

She lowered her head to the pillow. Though she could hardly wait until her xebec was rid of a male, sadness gripped her at the thought of Marko leaving. But he couldn't stay. She'd never asked but assumed the reason he wanted to go to Ragusa was to get commissioned as a captain of another ship. After all, he dedicated his life to sea.

Besides, when did she lose her head over this man? She had been and still was married to a man before God, and even if death had separated them, she had to remain chaste.

But that had been Carmen's life so long ago, when she'd lived enslaved by society, and her father's honor had been measured by her purity to the point of not letting her leave the house on her own. She had cast that Carmen away the day she boarded the *Strega,* and perhaps it was time to truly let go of her.

Bathed in morning sun, the ship's deck warmed the soles of Sirena's boots. Ropes and timber creaked on gentle swells. She squinted against the silver specks glistening on the sea and wrung water out of her freshly washed hair. Brushing the wet strands off her face, she caught a glimpse of Marko a few feet away. His muscles bulged as he lifted a cask over his head. The water cascaded down his body, caressing every well-defined muscle, soaking into his black breeches. Giggling pirates confirmed she wasn't the only one enjoying the sight.

For the past two days he'd kept busy repairing the rigging and sails. He had spent his evenings singing and drinking with the women. It was apparent by their quick acceptance he had become one of the crew members. Younger girls even started to pay attention to their appearance. Had he taken any of them? If he had left a trail of bastards wherever he went, it wouldn't surprise her. A man of such presence could seduce a stone.

But that should be the least of her concerns. Why did she feel such a prick of jealousy? The few short hours of each night before the dawn he had spent in her room, confirmed her suspicions—he avoided her. Why wouldn't he? She had abolished him to the floor.

Stone was what her heart had turned into. Marko's musky scent drifted to her on a breeze and woke her painful memories. Her late husband had loved her. And while maybe her affection had not been forthcoming in an overt way, she had loved him in her own fashion. Yet each time she had looked at him she never felt that tremor in her soul her mother had spoken of when she talked about Papa.

Marko's soapy hands on his torso ceased washing. He turned his head to her, but did not smile. Nor did he seem surprised or displeased by her stare. He studied her as if he was able to read her thoughts. His enigmatic blue eyes never left hers. A perfect, beautiful smile tugged his lips. Wet blond curls fell to his shoulders and called out to her to smooth them away. Enslaved by his piercing eyes, she swallowed the lust in her throat.

The call of a seagull caused her to push back her memories and Marko's hold on her. It was time for her to transform into a refined lady, not to reminisce or occupy her mind with nonsense. Today she'd use him to take her through the Pila Gates of Ragusa, and he would be free to go on his merry way. But she had to admit, the crew's attitude toward her had changed since the fencing match. It might be she proved to them their Captain was capable of letting loose to have some fun. The women seemed to accept her and took her orders with zeal now.

Feet resting on the wooden railing, rocking in her chair, with one hand on the helm, Marta nodded to her. "Need help getting into your frock?"

"I'll manage." Sirena strode past her, wiping her hair, and entered her cabin.

She wiggled trying to adjust the tight corset then smoothed the silk of her rose dress, yanking on the fabric to cover her cleavage. Good grief, this attire was for a harlot not a widow who should spend the rest of her life clad in a bombazine gown. But there wasn't one of those mourning dresses on board. How many years since she stuffed her ribcage into one of these lace-up cages? It felt good to bathe, but this gown choked the air out of her lungs. Who could wear this enclosure and call it fashion? For once, she was glad to be a pirate clad in man's shirtsleeves and breeches and not a lady who had to endure this torture her entire life. Suddenly, the itch and discomfort of clothes washed in salt water didn't seem bad at all. However, seeing her brother would be worth an hour of pain. What would he make of her appearance? Her mane of curls cascading down her neck, she pinned a small hat with two silk roses to her hair.

That should do.

The crinoline, long chemise, and two layers of petticoats presented a challenge stepping over the high sill of the doorway. As soon as she freed the multiple hems that had snagged in the doorframe, she staggered onto the deck, and into Marko's arms. His mouth dropped open as his eyes fixed on her ample bustier, he blew a low whistle. "You could almost pass for a lady."

The look he gave her sent tremors of desire down her arms. As he steadied her, locking his gaze with hers, warmth rushed to her cheeks.

"Almost, but not quite," he said with a naughty smile, pulling the brim of her hat carefully forward so it would hang slightly into the view of her right eye. "Now you look perfect."

His warm breath brushed her face. The glitter in his blue gaze hypnotized her. He leaned forward and Sirena had the distinct feeling he would kiss her.

"Why, thank you," she whispered, taking a shaky step backward.

From a safe distance, she scanned him from his boots to his face, stopping briefly at his casually opened shirt. Washed and dressed in a proper sailor's attire, he too resembled a gentleman. The trimmed beard accentuated his sensuous lips. She shivered with the thought of his mouth devouring hers.

The familiarity she'd felt around him since the first day had grown even stronger, yet she still couldn't place where she'd seen him before. "I see the women provided you with fresh clothing."

"Yes," he said, casting a glance down. "Your crew is quite versatile. Who knew one of them had this?" His eyes roamed over her while he nodded. "The dress becomes you. Many of the finest lassies would kill for such an outfit."

"Really?" She arched an eyebrow. "This dress will become my death. I can hardly breathe. And this is supposed to be the latest fashion?" The women had grabbed the dresses in one of the raids as if the silk frocks were hot cakes.

"The very latest." Leaning close to her, he whispered, "I thought your hair was black, but now that you washed all the grime out, it shimmers like honey." Curling an end around his finger, he pressed the strand to his nose and drew a long breath. "Lavender. Silk. Very beautiful, indeed."

Whether he'd meant this as an honest compliment or one of his flatteries, his words rushed another wave of heat to her cheeks. What would a man know? Sun drying the fragrant plant, indigenous to this area had been women's jobs for centuries. "I think you are getting a whiff from the dress. The dried flowers are kept to ward off moths."

The scent had opposite effect on him, as it seemed. She stepped to the open starboard railing and glanced down the rope ladder at the dinghy. "You should preoccupy yourself with less frivolous things than the color of my hair. Rowing this boat on your own, for instance."

"I can handle the boat." He lowered to the dinghy and held his hands out until she descended the ladder, but dropped them to his sides when she didn't reach for his help.

Sirena raised her glance to Marta, standing on the deck. "I shall return after the change of the guard."

"Aye, Cap'n." Arms folded over her bosom, the large woman nodded. "God's speed."

With one push against the ship's bulk, Marko had set them on the short journey to Ragusa. "Don't worry. The cliffs hide the *Strega* well."

Sirena shifted uneasily, unsure if it was the tight dress or Marko's wink that caused the rush of heat between her thighs. Lightning strike her, there was just no way to sit comfortably in this frock. She uttered a quiet cuss, sending him into rolls of laughter.

"How do you know your way around the ships so well?" He pulled on the oars. Under the rolled-up sleeves of his shirt, his biceps flexed and flooded her with additional lust.

She snapped open her fan and glanced at the green land, stark against the clear blue sky. "I'm from Sylba."

"Ah, I see." Another stroke of the oars propelled the boat farther and tightened his muscles. "The island of ship owners and captains. It's in your blood."

She gave him half a smile, speeding up her fan. "I'm the youngest of four. All my brothers are captains as was my father and his father before him."

"Your father didn't see to marry you to one?" With a jerk of his head, he flicked the blond curl off his face, but the light breeze of *Maestral* blew it back.

"No," she sighed, exasperated at her twitching hand that wanted to smooth his curl back into his low ponytail. "Each evening my mother, as my grandmother had before her, sat by the window and stared at the sea, waiting for the sails of her husband's ships to appear on the horizon, never knowing if he'd return. I didn't want to spend my life like that."

Pursing his lips, he nodded. "The sea is cruel. What it takes, it rarely returns. Neither ships nor sailors."

"I married a mill owner, hoping I'd grow old with him." Her voice trailed off, talking about her late beloved still caused her pain. "He died protecting my honor."

Marko's face turned grave. "The Duke's men?"

She nodded and cast a long glance toward the horizon. "Due to drought our crops were scarce that year." With a hard swallow, she continued. "When they came for collection, we could only give them twenty barrels of oil instead of fifty." Her breath quivered "They accused us of hiding provisions to help pirates, but they offered to overlook it if I gave myself to them...freely. My husband grabbed his sword and slashed the first two men. I—" Unable to continue, she shook her head and averted her glance at the floorboards. Resurrecting the memories stirred her guilt even deeper.

Marko stopped rowing. The boat rocked on the gentle swells. A deep crease formed between his perfect eyebrows. "Your husband stood up to them. He died protecting what he loved the most. You. If it was me, I wouldn't do anything different, even if I didn't stand a chance against them."

She blinked fast to keep the burning tears from spilling out. It could have been Marko's words of understanding, but talking about her husband had lessened her pain. Marko didn't need to know the rest. Only a few people knew about her son. And she had to keep it that way to ensure the safety of Nikola and his foster family.

Marko resumed rowing, pulling harder on the left oar to slant the boat toward the coast. She fumbled with her fan as an excruciating silence stretched between them until they passed through one of the three enormous arches of a large arsenal.

Seagulls encircled the wide harbor nestled between high defensive walls. Ships and boats of all shapes and sizes were tied to the piers and bobbed lazily on the water.

After tying Sirena's dinghy to the dock, Marko held his hand out to her. His forehead wrinkled when she placed two coins in his hand. "No need to pay me, my lady," he mocked, but she quirked her eyebrows and flicked her head, indicating a man in a bright red hose, a waist length, ribboned doublet, and velvety hat adorned with pheasant feathers who stood to the right of him. Marko straightened and turned to the clerk.

The man extended his gloved hand. "Two Ragusan Libertines for docking here."

"I barely finished tying the boat." The silver coins clinked when Marko placed them in the paper pusher's hand. "I see the officials are very efficient."

The man closed his fingers around the money and left. His breeches bounced at his knees with each ponderous step.

"God damn docking fees," Marko grumbled, extending his hand to Sirena.

"What are you complaining about? The money was mine."

Leaning on his strong arm, she steadied her footing on the rocking boat. With her free hand she raised the multiple hems of her skirts, stepped onto the dock, and wobbled.

He hastily wrapped his free arm around her waist, steadying her. "Easy there. It will take a minute until your land legs return."

"There's nothing wrong with my legs." She pulled back, but not before his sea fresh scent stirred simmering heat below her belly. Blistering barnacles, this was a trap she must not fall prey to. Why did she keep ending up in his arms? As she smoothed the wrinkles of her dress, she avoided looking at him.

He nudged her with his elbow and cocked his head, encouraging her to loop her arm around his. Reluctantly, she slid her gloved hand through the loop his arm made. His firm bicep budged under her palm. At the end of the dock, where the long pier met the lime-stone promenade, he halted and stared at her.

"There is Pila Gate." He pointed at the stone passage to the city. White flags with red trim and letters LI-BER-TAS flapped on the breeze. Two guards in colorful breastplates and oversized red berets manned the lowered drawbridge.

Marko resumed walking. She licked her lips, blinking fast, trying to steady her pounding heart. With her gaze fixed on the statue of Saint Blaise, the patron saint of the Ragusa, at the top of the arched way, she silently prayed no one would recognize her in this place.

Weapons clinked as the armed guards crossed their halberds in front of her and Marko. One of them peered at Marko. "What business do you have in the Republic of Ragusa?"

"We are here to pay the taxes." Tightening his hold on her hand, Marko's knuckles whitened. Yet he maintained the same frank tone of voice.

The watchman wiggled his nose, switching his glance from Marko to Sirena and back again. After an excruciating long gaze, he pulled his weapon close to his side. His counterpart followed suit. Marko led Sirena through the complex of multiple doors connected by the stone bridge.

"Relax and act normal. No one is paying any attention to us." He paused by the edge of the outer wall overlooking the harbor. . The Minčeta Tower dominated above the imposing Fort Bokar—both symbols of the unconquerable city

"The man I'm seeking serves on the frigate over there." She jerked her head in the direction of *The Four Winds* docked in the city's shipyard on the other side of the bay. "Your duty is fulfilled and so is mine. With thanks, I bid you farewell."

Hard as she tried to mask it, sadness edged her voice all the same. After two days, his cocky demeanor had grown on her. The dress felt even tighter around her neck and ribs. Would she ever see him again? Most likely not, and it was for the best. Once he disappeared into the crowd she should rejoice, not mourn his departure.

Sorrow reflected in his deep blue eyes. "May all saints watch over you." His small smile broke her heart.

They faced each other in complete silence. She should say something to make him stay, but what? Besides, all she could offer him was a pirate's place on her crew, but he was a captain. He would want to command the ship.

He reached inside his shirt and pulled out a tattered parchment. His big hands ripped the aged sheepskin in two pieces, he handed her one. "Here, take it. This way neither of us can find the treasure without the other."

She shook her head and arched her eyebrows. "I told you, these kinds of maps are of no interest to me." Nor did she have time trying to make sense of vague drawings. "I thought you would never part with it."

"I had this map for as long as I can remember. All the time I have had an urge to keep it a secret. Don't ask me how he knew, but Gaspar was after this. I cannot afford it to fall into the wrong hands again." After shoving one part of the chart in her small drawstring bag, he gave her hand a gentle squeeze. "I trust you." He bowed then took a quick leave.

As if deciphering old captain's riddles weren't enough. But if he was ready to protect the scrap with his life, it must be of some importance.

"Captain," she called before he reached the other side of the street.

He stopped and turned. One arm behind his back, he approached her with slow steps.

"I trust you wouldn't tell anyone of our existence. I prefer to stay a myth."

"Professional courtesy, Captain." He shrugged. "Besides, who'd believe me?"

She swallowed hard. "Many, I'm afraid."

"Fear not. It would destroy my reputation as a captain if I started believing in fairy tales." After a long glance, that sent prickles through her, he took his leave, striding away. Her eyes stayed on him until he disappeared into winding passageways.

"I would recognize your old dinghy anywhere, Carmen," said Carlo's deep voice from behind.

To hear her real name felt strange. Turning to him, she raised her head toward the dark bearded man. A smile stretched across her lips as she ran her hand on his soft facial hair. "When did you grow this?"

His big hand covered hers. "I started the day I took my first captain's post." A proud smile lit his face then vanished as his eyes scanned over her. "I am glad to see you out of mourning, but do you think this dress appropriate?"

"Don't you know it's the latest fashion?" Silk swished around her legs as she spun.

"Lord, what is this world coming to?" He chuckled and took her by her elbow. "Was that Cousin Jakov? I didn't know he enlisted in the Navy. I'd like a word with him."

"Enlisted?" Sirena's heart pounded. Marko wore a sailor's uniform. She must go on with this charade. In all these years existing as a pirate, lying to her brother had never come easy. "Oh, yes. I suppose he did."

"What men-of-war does he serve on?" Enthusiasm filled Carlo's voice. "I may know the captain and can pass on a recommendation."

"I, um—" she rubbed the side of her neck, heat waves flooded her and burned her cheeks, "I—don't know, he never mentioned it. Cousin Jakov has grown, but he is still like the wind. Who can catch him? As soon as we docked, he took off for the market. I'll tell him you send your greetings." She smiled at her youngest brother. In an instant, she forgot her uncomfortable situation, and her tight outfit, and became the lady she had been raised to be. The pirates' Captain Sirena seemed to fade away with the sight of Carlo. "It's so good to see you again, brother. It was too long this time."

He hauled her into a bear hug. The kind that always flooded her with peace. "By God, yes. Over two years, I reckon." The brass buttons on his sober captain's uniform glistened as he took her by her elbow. "Let's stroll along Stradun Corso and pretend we're still the young children who played hide and seek in the meadows. Tell me, how is my nephew?"

Thank god Carlo kept a strolling pace. Her pirate's boots would show under her dress with his usual marching strides. It wouldn't be good to reveal what was underneath her skirts in the middle of the Ragusa's main street lined with colorful awnings, shading the windows of small shops. The smell of freshly baked pastries made her mouth water. "Nikola is growing big and strong and with each day resembles his father more." At least she didn't lie about her boy. Odd, the truth deepened her pain. "Any news of our two older brothers?"

He nodded. "They fare well. I met with Miro last Christmas. He passed along the news from Paul, who had made it to a full captain now. They both miss you and send their love."

"Will any of you be taking a wife soon?" She shot him a teasing grin. His face reddened as always when she asked personal questions, but this time he lowered his head sheepishly. She winced. "You have a girl."

He halted, turning to her, his smile widened. "Veronica accepted my proposal of marriage."

"I always knew it would be her. You two are made for each other." Sirena wrapped her arms around him and leaned her head on his shoulder. "She is a lucky girl. Make her happy."

"It is my duty as her future husband." Taking his sister's hand in his, he continued walking. "I did not expect to see you here today. Have you not heard of the latest attack?"

Uneasiness made her tense. "No, where? When?"

"Survivors said it was Sirena and her crew of the *Strega*." His voice carried a hint of disbelief. "I've heard 'the *Strega*'s pirates did it,' more times than I can count. Every time misfortune strikes, someone uses that exact line as an excuse."

She rolled her eyes, releasing her breath. Her brother would not blindly believe in folk tales. "Sirena or not, I had to see you. There are so few of our family left. Our late mother, bless her soul, always said not to lose touch with one another."

Survivors. Could Gaspar be one of them? If he lived, he'd gather a force unknown to these waters and set out to find her, knowing his old adversary had died. Regretfully, her few short moments where she could be her old self, passed in a blink of an eye. "Humbug," she murmured.

Carlo snapped his head toward her. "What?"

"Hm?"

"You said something."

"Oh, it's nothing." She squeezed his arm to steady her voice. "Just thinking of that nice gown in the seamstress shop."

Chiming a low chuckle, he leaned toward her. "Don't you remember the porcelain doll Papa brought you from Venice? You stripped her of her dress and wrapped her in rags, then named her Sirena and pretended she was a pirate."

"How could I forget my favorite toy?" In an instant, warmth filled her chest from the fond memories. There were so few. Twenty years ago, she had merely pretended to be a pirate's captain. Who knew? Maybe in some strange way, her imagination had sealed her destiny. By her seventeenth summer, she had refused all of the ship captains who came asking for her hand in marriage. Her family had looked upon her with disdain when she had finally accepted a proposal from a miller.

"All the captains are commissioned to capture this Sirena and bring her to swift justice, but I know we'll be chasing the wind." Carlo cast a cheerful smile. "I am glad Cousin Jakov is with you. Nonetheless, brigands will attack ships. Do be careful on your voyage back."

Justice? There would be no fairness or mercy in her trial. "I can swing a sword. You gave me my first for my eighth birthday and then you taught me how to use it."

"Until you got better than me," he said, chuckling. "And then I convinced Papa to get you a proper teacher."

Fond memories brought a smile to her lips. She patted her brother's forearm. "You are right, brother. Chasing after this...Sirena is nothing but waste of time." One day her luck would run out. She would rather die in battle than see disappointment on her brothers' faces when she was brought before the authorities.

"I must return to my duties." From his belt, he untied a cash purse and placed the drawstring bag in her gloved hand. "For Nikola, I know it takes a good bit of coin to raise a child on your own." Closing her fingers around the bag, he said, "And for the dress you saw in the shop. Make sure no one sees you with the money."

"Carlo," she shook her head, refusing the purse. "You really shouldn't—"

He put his hand up. "I must. You work hard tending olive trees. It shows on your sun beaten face and I'm sure there'd be callouses on your palms under those gloves. "

She fell silent. He was right about one thing. She had been working hard, but not in the fields. After she had run away with a bundle in her arms, stopping one last time to glance at her husband's bloodied body slumped on the ground, their orchards and mills had been confiscated. Through the folks who'd hid her and Nikola, she had come in contact with Antun and eventually, the pirates.

Bristles of Carlo's beard brushed her cheek when he kissed her. "Fare well, sister."

Tears stung her eyes. She pushed them back and hurried on a fast trot to the dinghy. Her family had endured too much pain, too much loss to this sea. And all the crying over the hardships hadn't helped so far. The *Strega* and her crew waited.

Chapter 8

The bells from the church tower of Saint Nicholas, shadowing houses with red roof tiles, tolled the noon hour. The lime-stone paved streets of Ragusa were covered with cavaliers chatting with the ladies and their governesses dressed in starched black attire. Aproned servant girls, pages, and peddlers bustled around. Scholars in their square caps with scrolls in their hands debated in the deep shade of the old buildings.

Staying well out of Sirena's sight, Marko followed her rose silk gown through the busy city. Never before had saying farewell to a woman pierced his heart. If he hadn't known the very poised man whose candid expressions accentuated the family resemblance was her brother, jealousy would have ripped him to shreds. What kind of spell had she cast over him? He barely knew her. A nagging tug deep in his stomach urged him to find out more about this extraordinary woman. She could be the one who'd save him from getting caught in a rotten marriage.

Months ago Marko had set sail to Piraeus not only to deliver bales of silk but to postpone his wedding to Contessa De Montagne. Blessings upon the man who had raised him, not some pirate as Gaspar had stated. However, the damsel his father was forcing him to marry had passed her prime, and despite all her expensive gowns, she was unattractive. Marko didn't care to advance their family status from Nobile to Conte, but the prospect of the title blinded his father. The man couldn't see the bargain contained settling the Conte's substantial gambling debts.

Taking on piracy and living as a renegade held more appeal to Marko than becoming a Conte and a husband to a woman he had no desire for. He far preferred to sail the seas forever with Captain Sirena by his side. The woman shook him to his very core. Even the mere thought of the prospect of being with her for the rest of his life sent warmth to his chest.

But could a ship have two captains? A minor wrinkle he'd smooth out later. As it seemed his heart had made its choice. If life had taught him anything, it was never to settle for someone else's dreams. Even if his dream had vowed to love, cherish, and honor another man, till death had torn them apart. So it had and judging from her reaction, she would never stop blaming herself for the tragedy. What if her heart still belonged to her late husband? Marko halted when Sirena and her companion stopped by The Large Onofrio's fountain. With his back flat against the sun warmed smooth stone wall of the building, he peered around the corner. The man-of-war captain gave her a peck on her cheek and took his leave. Sirena straightened and stared after her brother for some time then climbed two marble steps to the round edge of the well. She pulled a coin from her purse. As per tradition, she placed a kiss on the Seguin to better her chance at good luck and flicked the money into the water pouring from the mouth of twelve carved masked faces. A long sigh escaped her and she scurried along the paved street washed in the early afternoon sunshine.

Keeping his eyes on her while staying out of her sight presented a challenge, but he couldn't afford to lose her in the crowd. At the top of Stradun Street, where the dome of the imposing baroque Cathedral of Assumption rose behind the houses at the end of the plaza, she turned toward the harbor and left the main city.

Great sea beastie, he'd struck a real booty by a sheer dumb luck. Never had he believed nor expected he'd meet the real Sirena and come across the *Strega* and her crew. The women's sad faces as he left the deck would stay imprinted in his memory forever. He missed them already. Would he ever get over their salted sardines soaked in olive oil and the best grog he had sampled? Even if the meals came served on the tarnished pewter, instead of fine china, they tasted better in such good company. His mouth watered. But it was the image of Sirena's gray eyes, bouncing curls, and her appealing bosom that urged him not to let her out of sight, ever. The way water had soaked into her chemise and molded the thin fabric to her breasts would not leave his thoughts.

Had he not lost his ship, crew and cargo, and then gotten captured, none of this would have happened. Nor would he have found out his parents had been pirates. He still couldn't fully grasp the fact. In two days of snooping around and talking to the crew he'd discovered there, in fact, had been an older captain Sirena who had passed away. Could that woman have been the one who had given birth to him? Possibly. While Sirena believed the words in the leather bound volume were just some riddle, he'd known them as a lullaby. The melody the funny dressed lady had sung to him many years ago was forever etched in his memory.

This new Sirena had saved his life not once, but twice. Had she not sunk Gaspar's brigantine, he would have been hoisted to the top of a main mast. And without water, he wouldn't have survived on that tiny islet for long. If it had been a navy ship that rescued him, he'd have to repay them and show his gratitude by serving for life.

But his rescue came at a price. He was a ship-less, crewless captain in a foreign city with no means to send word of his welfare to his people on a faraway island. In this situation he wouldn't be able to defend himself against a couple of muggers. He followed Sirena out of the city through the same gate. After she crossed the drawbridge, she headed for the dinghy. She would not get away without him. A quick scan of the street to make sure no men of law patrolled and he set out to stop the woman who possessed half of his map and all of his heart.

"Psst, Cap'n." A hiss coming from the darkness caused him to halt and turn in the direction of the voice. Out of the alley stepped a skinny man in tattered clothes and a long beard.

Marko's eyes widened at the sight of his quartermaster. "Rocco." He embraced the half-starved man. "Bless the Saints, you survived."

"Barely. Got picked up by fishermen." Rocco patted Marko's shoulders, raking a long glance over his navy uniform. "I knew Lady Luck was on your side. You didn't enlist?"

Marko grunted, dismissing Rocco's assumption with a headshake. If Rocco knew this time the Lady Luck was a real lady, he would not believe him.

"Long story." He patted his mate's back. "At least you are not a pirate or worse, serving on the man-of-war."

A peak around the corner confirmed the realization of his fortune. Sirena stepped inside her boat. He faced Rocco again and spoke fast. "Did anyone else survive the ambush?"

Rocco pointed to the stone house at the end of the alley crowded with buildings. "There are a few of us, but it's no use, Cap'n. We have no ship to set sail."

"There may be a ship." Marko pressed his finger to his lips and lowered his voice. "If we act fast."

Rocco gave him a suspicious glance. "Unless you already commissioned a ship, you're not planning to steal one, are you? We'd never get away with theft in this tightly run harbor."

"No," Marko grabbed him by the worn sleeve and dragged him along the narrow alley. "It's the *Strega*."

"W—what?" Rocco's laugh bounced off the walls in the narrow ally. "By all respect, Cap'n, but have you lost your precious mind? That ship is a myth."

"Shhhh, keep your voice down," Marko hissed and turned to Rocco. One could never know whose prying ears listened behind the half closed shutters. "It's real and so is her captain. Now go gather the crew and meet me outside the defensive walls."

Rocco tapped his finger on Marko's forehead. "Have seagulls picked your brain?" He took a long step back. "If what you say is true, the men will never serve under a woman, nor would they become pirates."

Such insolence would be met with at least five lashes of his cat-of-nine-tails, but without the ship and with the crew reduced to mere few men, Rocco was forgiven. "If I said it's true, it's true. No time to debate. Go!"

Marko ran toward the dock just to see Sirena weigh anchor. Her tight dress crumpled around her waist when she sat down and began to stroke the water with the oars. In the silk outfit she wouldn't make very fast progress.

He darted for the dock and leaped off the edge. Before he took the plunge, her eyes widened as she froze leaning forward to pull on the oars. Immersed in the sea, he was invigorated by the salt water cooling off his sweaty body. Surfacing, he shook the water from his hair and face. In two short strokes, he approached her dinghy and grabbed onto a gunwale.

The disbelief reflected on her pretty face was soon replaced by anger. "You sure know how to make a spectacle," she hissed.

"Drunken sailors tumble in all the time." He took a chance with his actions, and she certainly didn't need any attention drawn to her. An arm stretched to her, he pleaded. "Will you help me in or just stare at me?"

Sirena swung an oar toward him. He clutched the smooth wood and clambered into the rocking boat. The smell of seaweed and crabs, he had become accustom to, welcomed him. With both arms stretched wide, he gestured toward the harbor. "See, no one paid any heed to us."

Without breaking their locked gazes, she leaned forward. Her hand stopped above her right buskin. Most likely where she hid the dagger. "What do you want now, Captain?"

Asking a pirate for help wouldn't be easy, but he had no choice. The short moment of softness he had noticed at their parting could have fooled him into thinking she wanted him to stay. Not one to be in mercy of anyone, let alone a woman who could slit his throat in a heartbeat, he gulped. "Your ship."

She sprang to her feet, rocking the boat anew. Her deep laughter filled him with dread. "Never."

"Just hear me out." His drenched clothes clung to him, while beads of water dripped into his eyes. Twisting, he turned to the dock. A quick head count confirmed seven surviving men of his crew kept to the line of houses as they hastened toward the city's sea walls. He faced her again and swallowed. "There are a few of my men who survived

Gaspar's raid on the *Levant*. We need a safe passage to Vis. There I have my other ships. Your reward will be hefty."

Gathering her skirts around her slender hips, she returned to her seat. "What kind of reward?"

His shoulders relaxed. At least she listened to him, but what could be lucrative enough to a pirate? "Anything your heart desires."

One of her brows quirked, she chewed on the corner of her lip. If he knew her by now, this meant she was thinking hard. She surely must have a wish in her heart.

"You say 'a few men.' How many exactly?" Her voice carried a demand he wasn't used to hearing from a woman.

Captivated by her eyes, he absently replied. "Including me? Eight."

Annoyance flashed across her heart shaped face. "Eight men on a ship full of women will wreak havoc. Can't you commission another ship?"

"I can, but that would put me in the rank of mere skipper." Proud determination laced his voice. "A captain needs his ship and his men." He reached for the oars and turned the drifting boat around. The dinghy glided through the calm harbor waters with his rowing. "Will you help us? We'll be more than glad to take the cargo hold."

She shifted as if in discomfort. Her chest rose and fell with each long breath. Damn his hot blooded groin. In the midday sun, the silk shimmered across her bosom like spun gold. Someday soon, he'd fill her wardrobe with gowns of all kinds and grant her every wish. But taking down her citadel would require a lot more than pretty dresses. The woman who'd put his skills of seduction to an ultimate test had finally come his way, but as it seemed, it was him who had succumbed under her coldness.

"The rule on my ship is no men." She snapped her fan open and swatted a fly. "I'll put it before the crew. Just get us beyond the harbor before the guardsmen suspect anything."

With a hard pull on rows, he propelled the boat faster. "You will not regret this."

"Halt," the guard on the long pier shouted after them.

Marko swung the rows backward, causing the dinghy to stop and rock on the waves the boat had created.

The guard examined him, sending cold shivers up Marko's spine. Reaching inside his shirt, Marko squeezed the pommel of his knife. Sirena exchanged a glance with him and leaned forward, her hand stopped above her right buskin.

"Shouldn't you report to your captain?" Iron clinked as the guard pointed his halberd at Marko.

"I'm trying." Marko sneered. "My old ship is decommissioned and I must report to a new post on a ship anchored in another harbor. I even tumbled into the sea in haste and, frankly, you're in my way."

"In that case," the watchman said, straightening his red beret. "Be on your way."

Marko exhaled a relieved breath. The guard could have asked to see the proof of payment of their taxes, as they had claimed as their reason had been to come to the Republic of Ragusa. His hands clutching the oars, Marko pulled hard on the left and turned the dinghy in the direction of steep cliffs.

Puzzlement reflected on her expression as her jaw tightened. "You are very quick to spin a lie. Should I trust you?"

"My dear lady," he said in a husky tone, "*you* can always trust *me*."

Once out of the sight of any guards, Marko hoisted a small sail. After a short trip around the high defensive walls and battling the steady swells caused by the *Maestral*, he spotted the waiting group. Waving his arm, he signaled for them to swim out.

Men in tattered gray shirts and breeches braved the waves and waddled into the sea, swimming toward the dinghy. One by one, they grabbed onto gunwales and swiftly vaulted onboard, causing water to pool inside the small craft. Sirena raised the multiple hems of her dress to prevent them from dipping in the water. Wide eyed, the men pulled seaweed off their wet uniforms while their gaze switched between Sirena and Marko.

Rocco finally turned to him. "This is the pirate?"

"Don't you be fooled by her beauty," Marko assured him. "She is all pirate, from her pretty little nose to the dagger in her boot." Stroking his beard, he gave her a wink as a sign of his adoration.

Sirena's eyes traveled from one man to the next. Her silence and arched eyebrows made Marko's mind and body uneasy. If it wasn't for a slight blush in her cheeks, the woman would be impossible to read. When would she say something?

Chapter 9

Sirena reached the top of the rope ladder and climbed onboard. Not wanting to see Marta's face crisscrossed with fine wrinkles and a frown confronting her, she averted her gaze to the *Strega*'s freshly scrubbed deck glistening in the afternoon sun.

"Cap'n?" Marta croaked, shoving her face inches from Sirena's. "It's my understanding we got rid of one man, not bring him back with seven more."

Sirena leveled her gaze at Marta's disgruntled expression, which she'd anticipated, and then slowly glanced down at the dinghy tied to the ship, bobbing on steady waves. Marko and his remaining crew waited for their destiny. Some chewed their nails, but all had their eyes fixed on her. Tugging on the high collar of her dress, Sirena turned to Marta. The gown seemed to get tighter by the minute. "They are in peril and seek our help. I will declare this to the crew. First I must change from this...costume."

She scurried to her cabin and stopped by the door. Marko's comforting scent had faded, replaced by the smell of confinement and loneliness. A miserable feeling swept over her and she shuddered at the thought of the old captain spending her days alone in this room. Not the kind of destiny she'd foreseen for herself. The voluminous petticoats swished around her as she hurriedly changed. Her crew might not take her seriously dressed like this when she announced her decision.

The struggled to untie, unlace, unbutton, and scramble out of the corset, crinoline, and the chemise seemed never-ending. No wonder the ladies couldn't do this alone day after day. Glad to be free of the ridiculous dress and back in her pirate uniform of brown breeches taken in at the waist to fit her, shirtsleeves, and black jerkin, she stepped out, drawing a deep breath of salty air. The clamor of women reached her from the lower deck and tightened her stomach all over again, as if she'd never gotten out of her corset.

Marta stood in front of the helm, her hands in the air. "Settle down. Wait for the Cap'n to explain."

Accommodating these men meant violating the women's main pirate's code. Twirling a strand of her hair tied in a low ponytail and secured with a red bandana, Sirena turned her head. Eight men huddled next to the starboard railing. How could she bring them upon her crew? Marko's blue eyes met hers and worsened her perplexing situation. How could she let him down?

Marta turned to Sirena with a quizzical look and whispered, "The women suspected what is going on. I had to tell them, Cap'n."

"I take it the crew is not fond of my decision."

"I think they are. The problem is each of the crew wants a man, some are willing to share, but still there just aren't enough mariners."

Sure that the old captain was watching her from either Heaven or Hell, Sirena drew a long breath then exhaled deeply, but it didn't help lessen her tension. The fierce dame would have never succumbed to these stirrings. "The men are not joining us. We're merely providing them with a ride."

"They know that, yet they want the men to bunk with them." Marta ogled a skinny man, Marko introduced as Rocco. "That one I'll take. Nothing but bones and skin left on him, but I'll have him all the same."

One long and slow scan over the crew confirmed the unkempt women waited on their Captain's final decision with raw anticipation. Tension left Sirena. The women deserved to have some mirth and these men posed no threat to any of them. "All hands," she grumbled, turning toward the men. "Get ready. We'll set sail at nightfall." Her announcement spread cheer. Marko cast her a saucy wink followed by a victorious smile.

The women's voices carried a livelier tone in their singing as they welcomed any help the new crew of men offered, and the life on deck of the *Strega* resumed once again.

"They are happy, Captain," Marko's deep voice chimed behind her.

She looked at him over her shoulder. "I suppose." Then she faced her peculiar crew again. "Aren't you going to join them?"

He stepped next to her. "Are you?"

"No," she whispered. Her happiness had been forfeited long ago. "Marta knows my orders. She'll make sure they are followed." Sirena met his gaze. "I bid you goodnight." She retreated to her cabin, leaving him standing on the gallery, but she couldn't shake off the wish he'd stop her or offer to join her.

A few minutes later the faint knock on her door made her close her eyes. She knew it was him, and if she opened the door, she would be helplessly lost to this enticing man. Right now, she yearned to be with him. Her feet itched to spring from the chair and let him in. But the memory of her late husband kept her nailed to the spot.

I want you to be happy, Carmen, no matter what you do. His favorite saying surfaced in her mind. Death had separated them and her heart died with him. Yet, she had so much youth and life in her and no one to give it to.

After her ignoring the third knock, the door opened and Marko popped his head in. "I know you're in here."

A broken breath shook her chest. He stepped in and sauntered to her bunk. She turned to him and got to her feet. His manly scent enveloped her and clouded her mind. "Now is not the best time, Marko."

"It's never the time, is it?" His husky whisper, coupled with his gentle cupping of her chin, sent shivers of pleasant anticipation through her. "This could be the only time we have."

Like a butterfly's wings, his lips brushed hers and caused her breath to quiver. She wanted him to continue, to lay his hands on her, and pull her against his hard body. As if he read her mind, his arms wrapped around her waist. He deepened his kiss with a groan, tightening his hold around her. Her lips parted and she breathed him in, allowing his tongue to explore her mouth. For a moment, she tasted wine on his skin, deep and affecting, like his voice. The soft bristles of his beard teased her neck and made her wonder what their joining would be like.

God almighty, the man knew just how to handle her. Her legs gave out under her and she lost her balance, leaning into him. His tongue trailed over her chin and down her neck, coaxing a soft moan from her.

"Sirena of the Adriatic," he murmured, wrapping his arm around her shoulders. "Consider yourself claimed by me."

His words stirred her in a wrong way. She'd always belong to her husband, until the day they unite in death. Not this man, even if his kissing and busy hands fed her hungry fire.

"No." She scrambled from his hold and pushed him away. "I cannot be claimed."

His broad shoulders rose and fell with his fast breaths while his lips thinned in irritation. "Why do you refuse me?"

"I have a ship to run and this is not good for either of us." Pretending to be busy examining the map on the low table, she avoided looking at him. "Besides, once we've taken you to your destination and our obligations are fulfilled, we won't see each other again. Ever."

"It doesn't have to end there." His solemn voice carried a certain hint of sincerity, but who was he kidding? She was a tough woman, living a man's life, battling the sea each day, and he...though his hungry and long glances had not escaped her, she couldn't be certain of his intentions.

She dismissed him with a wave of her hand. "Leave."

"Why won't you look at me?"

She turned slowly and let her gaze drift over him. He stood rigid, his arms held to his sides. Hunger in his hard, piercing gaze flooded her with a whole new surge of passion. She had seen that crescent crease in the corner of his left eyebrow on only one face before, but could it be? A gulp of air forced into her clenched chest.

"Please go," she whispered.

He closed his eyes and shook his head. The same fire still burned in his eyes when he opened them. "Perhaps later tonight I'll find you in a better mood. I can see my pallet is still in the corner." After a deep bow, he left her alone in the cabin while the merriment abounded on deck.

She exhaled long and hard. She came too damn close to succumbing to him. No way could she ever afford to fall for his charms. Brushing her finger over her lips where just a moment ago Marko's mouth had sealed hers, she reveled in the sensuous tingles rushing through her. His kissing skills were impressive. Better than she had imagined. The way he pulled her into his arms, pressed her against his firm chest, seized her lips...she buried her face in her hands and drew a long breath. No point losing her head in the short moment of insanity. This would not happen again.

Peeking in between her fingers, she scanned over the items on her desk to shake the thoughts out of her head. The corner of the map Marko had entrusted her with poked from her drawstring bag. Spreading the patch out, she scanned the drawings. The other half tucked inside his shirt, next to his skin entered her mind. No, she must not think of him.

Upon closer examination of the drawing the corner of the depicted island appeared familiar. It could be the way he had ripped the map in half and stretched the soft cloth. She reached for her magnifying glass and searched the chart of the Adriatic Sea spread on her desk. Dropping the lens, she sprang to her feet. The chair clunked on the floorboards as she tipped the wooden seat.

In two long strides she stomped to the deck and exhaled in relief to find Marko at the helm. "Captain."

He turned to her with a stern face. "I see we are back to formalities."

"No time for pleasantries, I'm afraid. May I request you to step into my quarters?" She gestured with her hand for him to follow her.

A smug smile stretched his lips. He jerked his head at Rocco. "My presence is requested by the lady. Take over the helm."

Rocco climbed the three steps to the gallery deck with a heavy sigh. "Aye, Cap'n, but the ship is still anchored."

"Steady as she goes," Marko grumbled, then turned to Sirena with mocking smile. "I'm right behind you, my lady."

By the time he entered her room she was leaning over the table and tapping the ripped piece of the map. "I believe I know where this is, but to confirm I need to see the other half."

His glance traveled between her pointed finger on the table and her face. "Are you sure?"

Hand extended to him, she nodded. "Let me try something."

He reached into his shirt, pulled the scrap of hide out, and passed the roll to her.

"Whoever drew this is very clever," she said, unrolling the map. Smoothing the wrinkles of the two pieces on the table, she turned her half up-side-down, then covered it with his half, lining the edges. "Let's hope I'm right." She took both halves in her hand and pulled her dagger under the cloth, swiftly cutting them in half.

His eyes threatened to pop out and his mouth dropped. "Are you insane?" He roared, pointing at her hands. "You ruined it."

"No, Captain." She shot him a quick glance with raised eyebrows. "I'm solving it. See, there was no wonder no one could recognize this piece of land." Her hands worked fast puzzling the edges of now four squares in different ways and revealing a whole new picture. "Left was right and up was down." Straightening, she smiled. "Here, do you know it?"

He leaned over the table and examined the map. "No, I'm afraid I do not."

She swiped the rearranged map aside and picked up the magnifying glass. Examining the piece of land on the big chart, confirmed her suspicion.

"I know these things are not supposed to be clear, but there's no mistaking the two." She pointed to a dot on the big chart and handed him the round glass tool. "Had you not ripped the map in half, this would never have dawned on me."

With one eye closed and the other squinting through the lens, he slouched over the table. Realization flashed in his eyes as he leveled them with hers. "By God," he whispered in awe. "All the time I had the darn thing, I never knew it's just a stone throw away from my island." He pressed his eye on the glass and examined the big chart again. "It's the islet of Biševo."

She stretched two fingers, pointing to his island Vis and a scrap of land Biševo on the chart. "If the wind is on our side, we can make it in a day."

"I shall order the course." Marko strutted toward the deck.

"Captain."

He halted with one leg in the midair ready to step over the high door sill and cocked his head toward her.

"This is my ship. I give orders here." It could have been the moment of excitement that caused him to forget his place, but Sirena must not allow him and his men to take over.

His booted foot thudded on the floorboards. "Yes of course, Captain. But we may lose the wind by nightfall."

"Fear not." She pressed her palms on the table and stood, locking her gaze with his azure blue eyes. Once they set sail it would mean the beginning of a voyage that would end with them separating. He would disappear from her life, this time for good, and she'd never set her eyes on him again. No, there was no rush to reach the island even with the sky growing darker and shadows stretched. "This is a fast ship and her sails need little wind."

"In that case, Captain," he bowed, "I'll make myself useful on deck."

With a slight bow of her head, she dismissed him. Again.

The pale moon reflected on the dark sea surface. Sirena extended her telescope and pressed the narrow end to her eye for the sixth time. The sun bleached, barren cliffs loomed in the night as the *Strega* glided along the coast of the small islet of Biševo. No other ships appeared on the horizon, but in the middle of the night their luck could change in an instant and an ambush could come from anywhere.

She lowered the looking glass. Marko took the device from her hand and peeked through the lens. "We circled the islet at least four times. If there's anyone out here, we'd see them by now. Call for anchor down, Marta."

Marta glanced at Sirena and waited on her order with raised eyebrows.

Sirena turned to Marko, then to the land again, and finally to Marta. At least her quartermaster still had a sense of propriety. "Anchor down."

"Aye." Marta nodded and faced the deck. "Anchor down," she barked with her loud voice then turned to Sirena. "I don't like those clouds, Cap'n. That kind brings storms with them."

Sirena spun on her heel and glanced toward the sky. Flashes of lighting revealed a thick layer of clouds in the distance. "If a storm is coming, it's still miles away."

"Storms move fast at sea." Marta stuck her index finger in her mouth and pulled it out. With straight arm she held it pointed at the sky. The sea-adept woman waited with furrowed brow. "This one is moving very fast and it's coming from the east." She then raised her hand toward the sky. She turned in the direction of the thick cloud mass, tracing her glance at the moon. "We have an hour—two maybe—until the storm. It's coming straight at us."

Sirena turned to look at the islet surrounded by calm waters. In an hour or so, high waves would break against the sharp rocks. *Macchia* shrubs and scarce pines covering the islet would bend in the wind. "I trust you, Marta. You gave your best years to the sea. Your experience has helped us out of many perilous situations." Sirena forced on a smile. "We have an hour or so. We should use the time."

"The storm is packing a force to be reckoned with and none of the islet's coves are deep enough to sit the weather out. This is no time to be near the coast, Cap'n."

Marta's serious face filled Sirena with fear. "It's a small piece of land, some three miles long. You take the *Strega* out on the open sea where she can roll on the swells. We'll take a quick walk about just to see if..." Sirena shut her mouth before she revealed too much. "Lower the dinghy."

Always dependable Marta barked out the order without as much as a suspicious glance at Sirena.

"Marko and I are going. We'll give you a sign in case the storm approaches sooner." Sirena tightened the old-fashioned baldric supporting her cutlass and unhooked an oil lamp from the line under the foremast. "You know the signal. One flash all is well," she said, lighting the thick wick and closed the glass. "Two means do not approach the shallow waters."

"Aye, aye. Cap'n." Circling her finger above her head, Marta ordered to continue lowering the dinghy.

Sirena descended the rope ladder. Marko already waited in the dinghy with his arms stretched toward her. She paused on the lowest step.

He reached out to her and wrapped his hands around her waist. "Can't have you falling down."

Butterflies stirred in her stomach with his manly scent. A fuzzy feeling spread through her body. Her hands planted on his broad shoulders, she allowed him to lower her into the small craft. However, the time pressed upon them and she had to shake off the nonsense about getting soft.

"Marta may be wrong." Marko rowed fast, pulling hard on the oars. "These summer storms don't last too long. It'll be over before it starts."

"Marta is never wrong." The truth of her words brought an uncomfortable shake to her hands. Clutching the tiller, Sirena slanted the ship straight toward the coast. One glance over her shoulder confirmed the Strega's stern glided into the darkness. "A quick look around," she said, facing him. "If we don't find any signs of this treasure you're after, we're leaving. You can always return and search another day."

"Aye, Cap'n, but don't you want a share? After all you solved the map." Marko let go of the oars and moved to the prow. With a swift jump, he reached the rocks on the shore and tied the dinghy. "Can you get the anchor?"

Standing on the stern, she picked up the anchor. The broad bottomed device with a hook like arms clunked on its chain as she swung the cable. She hurled the iron as far as she could. A loud splashed filled the air and the sea foamed white. She had to admit a hefty share of the treasure would set her just fine for life, but first they'd have to find this supposed trove.

"Anchor down." After dusting her palms of dry rust, she grabbed the oil lamp and disembarked. She pulled the roughly-basted map from her shirt and brought the light over the chart.

"Your sewing is of finest quality." Marko mocked, pointing to the long, loose stitches done in black thread.

"This is temporary. I had to rush." While this excuse may fool him to think she was a skilled seamstress, she knew better. Her mother and grandmother had tried to confine her to a chair until her stitching had improved, but her love for the sea and her little boat had been stronger and called to her. "Here." She pointed at the darkened ink dot on the east side of the island's depiction. "There's got to be something there."

His eyes widened as if a realization had struck him. "Of course. The Blue Cave."

"Cave?" She brought the map closer to her face. "I don't see how you could recognize a cave in here. There's noth—"

"Shhhh." He turned toward the bushes. "Do you hear that?"

Frozen and breathless, she glanced from side to side. There were no armed men approaching the coast, as she'd expected so she gave him a puzzled look. "I don't hear anything," she whispered.

"Exactly." He faced her again. "When we first came I heard the crickets chirping, they stopped suddenly. This is the calm before the storm."

She inhaled deeply but still the sense of unease remained with her. With Marta and Rocco's skills, the two ship masters would lead the *Strega* out of the storm's path. What about her and Marko? "What do we do?"

"What the crickets did. Take cover. And fast." The lightning ripped through the sky as he ushered her into the boat. "We'll have to try to get to the cave before the water gets too choppy."

She hoisted the anchor from its watery bed and grabbed onto the tiller. The flame inside the oil lamp burned brighter as she opened the valve fully. Flicking the glass twice, she signaled to Marta. Sirena waited for the reply with rapid breath and eyes focused to the darkness. Two faint flashes appeared in the distance, followed by the illumination of another signal. The *Strega* was out at sea, braving the storm.

"The entrance is narrow, but I think we'll make it through." Marko rowed even faster.

A peal of thunder deafened her. She raised her voice to be heard over the howling wind. "I take it you've been here before."

"Once. A long time ago." He yelled back. "If my memory serves me it should be just around these rocks."

The first drops of rain fell and soon soaked into her hair and clothes. Waves propelled the little craft faster to their destination, but the swells were rising. At last, Marko slanted the boat toward some high cliffs. She couldn't make out the entrance to any cave. Another rumble of thunder opened the sky. Like a heavy curtain, rain poured down, washing the heat out of the air. The temperature plummeted. The chill soaked through. Shivers wracked her body.

"There!" Marko pointed, switching his seat to face forward. "We have only one chance at this. Keep the prow straight."

Her eyes widened at the sight of the small opening at the bottom of the high cliff, barely visible above the sea. "We'll never make it through."

"It's bigger than it looks." He shouted over his shoulder. "Duck your head!"

The nicked timbers of the boat's floor planks scraped her knees, her heart pounded, but she never lost her grip on the tiller. Marko raised the oars to the gunwales and crouched on the prow. Another wave pushed the boat closer to the cliff. He grabbed the rock and with a loud groan, his muscles rippling, pulled the skiff through the narrow opening.

Absolute darkness engulfed the little craft. Marko hung the lantern on the prow. Finally out of the howling wind and torrential rain, Sirena huddled on the floor boards in hopeless silence. The heavy downpour hit the waters and echoed thorough the cavern. The dim light of the lamp illuminated the silver veins in the looming dark rocks.

Her heart pounded madly against her chest. Since she'd become a pirate, there wasn't a day she hadn't come face to face with death. The danger of men had hardened her, but facing the death by god's hand, had presented her with whole new fear.

Marko leaned against the oars. The dinghy inched headlong through the water. "We made it," he whispered. "There is an underwater stone bar, connecting the walls of the cave. I'll stop there."

The boat wobbled as he hurried to secure the prow line to the rocks and get the anchor down. Sirena's teeth rattled as the cavern's cold penetrated her soaked clothes.

Shudders rippled up and down her spine. "S—so c— c—old. I'm—so—cold."

Marko wrapped his arms around her. Pressed to his chest, she welcomed the warmth that seeped from his body, but it only made her tremble more. He rubbed his hands rapidly on her back. "Me—too. We—must take these—drenched shirts—and breeches—off, before—we catch—our—deaths."

Chapter 10

The thick rocks of the Blue Cave muffled the sound of the howling wind. An occasional wave pushed through the narrow entrance and rocked the dinghy. The echo of slow and steady drops of condensation mixed with Sirena's laborious breathing. Marko buried his fingers in her wet and tangled strands, pulling her head to his chest. She wrapped her arms around him. Her closeness soon replaced his cold spasms with sensuous shivers.

By some sheer dumb luck the wave had propelled the dinghy straight through the entrance, but...Marko closed his eyes, shaking away the thoughts of what could have happened.

Sirena's eyebrows furrowed as she raised her trembling chin. "Un—d—dre—s—s?"

He drew in a sharp breath of frigid air. Instead of speaking, he nodded quickly, clenching his jaw to stop his teeth from rattling. The crease on her forehead deepened. After a long stare, she pulled away and sat up straight.

"There—are blankets under—th—the prow." She blew on her hands to get some warmth into them. Removing her baldric over her head, she stammered again. "L—let's hope they are dry."

Marko opened the small, square panel in the middle of the pane and crawled inside the tight compartment, holding the oil lamp in front of him. A musty smell inside the triangular area seeped into his nostrils. A dusty bottle of wine rolled toward him. The spot where the glass container came from hid someone's secret stash of sundried squids. He also found two dry blankets and breathed a relieved sigh, sending a thank you to God.

Rough fibers of stiff and tattered blanket scraped his palms as he spread the hard wool cloth over the floorboards and took the other to Sirena.

She'd removed her jerkin and yanked on the lace of her shirt. "I can't get this off."

"Here." He uncorked the bottle with his teeth and spat the stopper on the floor, then handed her the wine. "Take a sip first. It'll warm you."

She reached for the bottle with a shaky hand. "Someone has hidden provisions under there." Liquid sloshed while she gulped. Swiping her lips with her hand, she handed the glass container to him.

He examined the messy tangle she made of her shirt lace, pulled his dagger from its scabbard attached to his belt, and cut the string that held her shirt to her bosom.

She winced and shot him a stunned glance of surprise. If she only knew what she did to him with that candid look. His heart drummed, while blood rushed to his groin. Could the wine have gone straight to her head? Or could the pomegranate blush in her cheeks and hungry fire in her eyes indicate she wanted him. In either case he would remain a gentleman and not ruin his chances with her.

"There." He wrapped the wool blanket around her shoulders. "You can undress without me seeing you."

"Thank you," she whispered, wiggling out of her shirt. "Damn, the sleeves are stuck to me."

"Let me help you. Turn around." Tightening his hold on the blanket with one hand, he grabbed the collar of her shirt. He used the opportunity to caress her and moved his thumb in small circles over her slippery skin. Another shiver arched her back. Flinching, she shot him a desirous glance over her shoulder. His hands itched to wrap around her and pull her to him as her unlaced pantalets dropped on the heap. He had seduced countless women, but his desire for this one woman in his company tonight tensed his every muscle. If she refused him, he wouldn't survive a day without seeing her beautiful face, hearing her sultry voice.

Tucking the corner of the blanket under her arm, he gestured toward the prow with tilt of his hand. "I spread the other blanket for you." Helping her get out of the drenched clothes seemed to relax his clenched jaw and stop his teeth from clattering. In fact, the cold air inside the cavern soothed his hot blood.

She clutched on the top of her improvised outfit with one hand and gathered the bottom in the other. "Will you join me?"

A smile stretched his lips. The softness in her voice and longing in her eyes were unmistakable even with her stutter. She wanted him near. "I will. First I want to wring water out of our clothes and open the cover of the hatchway on the prow. We'll need some air under there. Go get cozy in our makeshift bed."

Her bottom swayed under the blanket as she crawled on all fours through the narrow opening. Once she disappeared behind the wood panel, he scrambled out of his wet breeches and exhaled in relief as the pressure on his engorged groin loosened. He must trust his fate and not rush Sirena into anything she may regret later. Tonight, he'd be hers only if *she* desired him.

He spread their clothes on the small boat, doubting they would dry by morning. By the time he lay next to her, Sirena still shivered, despite being wrapped in the blanket.

Neither of them spoke for a long moment. He flipped the corner of the bottom cover over his legs, but it barely reached his knees. Crossing his arms, he turned to his side, facing her. Her shuddering begged him to draw her closer to him and let his body warm her.

He reached for her. "We'll warm up faster if we snuggle."

She raised her arm, inviting him to her under the warm blanket. He shifted closer. Her skin brushed against his and hilt of her dagger strapped to her thigh dug into his leg. To his surprise she pressed her mouth to his and wrapped the cover around him. His lips responded to hers in an instant. He swiped his tongue over her tempting rosy lips and pushed them apart. While their tongues met in slow, soft union, he untied the scabbard from her leg and tucked her weapon under the blanket. Lowering her, he covered every inch of her body with his. She panted while he caressed her face as gently as he could and cursed his frozen fingers.

He took a hold of her hand, resting on his shoulder, and pressed a kiss on her fingertips. "Are you sure you want this, Sirena?"

"Carmen. My name is Carmen." Her hot breath brushed his cheek.

"Carmen."

"Yes." she licked her lips, causing them to glisten.

"I like your name." He slid his hand down her slender neck as her glazed eyes filled with desire. "It suits you."

The dim light of the oil lamp revealed a fierce hunger in her eyes. He wanted all of her, not just her body tonight, but her mind and soul forever. Threading his fingers in her curls, he pulled her closer to him and sealed her lips with another hard kiss. This time he could not suppress his vigor bursting in his veins. He nibbled and caressed her. The strength of her lust intensified his desire.

His other hand trailed down her torso and cupped her breast, teasing her nipple with his thumb. Her heart beat, strong and fast, pounding against his palm. A low moan escaped her. Her back arched and she pressed firmly against his hand. He traced her leg from the round curve of her buttocks to the crook behind her knee, feeling the downy skin, then he grabbed her calf and wrapped her leg around him.

She curled her fingers on his wrist and guided him along her thighs. "I never needed anyone like I need *you*."

His long fingers slid to her moist hair between her legs, and his voice was husky with need. "You have to promise me one thing."

"Anything," she breathed against his lips.

"You give yourself to me tonight. I want every part of you. Your body. Your heart. And your soul."

"Tonight, I will." She panted. The loose strand of her curls fell on her neck, begging him to brush it aside and press his lips on her delicate throat.

Aware of the low ceiling, he carefully pulled back. "Not only tonight. I want you forever."

To have a woman for a night of passion was part of his life at sea, but his outlook on love had changed the day he'd met this marvelous vision of beauty.

Uneasiness filled him when instead of answering she studied him in silence.

To his relief she dug her hand in his mane and pulled him to her bosom. "Just love me tonight."

He cupped her cheek and brushed his thumb over her lips. Perhaps he should take what she offered and try to persuade her again, once he ensured her of his love and noble intentions. She wrapped her arms around his neck and pressed her lips on his. Overwhelmed by her deep kiss, he had no choice but to follow her luring song to the depths of his soul. Her tongue met his in hot demand, sending his mind into a spin. He broke away from her lips and trailed his tongue down her chin and neck, stopping between her breasts.

Her nipples pebbled in an instant as he took one between his lips and teased another with his thumb, coaxing a deep moan from her. Oh yes, he'd heat her passion tonight.

Slender fingers kneaded into his muscles and slid down his back, stopping just above his taut butt.

Her legs spread open and invited him to enter her. One swipe of his finger explored her moist nest and made her spine arch again. Yes, she was ripe for taking and he'd enjoy her, but first he was going to satisfy her. Their gazes locked as he pressed his erection against her inner thigh. She sucked in a hard breath and let the air out as he slowly eased inside her.

He dared not move as her tightness closed around his shaft like a fist. With his eyes closed, he groaned in delight. Her hips swayed slightly, taking him along with her rhythm. His thrusts were shallow at first. Wrapping his arms tight around her shoulders, he pushed harder. Lips parted, her eyes closed, her moans grew louder with each of his thrusts.

"Ah, Marko...don't stop," she begged and he delivered what she craved.

"Carmen," he murmured in her ear, maintaining his eager rhythm. "My beautiful Carmen."

She tilted her head toward him and sealed his lips with hers. His tongue dived into her mouth, exploring and teasing. Grabbing a handful of his hair, she threw her head back. With her back arched, her thighs held him tight. Her hips rocked upward, meeting his thrusts, while her passionate cries echoed through the cave.

Her release brought on his. Thrusting harder, his climax mounted fast. Groans escaped him as waves of exhilaration rocked his pelvis. His body stiffened and an immense pleasure tore through him.

Sweat soaked his body while his mouth dried like sand dunes. He held her close to him. "What did you do to me, my sweet Carmen?" he whispered, kissing her sweaty breasts.

Her chest heaved, she raked her hand through his hair and the whiskers of his beard, but she remained silent until her breathing calmed. She cradled his head in her palms and pulled him to her. "Marko," she huffed. "I've never experienced anything as good as this."

He smiled and placed another soft kiss on her forehead. Yes, he'd recognized the look of a pleasant surprise on her face when she'd climaxed. "Good? It was amazing. You were amazing. You wait and see. It will get better."

"Better?" A smile stretched her lips and a long satisfied sigh escaped her.

"Oh yes," he murmured, rubbing her soft stomach. "There may not pass a single day if I don't show you my love."

Her expression changed with his pledge. She looked away. And her silence and stiffness pressed heavily on his shoulders. A single tear slid down her face and broke his heart. He wiped the droplet off with his thumb.

"I wish," she sniffed. "I wish this could be. I truly do." She shook her head slowly. "But it's...impossible."

He cupped her face in his palms, tilting her head toward him. "Don't say impossible. There are always complications, but don't give up on me—on us, Carmen. We'll find a way to be together."

Her forehead creased as her gray eyes examined his face. "I'm a widow and a pirate whose head can bring a hefty reward."

"And I'm bound to wed a woman I can't stand to look at." The bristly wool blanket brushed his skin as he rolled to his back, pulling her head to his chest. "I'd rather sail the seas with you for the rest of my life."

"You would become a pirate?" Astonishment laced her voice. "For me?"

He nodded. "For you I would do anything." He spoke nothing but the truth. But would she be brave enough to accept him?

Marko woke with numb fingers. Remembering the tight space, he turned to find his love. The beauty lying across his arm cut the blood circulation to his limb. He kissed her temple.

The heat below the prow of the dinghy was getting unbearable. In addition, his call of nature tormented him.

Carmen stirred but continued to sleep as he carefully pulled his arm out. Nettles shot along his skin so he shook his limb loose.

They would return to the *Strega* and she might become the cold, reserved Captain again. Either way, she would not get rid of him. Especially now that he'd discovered what kind of passion she possessed and was capable of evoking in him.

On all fours, he crawled out of the cramped space. The storm had passed and a single ray of sun penetrated the cavern from the vault on the ceiling, reflecting on the water and bathing the grotto in aquamarine light. A stone bar, connecting the walls of the cave, was clearly visible just below the waterline. Whistling the old lullaby, he checked on their clothes. They were mostly dry. He pulled his breeches on and placed Carmen's clothes next to the prow's opening. It would be a sacrilege to empty one's bladder in these pristine waters or anywhere here, however the steady dripping made holding impossible. He hurried to the stern.

The dinghy rocked and he looked over his shoulder. Dressed in her pirate's attire and with her hair pulled in her usual low ponytail, Captain Sirena had made her reappearance. Her cold eyes traveled from him to the high rocks encircling them. He traced her gaze to a dark tunnel in the rock at the depth of the cave.

"Under the vanishing star," she whispered.

"Where the lion's guards are," Marko sang the next line as he always remembered it.

Her eyes widened in astonishment and he continued, "Deep in the rock, of a hue,"

"And over waters blue." She finished the verse and pointed to a rock at the end of the cave's depth. "There. I saw a speck of light disappear. There it is again."

He scooted to her and followed her finger, but saw nothing. "Did it disappear again?" Before she could answer a spark of light blinked in the darkness. There had to be a natural hole in the rock allowing the light to shine through for a fraction of a second. This was too easy, but then again for almost twenty seven years he couldn't solve the map neither had he connected the lullaby as a piece of puzzle. "Lions keeping the guard are missing."

As if on cue, a pair of sea lions dived into the water. The animals' natural curiosity propelled them toward the dinghy. They circled the boat twice before vanishing in the depths. He tilted his head to the spot Sirena had pointed at and stroked his beard. "How are we going to get up there?"

"The wall shouldn't be hard to scale." She gave him a grin and without a word went to tie the end of thick rope around her waist.

To scale the walls here would be a dangerous undertaking. Maybe she had a pirate's trick. Nimble like a water nymph, she claimed the steep rock, leaving only a trail of rope behind her. Her foot slipped a couple of times, making his heart skip a beat. At the top, she attached an iron sheave to the rope and hooked the device to the nook in the rock.

His heart drummed when she crawled inside the tunnel, setting the debris of thick dust, pebbles and moss to roll down the rock face.

"The tunnel is about five feet long." Her voice echoed from the dark hole.

Eyes fixed at the spot, he waited. The steady dripping filled the silence. Time stretched. The *vanishing star* appeared again, briefly illuminating the tunnel, but he couldn't spot Carmen.

"I've got it," she announced triumphantly, holding the wooden box over her head, as she reappeared after a several long and excruciating minutes. . "Bring the boat here, I'm coming down."

With two short strokes of the oars, he rowed to the edge of the wall. The rope whizzed as she descended. Marko exhaled in relief once her feet thudded on the wood of the dinghy. With a hard yank, she released the pulley. The iron wheel splashed in the sea and she reeled the device and the rope in.

"Let's see what's in here." She set the chest down and examined the rusty lock. "Blood and ashes, this still holds tight."

"Let me." He pulled his pistol from his waistband and aimed for the iron clamp.

"Don't!" She put her hands up. "The wood looks very brittle. You may shatter what's inside."

Lowering the weapon, he quirked his eyebrows. "What do you suggest?"

"You need some leverage." She darted to the stern. From under the bench, she pulled out an iron lever. "Try this."

He took the bar from her hand and pushed the flat end under the lid. The wood creaked and splintered under the pressure and the rusty lock completely gave in. The iron clinked on the floorboards. Marko opened the box.

They exchanged the puzzled glances then gaped at the detailed top of another chest placed inside the plain wooden box. Gold leaves decorated the corners of deep, red leather.

"Looks like it hasn't seen daylight in decades. Do you think this is the crest of the Marquis?" She pointed to encircled winged lion bearing the letters DG.

He slowly pulled the leather box out of its protective covering. "We'll find out soon."

Her face lit up with the sight of the whole chest encrusted with leaves of the same gold along its edges. "It's truly beautiful."

"Not as beautiful as you are." He gave her a wink. A quick glance at the solid lock in front of the leather case told him, this would be impossible to pry open. "Damn, I don't want to ruin this chest, but..." He stood pulling his knife out.

She played with the small key pendant hung from the chain, then yanked the necklace over her head, and passed the key to him before he cut into the lid. "Here, try this."

The intricate piece of metal fit perfectly inside the lock. With one swift turn of his hand, the lock clicked and the lid popped up. The pungent smell of stale leather made him grimace. A folded, white crocheted square on top drew his attention.

He cut a puzzled look to Carmen. "What kind of treasure is this?" Soft cotton caressed his palm as he picked the item and examined the embroidered MVDG in the corner of the silk trim.

She reached for a lock of blond hair tied with a thin blue ribbon. "That's a baby blanket you're holding. This is a mother's trove."

"God almighty." He stared at the chest's disappointing contents. "This cannot be the Captain Sirena's treasure. People have been searching over two decades and for what?"

"This *must* be her treasure." Carmen pointed to the key sticking out of the lock. "She gave me the key the day she named me her successor. Minutes later, she died." After carefully replacing the bound hair, she picked up a small box with a wind up key at the back. "A music box," she said, turning the dial. "I always wanted one of these."

When she opened the lid to discover two sea lions made of silver spin around each other, a soft melody filled the cavern with the chords of a lullaby. Her wide eyes met his. "You know this song, don't you?"

Dumbfounded he could barely manage a nod. The music stopped and she placed the box back on the floor planks and picked up a round container decorated with red and gold threads and tassels. The lid popped and she pulled out a scroll. Her eyes traveled over the aged waxed paper as she read. Holding the document to her chest, she looked up at him with sparkling eyes. "Do you have a middle name?"

"Why do you ask?" He had made sure no one discovered it and always wondered how anyone could be so cruel and give their child such name. At the quirk of her eyebrows, he pulled a wry face and said, "Valerye."

"Oh my god." Mouth agape, she stared at him as if she just saw a ghost. Her chest heaved and she licked her lips. "Your Grace," she breathed, lowering to her knees.

"What are you doing?" Puzzled he reached for the scroll in her hand. "Give me that."

His knees weakened as he looked on the familiar handwriting.

> *I, Teodor Breda, the royal physician entrusted to the Marchioness Ondine De Genasi, am the sole witness of a birth of her heir, Marko Valerye De Genasi.*
>
> *Coming after the request the biological mother, Marchioness Ondine De Genasi, I am delivering the mentioned infant to the loving care of family Nobile Lucin on the island Vis, where I am to remain and ensure our young Marquess's wellbeing.*

Teodor Breda, March 8, 1764

His hands shook by the time he finished reading. The letter had been written by his physician. Though questions swarmed him, one was answered. The physician's annoying and overwhelming concern for Marko's health. There would be plenty of time to find answers for all of his queries. Right now he must not let Carmen kneel in front of him. He crouched and took her by her arm.

"Don't you bow before me." Pulling her up with him, he shook his head. "You bow to no one."

And just like last night when he'd promised to show her his love each and every day, her expression changed. She appeared scared as her chest rose and fell with her rapid breathing. Did she think his love for her would fade in an instant just because of this scroll? If any of this held any truth, there were those who'd dispute his claims and stop him from reclaiming the rank. Marquis had not existed in decades and over the years the title diminished.

He wrapped her in his embrace. "If anything, it should be me who will bow before you."

Brushing her lush lips with his, he nibbled her soft skin. She sucked in a breath and welcomed his kiss. Her mouth took his mind on a whirlwind of pleasure and he let the scroll slide from his fingers. He dug his hand in her mane and continued to tease her tongue with his.

The pressure building in the crotch of his breeches urged him to lay Carmen down on the nest of blankets once more. He'd thought he'd satiated his hunger for her with last night's love making, but in fact it only had left him yearning for more.

"I want you, Carmen," he breathed against her lips, and her surrendering sigh confirmed she was willing to be his again. He would satisfy her with all the pleasure she deserved, hour after hour.

"Cap'n." Marta's raspy bark echoed through the cavern.

Chapter 11

Sirena scanned the cave painted in blue luminescence. Thick rocks shielded the heat of the mid-summer day while the ceaseless drizzling filled the silence. Last night's storm had sent her and Marko here in a hurry, but she certainly had not expected to discover old captain's treasure. And what trove it was, a few items only a mother would cherish. It was evident the trunk protected the most precious piece—Marko—or should she think of him now as the young Marquis.

No matter how many times she repeated to herself their discovery should not change the way she felt about their coupling last night, all she could think of was how a moment of weakness would cost her a lifetime of heartache. Marko would try to inherit the rank and the status he was entitled to by birth. And what man wouldn't?

Yet he must not forget, with the title came the responsibility. A few people still held onto a dream that one day a Marquis would return and continue the legacy of old. A member of the nobility who'd fight for the rights of the common man, but thirty years had passed since the slaying of the old Marquis and the dream was at the low ebb.

"Cap'n?" Marta called again. "Are you all right?"

Sirena turned to the opening which appeared bigger now that the calm waters lazily hugged the rocks. Blinded by the light she could only make the shadow of the quartermaster crouching on the stern of a small boat. The backs of two crew members, clutching the oars behind her, swayed with the rocking craft. "Thanks to all the angels, the *Strega's* made it through the storm."

"We made it just fine, Cap'n. Got out of the storm's path when you sent us away." Marta swatted a fly. "Do you need our help getting out of there?"

"No." Sirena stepped in front of Marko, trying to hide his bare chested appearance and the trunk with *treasure*. "We'll be out in just a moment."

"Aye, Cap'n." Judging by Marta's slow nod and questioning tone, Sirena wondered if the woman knew more than she was willing to show. "The *Strega* is anchored a few yards out. No other ships are about."

"Aye." Sirena's cheeks burned. Marta would have to be blind not to notice Marko's half naked presence. Women had seen him shirtless around the ship before, so why was Sirena worrying her mind with this now? She didn't have to justify her actions to anyone.

Turning to Marko, Sirena caught him carefully returning the items and closing the lid of the chest. *The young Marquis.* The fact didn't seem to disturb him, but in truth, it complicated things. How would she fit in his life? Their sweet love making of last night, still sent quivers of desire to her womb. She would give anything for him to hold her again, as he had last night.

With the same blanket he'd wrapped her into, he covered the trunk. "This should keep it hidden from curious eyes on the *Strega*." After stashing the box under the prow, he grabbed the oars. "Ready?"

She placed her hands next to his. "Perhaps I should row, Your Grace."

Eyebrows quirked, his head cocked. His funny frown suggested he was joking with her. "Are you mocking me?"

Her spine rigid, she kept her hands next to his, but shook her head. "I would never dare of such insolence, Your Grace."

"Then for Christ's sake, stop addressing me like that." The soft smile of his—she'd come to adore—appeared on his handsome face. He tickled her hands, coaxing a chuckle from her, and she let go off the oars. "That's better. As you see, I'm still the same man." Pressing his hand on his chest, he leaned forward. "Forever yours, Marko."

During the five minute trip to the *Strega*, Sirena got lost in her thoughts. This was the end of their voyage together. The outline of the island Vis stood less than four miles south, and he would without doubt pursue to establish his title and rank. Reclaim his lands and possessions. His wish, to become a pirate and sail the seas with her forever, had been most likely forgotten.

She snapped out of her mulling when his hand clutched hers. His adoring eyes and his soft expression met her glance. "The *Strega*'s just there." He jerked his head. "Before you go back to your life, I'll have you know, our discovery doesn't change the way how I feel about you."

The sincerity in his voice left her speechless. Sirena wanted to believe him. Instead, she gazed over his shoulder toward the barren rocks, a clump of land where just a few hours ago, he'd been a common man and had shown her how sweet his loving was. No matter what he said, the fact remained, he was someone from the royal class and she...well, didn't belong in his world.

With skilled rowing, he propelled the dinghy next to the *Strega*'s bulk. She stood and took hold of rope ladder. He sprang to his feet and grabbed her elbow.

"You promised to be mine." Desperation laced his whisper, reflected in his eyes.

Her heart broke but she squared her shoulders. "I'll always remember our special night with fondness."

"Carmen." He pulled back, releasing his hold on her arm. His forehead creased. "Don't give up on us."

His words brought tears to her eyes, but she swallowed the lump in her throat. "You have a huge responsibility ahead of you and so do I." She climbed to the deck, leaving him standing on the dinghy and feeling his stare burning a hole in her back.

"The *Strega* suffered no damage, Cap'n," Marta informed her in front of the assembled crew.

Sirena paused on her hurried way to her cabin and faced the deck. "I'm proud of you. All of you." She turned to Marta. "Double the rations tonight."

Marta gave her a grin with blackened teeth. "Aye, Cap'n."

In front of the cabin, Sirena waved to the cheering crew and stepped through the door. Once out of their view she paced the floor. Her racing mind wouldn't allow her to return to her duties. Or to sit.

What had she done? Dropped her guard for a moment and in the next instance, bereft of all common sense, she had crumbled under Marko's seductions. The prospect of finding the treasure had clouded her mind. If only she'd stayed on the *Strega* last night, none of this would have happened.

What had he done to her? She was brought up to keep her stirrings to herself and not to provoke a man with words or actions. Certainly, she had never spoken anything of the sort to her late husband. Nor had she looked forward to his nocturnal visits, but she had fulfilled her wifely duty without a single complaint—or enjoyment. Marko's hands gliding along her skin taunting her, flashed in her memory. Could it be possible that she had not loved her late husband, rather only tried to convince herself she had? A woman could love a man without the physical pleasuring. Sirena shook the thought away. It wouldn't be fair to compare a simple man like her departed husband to a man such as Marko, skilled in the art of seduction.

Now the familiarity she had noticed about him when they'd first met was clear. Marko was the deceased captain's son. Obviously, no one had known about her true identity. Or did they?

Three short knocks sounded on the door followed by Marta's voice. "Cap'n?"

Sirena halted. Marta had been serving here for years. If anyone knew a thing about all this it would be her and by God, Sirena would make her talk right now. Marta hid behind her expressionless face and few spoken words long enough.

Stepping to the door, Sirena paused, her hand on the knob. If she found the truth, where would it lead? Deeper into trouble, but perhaps this could be one of those things that had to worsen before it turned better. A tug on the nicked wood and she pulled the door open.

Marta stood on the other side her fist in the air, ready to knock again. Her eyes mellowed. "I need a word with you."

Sirena stepped aside opening the door fully, then closed it after Marta had passed through, pulling her black bandana off her head.

The old woman's eyes bored into Sirena's and she sensed the things were about to take a disturbing turn even before Marta spoke. "You found the chest, didn't you?"

Sirena did not answer. Her first instinct was to deny, but unsure if Marko had talked, she stepped sideways and examined Marta's face. "What do you know of the chest?"

Marta's shoulders relaxed as she exhaled a long breath, lowering her glance to the scarf in her hand. She cleared her throat and looked Sirena straight in the eye. "I hid it there. In the cave, thirty three years ago."

Sirena kept her stare on Marta, not blinking. She had put the chest there? So Marko had not opened his mouth about this. How could he stay so calm? As if the scroll meant nothing at all. But the question sparkling was how much Marta knew?

"Cap'n," Marta croaked. "I have nothing but my sword and my honor. I gave my word to our departed Sirena." She reached inside the deep pocket of her tattered skirt. A yellowed piece of paper crinkled as she pulled the parchment out and extended her hand. "She made me promise not to give this to you before you found the chest."

Sirena stared at the letter in Marta's hand for what seemed like an eternity. Slowly she took the sheet and, unfolded the paper. Perhaps all of the answers would be in there.

The familiar handwriting of the deceased captain sprawled on the page.

> *Carmen,*
>
> *You are reading this because you've done well and succeeded in what I've asked of you. If luck is with you perhaps someday soon, you may find my*

son, Marko. The last time I looked upon him he was just a boy. He'd be a grown man by now.

And just what a man had he become. Sirena paused at the thought, turning away from Marta's curious face. She returned to the elegant writing.

His rank and title were forfeited when I and my husband were forced into hiding. The slain couple found in our nuptial bed was that of our servants.

The saddest day of my life was the day I had to leave my newborn boy. I got to hold him in my arms for a few hours. I relived the same sorrow each time I looked at you. As it seems, Carmen, destiny presented us with the similar path. Though I wasn't with Marko through his life, I was always informed about him. I know his father is forcing a marriage of convenience upon him. Carmen, if there ever was a young man in need of saving, it is Marko.

Marchioness, Ondine De Genasi

Sirena shuddered with the reminder of when she had left her Nikola in the care of another family. The old captain had recognized the same pain in Sirena. The kind of hurt no woman should ever have to experience—giving up her child.

But what had the deceased captain wanted from her? She couldn't expect her to stop Marko from entering into this marriage of convenience? So what if he had said he couldn't stand to look at the woman? He would, in time. No, although Sirena's heart broke, she must not stand in his way to his title and rank. Even if it had been forfeited, no man would let go of what was rightfully his. And for herself, she promised she'd do the right thing by these women. Honor, she wouldn't forfeit.

She glanced at the letter in her hand. "Did you know who she was?"

"No, Cap'n. No one did. She was the Cap'n when I came aboard." Marta stepped to her. "I don't know what was in the chest, nor could I read the letter, but I could see from the first moment that he's her son. Did you not notice the resemblance?"

"He appeared familiar." Sirena closed her eyes. If Marta had said this before today, she wouldn't have believed it. "But I couldn't figure out where I've seen him before. Had she never spoken of him?"

"She did mention him in her own obscure way, but at the time it didn't make sense to me. Now I know what she meant each time she said *her blond curls*. Her strands were straight and of chestnut color before they turned gray." Marta gave Sirena a reluctant glance. "So, who was she?"

Never before had Sirena heard Marta utter so many words. She raked her brain, searching her early days onboard the *Strega* when she had feared Marta. The order-barking quartermaster had taught Sirena a good lesson and she had strived to become the untouchable, tough woman she was. Eight years of hard work to detach herself from her emotions had crumbled under Marko's longing gaze in the cave that had sheltered them from a storm.

"She was—" Sirena rubbed the side of her neck, but the tension mounted. What she needed was a good sword fight to empty all this pent up anger she couldn't unleash elsewhere. "The Marchioness Ondine De Genasi."

All color drained from Marta's face. Sirena feared the old woman would collapse in front of her. "The Marquis and his wife were slain in their bed." Marta's whisper, though barely audible, filled the long silence.

"The bodies of two servants were used as decoys." Sirena cringed at the thought. The two innocent people had died in place of their royal masters. The Marquis and Marchioness had continued on their noble cause as pirates and helped the people by spreading the booty, but their actions had not justified the murder. "Marta, not a word of this outside this cabin. Understand?"

"Aye, Cap'n." Marta pressed her hand to her heart. "Many of our women have left their families behind. I guess she was no different, after all. I left my daughter on the steps of an orphanage. She didn't survive her first week there."

For the first time Sirena noticed sorrow filled Marta's eyes, but then the pain was quickly replaced with her well-known hard stare.

Perhaps encouraged by Marta's confession, Sirena couldn't hold her secret any longer. "I too have a child I left behind," she said, glancing away as if Marta would see her decision as cruel.

Marta's nod followed by long and loud exhale told Sirena the quartermaster had known of her son. "Do we have a heading, Cap'n?"

Sirena stepped in front of the small window overlooking the deck. Each time she had glanced upon Nikola, her love for him must have shown on her face. How many other crew members could have noticed the pain in her eyes?

Through the pane she glimpsed Marko tying the lines of the hoisted dingy. The blanket wrapped around the small treasure chest, flapped in the wind as he swaggered toward the gallery deck. A heading? No, she didn't have a clear direction, but maybe he could give her one. "Have Marko come in."

"Aye." Marta opened the door and left.

Salty air carried on the afternoon breeze and filled the cabin. Sirena read the Marchioness' letter one more time. Had the old lady somehow planned all of this? Oh, if she watched from wherever she may be, Sirena was positive the dame had a good laugh.

"You have sent for me, my lady?" Marko stepped in, his arms wrapped around the box.

His blue eyes, sensual lips, broad shoulder, narrow hips and strong long legs clad in his black breeches sent a wave of sensuous shivers through her. How she longed for him to wrap his arms around her, instead of the box bundled in the blanket, and have his way with her. She stood in silence, facing him.

He cleared his throat before he spoke again. "I want you to hide this for me. Please. Keep it safe."

Reluctantly, she lowered to her knees. Safekeeping this trunk for him was not something she'd like to commit to, but she couldn't ignore the plea in his voice.

Pouting, he gave her a scolding look. "Didn't I tell you not to kneel in front of me?"

She expressed her annoyance of his comment with a click of her tongue. Would his true identity intensify his arrogance? With her hands around the slots on the planks, she pulled the loose floorboard and revealed the hiding spot slightly bigger than the trunk. "It should fit in here."

He kneeled next to her and inspected the hole. "Is it dry down there?"

"As dry as inside a ship can be."

He lowered the chest inside the hidey hole with care, she noticed. When he first had set his eyes on its contents, he had believed they discovered someone's junk. She was right—he had changed his priorities and was now thinking of this as a true treasure.

After replacing the floorboards, he dusted his hands. She wished he'd pull her to him and tell her this was all one big mistake. But he didn't. Of course, he was the Marquis.

He caressed her shoulder. "I'm in no hurry to return home. The only two persons waiting on me are my aging father and an older woman hungry for our family's fortune."

"Don't you wish to reclaim your rank?"

He blinked and turned to gaze at the wall. His shoulders rose and lowered with his deep breath. "There are men in high places that would dispute the evidence and fight my claims."

She cut a stern glance at him in disbelief. "What about the people who still hold onto the hope that a caring Marquis would come into power?"

"A very few feeble minded people whose coffers are drained. The Marquis they are expecting to put the end to all this injustice and oppression is not me. I can't be. How am I to stop an insatiable machine that devours taxes?" His pause stretched into longer silence. He drew a sharp breath before he continued. "I'm a sea captain and a swordsman, not someone who is schooled in finesse of diplomacy. The scroll won't prove I'm a Marquis when my parents supposedly died two years before I was born. No one would believe me."

"Your physician holds the proof."

Shaking his head slowly, he blinked and gaped at her. "He'd be ridiculed. Besides, it is not safe. The same people who organized the slaying of my parents would come after me. "

She tried to ease the lump in her throat by swallowing, to no success. "So what now?"

"As I said last night, all I want is to sail the seas with you. Forever."

"What about your men?"

He glanced toward the deck then at her again. "I cannot expect them to follow me. They are free to go if they wish, but I doubt any of them will leave my side."

"You know what will become of you if you stay here?"

Though he had said so, she just couldn't accept his words. No one chose this kind of existence for something as foolish as love.

A grin spread on his lips. "A pirate. I made my decision, and nothing will change my mind."

She sprang to her feet as anger flared inside her. Maybe he didn't understand a pirate's life. He'd only seen the positive. "This is not an adventure. I was forced into this life. All of us here were. Don't you think that perhaps I would love to live on land, instead, and grow my own garden? And feel firm soil under my feet rather than the shifting boards of the deck. Do you think I enjoy exposure to the sun, heat, rain, damp and cold nights at sea?"

He stood too. "Then stay with me on the island. I can give you what you want and more."

Raising her hand, she pointed at the deck. "I can't leave these women. I gave my promise to...your mother."

With a step toward her, he backed her against the wall. His longing gaze, coupled with the brush of his knuckles on her cheek, stirred a fierce desire in her. "Can't you see? We belong together," he whispered in a husky tone.

"Don't." She closed her eyes. "Please."

His soft lips and whiskers brushed her neck. "Stop me."

"I—" forcing a long breath from her chest, she arched her back. She couldn't allow him to go farther, but how was she to stop him when she longed for his embrace? Blistering barnacles, he knew how to touch her. His lips crushed hers, parting them with his tongue. He teased and explored her mouth, while his moan stirred her desire deeper. She tightened her hold on him.

"I'm here my love," he breathed, not taking his lips from hers. "Here for you."

A loud skirmish on the *Strega*'s deck brought their moment of passion to an abrupt end. Pulling back, he turned to the window. Sirena scurried past him, but he grabbed her wrist and with a hard tug forced her to face him.

"I'm sure it's nothing. Let Marta handle this." The corner of his lip twitched, filling her with an incredible urge to kiss him again.

"No—" She spun her head toward the deck, as the voices grew louder, then back at him. "I think I should see to this."

Straightening her bandana, she stomped to the door. Knob in her hand, she paused and turned to him. "In the future, there'll be no displaying of affection on board where any of the crew could see us."

Disappointment flashed in his eyes. He nodded. "Aye, Captain."

Her heart pounded as she stepped on the gallery deck. God knew how far she'd have let him go had the women not gotten in a fight.

"Break it off," Marta growled, pushing a handful of gathered women out of her way and stepping inside the circle where two of them pounded their fists on Angelia.

"She is lying, Marta," the taller woman shrieked, her arm hovering above Angelia's head.

Angelia swiped her hand over her bleeding lips. "I'm telling the truth. Gaspar's ship will pass through. Tonight."

A burly woman stuck her fist close to Angelia's face. "How come you didn't inform the Cap'n of this?"

"Angelia!" Sirena's stern voice made the crowd spin their heads toward the gallery deck. "Not another word. Come forth."

The crowd parted and Marta jerked her head at Angelia to follow her. With their wide stance and narrowed eyes, the women tracked the movements of the two pirates. They climbed the three steps and Marta pushed Angelia in front of Sirena.

She scanned the girl's red face. If she was willing to get such a beating, then her information must be true. "You should have come to me first instead of giving the details to the crew."

Angelia lowered her eyes at the floorboards. "I'm sorry, Cap'n. Not going to happen again."

Sirena nudged her chin. "Tell me what you know?"

"It—it c—came to me last night," Angelia stammered. "Something Gaspar said. H—he has another ship passing through here."

Marko, who had been leaning against the wall until now, stepped forward. "How do you know it's tonight?"

Angelia licked her still bleeding lips. "Gaspar mentioned it would happen the night after *Assumption of Mary*."

Guilt stung Sirena at the realization she hadn't said her prayer to the patron saint of all sailors and therefore pirates.

Stepping next to her, Marta tilted her head and whispered in her ear, "Should we trust her?"

"I don't know," Sirena answered and sighed. "Her previous lead proved right. I'll let the crew decide this one."

Marta uncorked the rum skin with her meaty hand and drew a long swag. "Could this have slipped her mind when she escaped the pig who beat her?"

Sirena shrugged. "Possible." She shook her head when Marta passed her the skin. "An unguarded and unarmed merchant ship travelling at night is our specialty. The job would be easy. Think of the booty. It would set us all for life."

"But, Cap'n." Marta rasped after another long swig of rum. "This could be a trap."

"We take our chances each time. How is this different?" Sirena pounded her fist on the wooden railing. Descending one step, she scanned the deck. The women's hungry faces waited on her announcement. As noble as the old captain's attempts had been to help the people, the Duke's heavy taxation only made them more destitute. And the kind of treasure she'd left behind refused to step up to the job. But she could not blame Marko for the hard times and the people's suffering.

One last raid for the old times' sake was in order. They'd keep all of the booty, disburse to the islands and live modest lives. Yes, this one would be just for them. "Corsairs of the *Strega*, we sank Gaspar's brigantine with ease and the booty we gathered will provide many of the people on the mainland with food enough to live through another winter. This raid could set us all up with riches to end this kind of existence. What say you?"

The crew cheered, filling Sirena with pride. Unsheathing her cutlass, she joined the women in shouting and waved her sword in the air.

"Sirena."

At Marko's sober voice, she snapped her glance to him and met his austere gaze.

He held the door to her cabin open with one hand and with the other he gestured for her to follow him in.

Sirena turned to Marta. "It seems Captain Marko wants a word in private." A hint of humor laced her voice.

Marta nodded. "Aye, Cap'n."

Sirena stepped inside her cabin with Marko behind her, his expression still grave.

"I told you on my first day here," he said as he shut the door behind him. "You may be harboring a traitor."

Sirena folded her arms, pursed her lips, examining his face. Though she had suspected something not quite right with Angelia the first time she'd seen her, the girl had come around and proved herself with hard work and training. "And you think it's Angelia?"

He grabbed Sirena by her shoulders, his stare hard. "Gaspar expected your attack, only at a different place and day. When you ambushed him, he called someone a betraying wench." Pointing toward the deck, Marko continued. "That girl may be feeding you information."

"That is what being a pirate is all about. Ambush, take what you can, and sink what you can't. You want to be one of us? So stand up and be counted." At another loud cheer on the deck, she spun around. "The crew has made their decision. Make sure your pistols are well oiled and your blade is sharpened."

"Carmen, listen to me. This is a trap." The desperation in his voice bounced off her back as she scurried out the exit.

Pausing by the door, she turned to him. "Everything is possible, but with your men well rested and satisfied, we stand better chance. Will you help us?"

"Of course we will, but I see greed in your eyes. Careful, Sirena, rapacious desires have led many to their deaths." With a single nod he left her company.

"Going back to those experienced girls?" she shouted after him not believing her words.

He halted outside her cabin and turned to her. His familiar smug smile spread across his face. "Yes, I am."

Pain stabbed Sirena's chest. To her surprise, he strutted to her. Lowering his head to her ear, he whispered, "Just so you know, I'd rather sit alone on the stern."

His closeness tightened her chest more than the corset of the dress she had worn two days ago. The desire he stirred inside her packed a raw power that she planned to use in the fight tonight.

He took a step back and squared his shoulders. "We must prepare for the battle then."

Chapter 12

Anchored a few miles south of Vis, the *Strega* drifted on the calm sea. The lush green island loomed in the distance, stark against the blue sea and the last of the redness in the sky. A strong desire to return home gripped Marko. He could go back and do what his father bid of him. Spend the rest of his life as a miserable man in a loveless, passionless marriage. And wonder every passing day what it could have been if he had stayed and fought alongside the woman who held his heart.

The thud of his knee-high boots on the weather beaten planks of the *Strega* slowly calmed his temper. In the past half-hour he had covered at least ten yards in an anxious pace back and forth across the stern. Halting, he glanced toward the dipping sun and drew a long breath. The smell of brine filled his lungs. His decision to become a pirate made perfect sense. He belonged here on the seas with Sirena.

If anyone knew the pirate's business, it was these women. He uttered a curse he had not known a week ago and rounded the corner of Sirena's cabin to the main deck. It was two, maybe three hours before the dark would engulf the islands and the sea. He had better prepare for the ambush.

The deck of the *Strega* bustled with activity. Cannonballs were counted and restocked, daggers, scimitars, cutlasses, rapiers sharpened. He scurried down the three steps of the gallery deck and found Rocco slouched over a makeshift table of an overturned bucket.

Marko sat on the spiral-coiled halyard, facing his quartermaster. "This isn't your fight. I don't expect you to stay."

Rocco cast him a quick glance, but did not stop oiling his pistol. "This is my fight as much as it is yours."

Sighing, Marko stroked his beard. "What did Marta do to you?"

A peculiar smile lit Rocco's suntanned face, setting deep lines around his mouth. "Everything a lanky man such as me could only hope for."

Rocco's mind had been set to the adventure. Marko leaned forward, bracing himself on his elbows. "This could be a trap."

"These women are certain this raid will go smooth, just as many before." Rocco raised the assembled pistol and aimed at the distance, testing the primer then lowered the weapon to the table. "I told our men they're free to leave if they wished, but none do. They want to avenge the sinking of the *Levant*."

Marko nodded. He didn't think any of his men would abandon their Captain. Add to it these luring mermaids calling themselves pirates and the prospect of a bountiful booty, it was no wonder they opted to stay. Shielding his eyes against the late afternoon sun, he raised his head at the silhouette of a stout woman approaching.

"It's time to weight the anchor and get into our positions," Marta informed them, patting Rocco's shoulder. "No worries, I'll be watching your backs."

Whirling, Rocco glanced at Marta over his scrawny shoulder as he assembled another pistol. "That's my woman."

A short chuckle escaped Marko, while he scanned the busy scene, searching for Sirena. With her stance wide, she stood on the gallery deck, one hand on the helm. She turned her head toward him and met his gaze. Transfixed, he got to his feet and tapped Rocco's bony shoulder. "Good luck tonight."

Wiping grease off his hands on a filthy rag, Rocco nodded. "Same to you, too."

Marko's legs carried him in the direction of the mesmerizing woman. God help him, but seeing her again, so beautiful and fierce, brimming with pistols and swords, eased all his doubts of tonight's battle.

He leaned against the portside. If they were all destined to die, at least he'd fall beside the woman he loved.

Sirena let go of the helm and sauntered in his direction, stopping inches in front of him. Her corkscrew curls resting on her shoulders sent tingles to his fingers. He'd survive anything but losing her. Despite his gloomy thoughts a smile crept to his lips.

"I'm well protected with Marta watching my back and you holding my heart." Curling an end of her hair around his finger, he continued. "I'm not going to let you out of my sight at any time tonight." How he wished to pull her in his embrace and hold her there forever. But he respected her request of no displaying his affection in front of the crew. Hoping his silent gaze would persuade her to reconsider her demand, he held her stare. Her unreadable, cold, gray eyes stirred his desire for her deeper. For the first time a surge of envy rippled through him. Rocco and Marta had, as did all of his men, an uncomplicated relationship, open for everyone to see.

As Sirena stepped back, her silky strands slipped out of his fingers. "You don't have to watch over me. I can hold my own."

"You are skilled with the sword, better than many men in fact. However, overconfidence will get you killed faster than the adversity. Stay where I can see you."

"Your pistols, Cap'n." Rocco approached with iron guns handles facing Marko. "Oiled and primed."

Marko took the weapons and after testing the primers, he pushed the pistols inside his waistband. Scrambling into an old buffcoat, he felt for his sword and dagger to assure they were where they supposed to be.

"Let us all kneel for a prayer," Marta announced with her loud bark.

The nicked wood prickled his knees through his breeches as he lowered next to Sirena and laced his fingers with hers. To his delight, she didn't pull her hand out of his but granted him a soft smile that warmed his soul.

"*God of power and mercy, maker and love of peace, to know you is to live, and to serve you is to reign.*" Marta's voice carried over the eerily silent crew. "*Through the intercession of St. Michael, the archangel, be our protection in battle against all evil. Help us to overcome war and violence and to establish your law of love and justice. Grant this through Christ our Lord.*"

"Amen," he replied in unison with the rest of the crew and, with his free hand, quickly crossed himself.

Returning to her post, Marta paused by him. "If I didn't know you better, I'd say that's fear in your eyes."

Marko glanced toward Sirena busy scanning the deck. "Fear I'll lose her." He faced Marta's hard stare. "I trust you'd leave us a way out?"

"We weren't born yesterday." Marta patted his arm and hurried along the gangway to the ship's head.

The ropes whizzed hoisting the lateen sails, followed by the creaking of the anchor-ring. The easterly wind ruffled the waters and filled tattered sail-cloth, sending the old ship gliding to its hiding place where they'd wait for the right moment to strike.

Hidden in the darkness between high cliffs, the *Strega* must appear like a ghost ship with her flat and ragged sails, Marko thought. Clutching his dagger in his right hand, he stood on the deck. Minutes passed by, then hours and no ship broke through the clouded night. Perhaps the information was false and Gaspar's vessel wasn't going to pass by at all.

"Ship ahoy," a crew member nearby whispered, passing on the message along and quickly extinguished his hopes.

He pressed the looking glass to his eye. A large vessel peered through the veil of darkness. Numerous oars on both sides stroked the surface as one. Lowering his telescope, he cut a glance to his left. Sirena's baffled expression confirmed she saw it too.

"This is a slave galleon," he whispered. How typical of Gaspar to line innocent people as a buffer between him and the cannons.

Sirena stood rooted, bewilderment written on her face. Marko stepped to her. "*You know* what will happen to those poor slaves if you sink this ship. No one would bother to unchain them."

"They'll go down with the ship. I..." She shook her head. "I can't do this."

Many of those men chained to benches and sentenced to row for the rest of their lives, would welcome death in exchange for another flogging by the galley masters. Neither Marko nor Sirena had a right to act as executioners.

"Cap'n!" Angelia's desperate cry ripped the silence. She ran to Sirena and fell on her knees. "I beg you, don't sink this ship. Please have mercy."

Sirena stood transfixed. Her eyes focused on Angelia's tear streaked face.

The young girl's face crumpled in grief. "Gaspar sent my little brother as a slave on this galleon." Sobs jerked her body and choked her words. "Janko is all I have left. He's only twelve years old. Gaspar promised to free him if I brought you here."

Sirena glanced at Marko. Her mouth opened as if she'd say something, but she closed it again, scanned the crew, then returned her gaze to Angelia. "How do you know your brother is on this ship?"

"He managed to send me a word last month. The man who delivered it told me to wait on the point where the galleon would pass, but Gaspar's men captured me."

A tight knot constricted Marko's chest. Either the girl was lying, or she truly believed her brother was alive. Whatever the case, Gaspar had used her to infiltrate Sirena's crew. Getting captured might have not been in pig's plan, but the first attack had been easy to make her believe he could be an easy target. Tonight he'd strike with all his might.

"Angelia." Marko crouched in front of the kneeling girl. Her eyes wide and round as plates, set on him. "You'll meet your brother again, but not in this life. I'm afraid."

The crew women yelled and spat at her. "She steered us into a trap."

"I'm sorry, Cap'n, I didn't know what else to do. Please forgive me." Angelia sobbed, clutching Sirena's ankles.

"I still expect you to fight to your last breath and defend this ship and your sisters." Anger laced Sirena's voice. She jerked her head at the women closest by. "Take her away." Marko pulled her aside when the wailing crewmember had been dragged off. "I will not waste cannonballs on a slave galleon," she said. "No doubt, there will be at least one ship escorting it. Our only chance is to outrun it."

Marko tilted his head toward the flat sails. Without wind their escape was a slim gamble, but at least it was a chance. Fighting in between sharp cliffs and an unapproachable coast would be worse. If good fortune was with them tonight, the escorting ship would be far behind. He leveled his eyes with hers and nodded. "Let's go for it."

"Hoist the colors. The rest of you, to your oars," she shouted and the crew sprang into action.

The sound of rope raising the flag whizzed through the heavy air. A black banner with white skull and crossed bones flapped on the mainmast. A peculiar smile appeared on her face as she stared at the waving cloth, confirming Marko's suspicion, she wanted to fight. As if on cue, the winds picked up and filled the sails.

Hands clutching the helm, she steered the *Strega* out of its hiding as the oars of the slave galleon left ripples on the dark surface. The sharp sound of a whistle pierced the still of the night. A thirty guns frigate sailed through the curtain of the moonless sky.

"To your posts." Marta's order boomed across the deck.

"Sirena," Marko called over the commotion caused by Marta's command. She raised her head over the helm, her beautiful eyes lit with the heat for battle. "Do not fire first."

"I will not start the fight, only return the fire."

The cannons on the privateer's frigate thundered, filling the air with white smoke and the smell of burnt powder. The sea foamed around their xebec as most of the cannonballs missed. The enemy didn't seem to want to sink the *Strega*. Sending a few warning shots only meant they wanted to board her. And judging by the speed they approached, their helmsman appeared to know his business well.

"Blood and ashes! Perhaps, this night is a good one to die." Sirena spun the large wheel, causing the *Strega* to tilt dangerously to the left.

"All port guns—fire!" She roared against the cries of battle. Her well trained crew returned fire with accuracy, sending projectiles ripping through the attacking vessel. Despite the damage, the frigate drew closer in the narrow passage between the two islands and fired again. At the sight of a head size iron ball hurling straight at him, Marko grabbed Sirena's shoulders and pulled her to the planks, covering her body with his. The sharp splinters flew around them, while the screams of the crew mixed with the battle sounds. He stood and pulled her up with him. A splinter stuck in his forearm caused him some pain, but he yanked the shard out.

Sirena grabbed his arm and inspected the wound. "You are hurt."

He grinned, trying to ignore the stinging and blood soaking in the sleeve of his buffcoat. Unsheathing his rapier he shouted, "It's nothing."

Just as he suspected, the privateer's ship boarded the *Strega* on the beam. The sound of swords crossing cut through the night as privateers poured overboard.

Marko craned his neck to scan the *Strega*'s deck. Their ship was in trouble. Broken off at the rig point, her stout mainmast and most of her rigging now hung in tangled mess.

Sirena pulled two pistols from her waistband, thumbed the hammers and fired one after the other at close range. Two privateers clutched their chests and slumped to the floorboards of the slippery deck. Since the matchlocks were useless to her after firing their solo shot, she discarded them and, pulled her swords out. As if she was desperate to clear a space for herself on the crowded deck, she slashed indiscriminately through the bodies in her way, keeping up her relentless pace. Though worried about her every move, Marko admired her strength and courage.

The enemy was lightly armored. Had they been attacked by another pirate's ship, the crew of the *Strega* would mix with them and it would be impossible to distinguish between the two crews. Thankfully, these men wore helmets and corselets, so Marko aimed to thrust through the side where the corselet was hinged.

By crouching, Sirena narrowly avoided the sword slashing her throat. However, a tip of the blade nicked her face, sending drops of blood racing down her cheek. At the first chance, Marko grabbed Sirena's arm. Raising her swords, she whirled around, halting them an inch above his head and giving him a puzzled glance.

"This is carnage. Order to abandon the ship. Swimming for our lives is the only chance at survival."

"No. They'll kill us one by one." At the battle cry of a man hurling at her, she spun around and thrust her blade in his abdomen.

Sirena was right. If they floated on the water, they would be easy targets for the privateers.

The second boarding party reached the bulkhead, where the last of the pirate's crew still fought. Keeping a watchful eye on Sirena, Marko yanked a lance from the hands of a dying privateer. He charged at the enemy, cutting them down in his wake. Still, the attacking men advanced and pushed him back. Damn, they'd all get killed here by these merciless soldiers. Backing against a broad body, he spun on his heel and faced Marta.

"I told you, I'd be watching your back."

"Marta," Marko shouted over his shoulder, parrying the blow of the blade. "Save your women. Jump overboard and swim." The cold metal of his sword clinked as it continued to cross with his enemy's. "Pass the order to Rocco. I'll get Sirena."

Marta yanked her rapier out of the chest of a privateer. "I don't think she'll like this order."

Whirling around, Marko dealt a swinging blow to a man charging at him. "She'll have no choice. Is the dinghy lowered?"

"Yes. Skiff too." Thrusting her dagger into the neck of a man who was about to slash Marko's chest, Marta nodded. "I'll shove those who still stand toward the nearest escape boat." She then let out a loud cry, heard over the clamor.

A few feet away from him Sirena paused, her swords poised in midair. She cut him a stern glance. "Who ordered the retreat?"

"I did," Marko shouted, thrusting his spear at the man ready to slash Sirena's throat.

Led by Rocco, both women and men quickly scurried to the shattered railing and slid down the ropes then boarded the small crafts. Marko shoved Sirena in front of him, but just like every captain destined to stay with the ship until the end, she resisted.

Marko's heart pounded. He'd take her place and die with the ship if need be. "Damn, I'll go down with the *Strega*, you save yourself."

"No! She's *my* ship. I will not abandon her." With a swift movement, she cut the ropes tying the small craft to the *Strega*'s hull. "Go," she shouted at the crew of about twenty five members.

Rocco nodded, his face grim, and after a short hesitation he pushed the oar against the hull. Rowing fast, the members and the boats disappeared into the darkness.

"What did you do, Sirena?" Marko pulled her in his embrace. For all he knew this may be the last chance he'd get. "Why didn't you save yourself?"

She pushed away from him. "The dinghy was loaded beyond the gunwales. The captain and officers must not abandon their ship." Her face crumpled. "And I couldn't leave you."

Men surrounded them before Marko could pull her to him again. Facing the enemy, he shoved her behind him while Marta panted a few steps to his left. All three waited for the swords to strike.

"Stop the killing." Gaspar's deep voice carried through the night. "These women are worth money."

Sirena's bloodied and bruised face showed no surprise as the captain clad in black approached through the parted crowd.

He pressed the blade to her neck. "You should've killed me while you had a chance."

Anger flared in Marko, he pulled his unfired pistol out and aimed at Gaspar. "And *you* should have killed *me* when you had *your* chance." In a frantic rage, he pulled the trigger. But Gaspar jerked away at the same time, and the single shot pierced the man behind him. The privateer's face went blank before he sank to his knees and toppled over.

Gaspar didn't turn around to see what became of his man. "But I will kill you now. You played your part. She solved the map for you and found the treasure. Where did you hide it?"

More anger rushed through Marko with Gaspar's confession. This had been a clever plan. The pox marked faced captain only had to wait for the events to unfold.

"Cap'n," one of the armed men called, pushing Angelia in front. "There's one more."

Gaspar jerked his head. "Bring her here." His face lit up at the sight of Angelia. "Ah, my conspirator."

"Where's my brother?" Angelia's sneer sent privateer's into roars of laughter. Blood soaked through her shirt as she tried to yank herself free from the iron grip of a man. "I did what you wanted. You promised," she said, gnashing her teeth.

Gaspar snorted. An awkward grimace turned his face grotesque. "Did no one ever warn you not to trust a man who fights for those with bigger purses? Your brother didn't last two months on the galleon. Fish nibbled his body long ago."

Tears spilled from Angelia's eyes, but rage flashed across them all the same and she yanked herself free. She slipped a dagger from her sleeve and lounged at Gaspar. "You filthy pig!"

Slashing his forearm, she let out a loud cry as Gaspar thrust his sword through her. Blood poured out of her mouth, life quickly drained out of her while she slumped to the floorboards. "You and your goddamned brother cost me enough," he spat before he released her lifeless body, not bothering to retrieve his sword.

Mouth parted, Sirena panted and shook her head. "No, no...she was but a child."

Marta's lips thinned as if she tried to keep tears at bay.

"We got the chest." The voice of another man broke the snide laughter of the crew. The men whirled in the direction of two of their comrades holding the box. "It was hidden under the floorboards in her quarters."

"What are we waiting for?" Gaspar shouted. "Open it."

Prodding the lock with a tip of the knife, the lid popped and all of the men stared at the contents in bewilderment.

"Hell, what kind of treasure is this?" Gaspar examined the knitted blanket, then threw the item in the pool of blood and spat. He picked up the music box in his hand and opened the lid. A sinister laugh shook him. "This is junk."

The fact that these dogs ransacked through his mother's trove—the sacred items she stashed away from prying eyes so long ago, made the blood boil in Marko's veins. These were the only treasures of her son that she had. He reached inside his shirt and curled his fingers around the pommel of his dagger. The scurvy dogs would not get away with this. Snatching the opportunity when Gaspar stomped on the music box, roaring in laughter, Marko pulled his dagger and dug the blade into Gaspar's doublet, slicing off buttons as the swine withdrew.

"That belonged to *someone*," he sneered through gritted teeth.

Gaspar stepped so close that Marko felt his breath in his eyes. Then he spat into his face. Disgusted and surprised, Marko jerked his head to the side. An instant later, excruciating pain in his left hip sent cold sweat to his nape. A hoarse cry ripped from his throat and he doubled over clutching Gaspar's blade that stuck deep into his flesh.

Gaspar pulled his arm back and Marko slumped to the planks. "Throw this dog overboard. If he surfaces, shoot him."

Warmth soaked Marko's breeches as blood seeped from the wound. Two men dragged him by his arms toward the railing. He lost the planks underneath his feet as they hurled his body over the side with one hard thrust. He only had a second to suck in a lungful of air. As he plunged into the icy cold sea, his only chance was to hold his breath. The wrenching pain in his injured hip intensified with the sting of salt and made it all but impossible not to cry out even under water.

In the heaving sea, his lungs screamed for air, but if he broke the surface, Gaspar's men would shoot him before he could take the first reviving breath.

And a dead man would be of no help to Sirena.

His hip revolted in agony the moment he paddled deeper, hoping to find the dinghy somehow.

Chapter 13

At the approach of dawn, thick fog bound the *Strega* in an eerie mist. Splintered wood, messy rigging, discarded weapons, and dead bodies of pirates and Gaspar's men sprawled on the deck. The stench of smoldering wood and spilled blood churned deeper in Sirena's stomach.

Two privateers aimed their harquebuses at the sea. With weapons pressed against their cheeks and their fingers on the triggers of guns, they waited,

A tall ruffian leaned over the shattered railing. "He's not coming up for air, Cap'n."

"Good," Gaspar sneered, grim resolve in his eyes as he glanced at Sirena. "Cap'n Marko is dead." He turned to his men. "Have these two chained and delivered to the frigate."

Though Marko was an excellent swimmer, no one could hold his breath for this long. Especially not with the kind of injury Gaspar had caused him. Determined not to show any emotion, Sirena hardened her expression, but tears stung her eyes all the same. The privateers had not found the scroll in the trunk when they ransacked through its contents. It made no difference, Marko had been killed and the world would never know he'd been the Marquis they'd waited for.

Marta hummed one of the *Strega*'s well-known ballads. Sirena kept her eyes on Angelia's body as Gaspar's men hurriedly fastened a set of iron shackles around her neck, wrists and ankles. Angelia's empty eyes pointed at the sky. A dark blood stain had appeared under her torso and slowly spread over the *Strega*'s boards toward Sirena's feet. Reminded of an old belief that touching those who died with their eyes open was a bad luck, she couldn't help but take a quick step back.

"Nothing would give me more pleasure than to keel haul you right now," Gaspar spat. The redness of his face made the pox marks appear deeper. "I would if not for the fact that your hide is worth more alive. And I'll prove to the world I wasn't mad when I said you existed." He raised his chin and his voice. "Sink this Satan's ship."

"Aye, Cap'n." The shouts came from every direction.

The rusty ring rubbed Sirena's neck raw, while the fetters and manacles dug into her skin, making the burn unbearable. She refused to move and two privateers shoved her toward the frigate. Each time they gave her a push on her back she'd dug in her feet and dared them with an impudent smile. Which only infuriated them further, and they yanked her harder. She'd lost her ship and most of its crew, got captured instead of killed in battle, and worst of all, Marko had died because she had refused to give his warning of a possible trap any consideration. The authorities would be dammed to get a word out of her on who their contact was. Protecting Nikola and his foster family together with all the people who supported them was the last thing she would do before the garrote was placed around her neck. Not even the Pope of Rome would make her confess a word that would endanger her son.

The hulking brute, with eyebrows so thick they looked like one straight line, shoved her again. "You'll wipe that smile right off your face when you stand on the gallows."

She lost her footing on the slippery deck and fell to her knees, but his kick in her ribs sent her to her elbows. Without a sound, she swallowed hard, hoping the two guards wouldn't notice. A booted foot in mid-air ready to strike again, the first guard halted when his comrade spoke.

"Damn you, man. The cap'n will blame us if she's dead. You know he wants the bloody reward down to the last Seguin."

The other ruffian angled his demijohn over her head and poured. "Get up."

The red wine soaked in her hair and mixed with splatters of dried blood on her cheek before it dripped to her lips. Stifling a moan of pain, she stood and cast him a long, silent stare. He replaced the cork on his bottle encased in wickerwork and looked away. It was a small, insignificant victory, nonetheless, Sirena reveled in it.

Two thick beams held the hatch of the frigate's belly propped up as the two women crossed to the enemy's ship.

"Watch your ship now, wenches." Gaspar's voice laden with victory stopped them on their way to the brig. "Port guns—fire!" he barked.

Fifteen cannons, aimed at the *Strega*, thundered at once, blowing the old xebec to nothing more than a hive of driftwood on the waves. Sirena's heart sank, her stomach dropped, but it was Marta's look of grief and yelp of sorrow that stabbed her. Their ship had been the old woman's home for most of her life. Perhaps in Heaven she'd get to command a vessel of her own. Then again what made her think the God's realm waited with gates open wide? Wherever Sirena ended up, she hoped not to come face to face with the old Captain. How was she to explain that she wouldn't listen to reason? She had given her word to the dying woman she'd do her proud. The departed Captain would not be pleased at this moment.

Turning to the bound women, a grin spread on Gaspar's face as he ordered, "Enough wasting time. Lock them below. We must look for captives."

The two women knew better than to flinch at Gaspar's words. Any reaction would have confirmed a small part of the crew had managed to get away from the carnage. Shackles clunked on the wooden stairs and the hutch closed behind them. The musty smell of the brig's air insulted her nostrils. The guard unlocked the cell and opened the screeching door. Shoved hard, Sirena entered the prison. With her back pressed to the dry planks of the wall, men raised her hands above her head to chain her wrists to the iron ring hanging from the low ceiling. Marta met the same treatment on the wall opposite from her.

Once left alone, Sirena's eyes slowly adjusted to the darkness. Certain of prying ears on the other side of the door, she whispered, "They'll never find the dinghy."

After considerable delay, Marta finally replied, "Thank you, Cap'n."

Stupefied, Sirena stared at her prison mate trying to make out her silhouette in the dark. Misery stirred deeper as the realization sank in. She had failed the old captain. "What are you thanking me for? I brought the death to us all, and not the good kind."

"But you also allowed those men to stay on the *Strega*. For once in my life I've known love, even if it only lasted for a few days."

Sirena fell silent. Guilt washed over her for bringing the legend to an ugly end and for the slight twinge of envy at Marta. At least she'd die knowing her Rocco was alive. Marko...Sirena's   head   slumped   forward   as   grief overwhelmed her. She only hoped her trial would take place soon, so she would meet him in the afterlife.

Dazzled by the sun over the water, Sirena squinted and straightened. Fresh air replaced the foul smell of the soggy straw in the dark brig. After two days chained in the ship's belly without a morsel of food and only scarce rations of brassy water, every part of her body screamed with agony. A throng gathered in the small port of Ploče as four guards escorted the two women off the ship, muskets pointed at their prisoners. Sirena was shoved toward the iron cage hoisted on the cart. Disbelief and disdain showed on people's bewildered faces.

"Beg for mercy." Cries replaced the curses they shouted. Guards hurried to lock the door on the cage, dodging foul vegetables. Little did the populace know, her fate was beyond remedy.

Straw crinkled under her while she dragged on her hands and knees to the corner and slumped against the iron bars.

Marta sat facing her. "Pay no heed to the folks, Cap'n. They mean well and are sad to see us captured."

Sirena nodded and swallowed through her dry throat. Caged and put on display like some wild animal to entertain the masses with the spectacle of her capture was demeaning and humiliating. If luck was with them, they wouldn't have to endure a long interrogation and imprisonment only to die from rope fever. "I want this charade over and soon."

A whip cracked and the two mules pulled the cart with their cage. People followed a few paces behind. The masses grew larger as they trotted through the narrow and bumpy streets lined with crowded houses. When the mules passed underneath the high walls, the guards shut the iron gates. The people's shouting continued.

The cart came to a stop in the dismal inner courtyard that appeared shadowy in the dusk. Another soldier unlocked the cage door.

"Get out," Gaspar barked, standing two feet from the cart, fists pushed onto his meaty hips.

Sirena followed Marta out of their mobile prison. A sly smile spread on Gaspar's face, and he grabbed hold of the chains binding her to Marta. Iron rings clunked against the stone paved courtyard as he yanked the restraints and dragged the two women like a pair of bulldogs toward the long table. Men in naval uniforms sat along one side, their backs to the wall of the large stone building.

Military officers scanned their gazes over Sirena and Marta, their eyebrows cocked. A few had their mouths hanging open.

"My reward should be doubled. They cost me many men." Gaspar's greed laden voice caused the officers to turn their heads toward him. Some of them frowned, but mostly everyone appeared disgusted.

The officer in a red admiral's uniform jerked his head at the two armed guards. "Seize him."

The guards scurried to Gaspar and aimed their muskets at his well-fed belly. Dropping the chain from his hands, he raised his arms over his head. "What is the meaning of this?"

The Admiral stood. "She exposed your scam when she sank your first ship." He nudged his chin toward Sirena and continued with bone-chilling indifference. "We let you carry on so you could capture her alive."

Gaspar cast a stern gaze at the Admiral. "What bloody scam?" Fear shook his voice.

The Admiral's unbuttoned doublet opened as he propped one hand on his hip, exposing the gold crusted hilt of his pistol in his waistband. "Have you not charged merchants insurance for their cargo?"

With a hard swallow, Gaspar nodded slowly. "Well yes, as it's required."

Leaning over the table, braced on one hand, the Admiral peered at him over his round spectacles. "But have you ever purchased the policy?"

Gaspar hung his head and pressed his lips tight.

"Have you, Captain?" the Admiral repeated with a raised voice.

Gaspar's eyebrows quirked, but he remained silent as a stone.

"Very well, your silence answered my question. The reward money will hardly pay a few of the victims of you scam. You are in debt to the Duke's Navy." Straightening, the Admiral glanced at the soldiers with their muskets still aimed at Gaspar. "Lock him up."

They lowered their guns and seized Gaspar by his arms.

"I would've captured more of them, but these pirates are swift. They escaped. This is an abomination!" Gaspar yelled, turning his head from side to side. "I'm not the one who should be arrested."

His feet scraped the flagstones of the courtyard as his captors dragged him toward the double pane doors.

"Pox on you all!" he squealed. His protests grew fainter and eventually ceased when the heavy door shut behind them.

Well, who knew God really existed and justice would prevail in the end, Sirena thought. Though the unexpected turn of the events wouldn't change her or Marta's situation, it still filled her with a flash of satisfaction.

Four constables led the two captive pirates down the worn stone steps to an underground room then removed their shackles. Spreading their arms wide, the men chained the wrists of the two women to the wooden beams on the wall. Sirena's feet barely reached the dirt floor. One of the men grabbed her chin and jerked her head from side to side. A slow smile crept across his face as he swiped his thumb over her lips and forced it into her mouth. His vile taste of gun oil and dirt made her gag. She bit his finger hard. He howled, pulling out his thumb.

"You filthy bitch!" He struck her with his fist. Her cheek burned with pain. She spat a mouthful of blood at him, but he'd stepped back in time to evade it.

Laughing scornfully, the man left.

Judging by screaming muscles in her arms and shoulders, many hours must have passed as they waited in the damp cell. Marta had stopped talking after a few minutes. Wanting to rid her thoughts of the turmoil of losing everything she had worked so hard to keep, even the company of a rat peering at her from a dark corner seemed appealing.

A screeching sound made her turn her head slowly toward the door. Two constables stepped in and unchained her from the wall. Leaving Marta behind, they led her through a maze of corridors and into a room similar to her cell. But in this one a chair faced a small table and a bucket of water was placed next to it. A large candelabrum cast long shadows that danced on the walls and ceiling.

The guard ordered her to sit and then proceeded to bind her wrists behind her back.

"You're tying my hands so I can't cradle my head from the blows, aren't you?" she said in a frightful whisper, but the man didn't comment. She was right. They would beat a confession out of her. Or they would try. But they could tear her joints out one by one. She would not give them the answers they wanted. Troubling question was how much they already knew?

A man in uniform took the seat opposite from her. Blank papers in front of him crinkled and from the way he poised the pen over them, Sirena concluded he was an *ilustrisimo*. In a routine tone, he demanded to know her name, age, and the names of her family members. She remained silent. When her questioner persisted, she dared him with a smirk. The scribe tilted his head, and as if he had hoped she would not co-operate, he put his quill to the paper. Scratching of his pen filled Sirena with fear of what he could be recording when she had not said a single word. He put his quill into the inkwell, dusted powder over the page and put away his sheet.

He stood and leaned over the table. "Who assisted you?"

She locked her glance with his cold eyes. "Assisted me, *Ilustrisimo*?"

"What do you know of a man called Antun?"

So, his question at least answered one of hers. What they knew wasn't enough to connect the dots. And she'd be damned if she'd say one word that would solve their puzzle. By now Antun would've heard of her capture and would have moved his family away.

"It's a common name, *Ilustrisimo*."

The scribe rounded the table and sat on the edge, his receding hairline gleamed in the light of the candelabrum. "You deny that you know this man?"

A dizzy feeling swept over her. She had not eaten a bite in over two days. Exhausted and starved, she felt the room spun in front of her.

"Answer the question," he ordered.

She did not. Instead, she gave an audacious laugh and concentrated on the floor before her. Obeying an order issued by the scribe, a constable stepped forward and struck a ferocious blow to the nape of her neck. The chair underneath her wobbled as her body slumped, but she steadied herself, choking on the scream that tried to escape.

"Answer the question," the scribe repeated, his voice uncompromising.

She kept her eyes on the flat stone stuck deep in the dirt, just like her in these dungeons. Another blow to her neck followed and stunned her by its force. Blood and ashes, if she wasn't tied to this chair, she'd show them both who to fear. Tears of pain welled up in her eyes despite her attempt to contain them, and she couldn't even wipe them. Damn, this was no moment to cry.

"Who assisted you?"

Her head swam with another blow. The chair shifted and toppled over, taking her to the cold floor. The constable bent over her and continued his torture by taking his whip to every part of her body he could reach. She bit her lips, but could no longer hold the scream in her throat.

"Answer."

Like echoes in a bad dream the shouts came from a distance. She was no longer in the underground room facing her inquisitor and a woman-beating constable. A green pasture sprinkled with spring flowers opened before her. Nikola ran toward her, his arms opened wide. Marko ran right behind her son.

Cold water splashed over her head, ceasing her dream. When the constable jerked her up, she could not contain a moan of desperation. Her tormentors had all the time in the world to take her to hell, but she would remain tight lipped.

The scribe hurriedly gathered his papers. "Enough for now. Take her back to her cell."

The constable gripped her arms and pushed her in front of him through narrow corridors. Her battered body screamed in protest with her every move, but she refused to show her pain and weakness. Darkness swallowed her again as she waited in front of the cell's door.

Sirena woke with a start at the sharp nails scratching at her bare feet. Screaming, she kicked her feet, and the sound of the rat skittering across the cold floor drifted to her. Her swollen eyes refused to open. The heavy chains rattled as she tried to ease her aching arms and shoulders.

"Stay still, Cap'n. I'll get that rat soon." Marta pressed a wet cloth over her forehead. The coldness seeped through her hot skin and eased some pain. "They beat you good. Animals."

Sirena licked her lips caked in dried blood. "You're not chained?" she asked with faint voice.

"I am. By my ankles. They ordered me to tend to you." Marta brought a ladle to her mouth and urged her to take a few sips of water. She lowered her voice to a whisper. "Not to worry, Cap'n. They didn't get a word out of me. Though they tried. Josef and Mary, did they try."

"Good," Sirena croaked. "How much time do we have left?"

A long silence came from Marta's end. She sounded grim when she answered, "Longer than either of us want. By my reckoning, they are speeding up the trial but I haven't heard when."

"I want this hell finished and fast."

"Me too, Cap'n." Marta tried to adjust Sirena's arms. Maybe her screaming muscles would find some rest. "But there has to be a good reason why the Lord wants us alive."

"I hope you are right, Marta. I really do." Discomfort, fatigue and pain spun Sirena's mind into unconsciousness again. Her feet pounded the lush grass as happiness filled her. With each step she came closer to Nikola and Marko.

Chapter 14

Dim moonlight cast an eerie glow on the rugged path in front of Marko. Crickets chirping and the scent of pine sap filled the moist summer air. Propped between skinny Rocco and another surviving sailor, Marko limped, struggling to ignore the pain searing through his hip and shooting down his leg. They approached the village—a cluster of houses, built high up, away from the shore, as a precaution against attacks. Nothing had changed in the year since he'd last seen his island, where everyone knew one another.

Panting, Rocco asked, "Shall we rest again, Cap'n?"

A large stone house surrounded by fortification walls on top of the imposing hill, watching over a sleepy fishermen's village, brought a sigh of relief to Marko. A few more steps to the front door stood between him and the only man he could ask for help. "We must keep moving."

"Are you sure, Cap'n?" Rocco adjusted Marko's arm on his skinny shoulder. "Your hip barely stopped bleeding."

"But the pain won't give me a moment's peace." Holding his leg propped on a rock, Marko cringed at the thought of taking another step. "Perhaps we should rest for a minute."

The two men leaned him against the waist high dry wall. He pulled the bandana out of his breech's pocket and mopped his forehead. "I meant to ask you, how did you find me in the water?"

Rocco shrugged. "We saw Gaspar's men hurl someone overboard. When a head bobbed to the surface in the dark, I knew it was you. No one else can stay under as long as you. I jumped out of the dinghy and swam."

"You gave me a fright when you grabbed me from behind. Don't ever sneak up on me like that." Pushing away from the wall, Marko lifted his chin and straightened his spine. "Shall we continue?"

"Aye, Cap'n." Both men wrapped his arms around their shoulders and grunted under his weight.

Clenching his teeth, Marko dragged his leg behind. "How did you know to hide me in the fishermen's hut in the cove of Srebrena?"

"Where else could I hide you so your father wouldn't know you're back? In two days since we got to our island you don't want to return home. Why do you postpone? All of the men went back." Rocco's bony shoulders slumped under Marko's arm. "I hear your father is grief-stricken with the news of your death."

Guilt stabbed at Marko for keeping his father in the dark, but his intuition told him his supposed demise would work out to his advantage. "He thinks I died with the sinking of the *Levant*. Let him think so until it is safe for me and him to announce differently. Sailors have been known to come back from the dead."

Rocco gulped the heavy air. "At least I was able to talk some sense into you. Rushing hot headed into saving our women will do no good for anyone. We need to plan this rescue carefully."

"You are right." Though being in love left him deprived of his sanity, Marko had no choice but to hang onto the fact Sirena and Marta were worth a good coin and that was all the bilge rat who held them cared about. "Are you sure there were no more sightings of Gaspar's ship?"

"Aye, Cap'n. Last we saw of him was two days ago through the looking glass at a great distance." The mariner holding Marko's right arm helped him climb the high step.

And yet Marko couldn't wait any longer. He had to act and call on someone who could help to save Sirena and Marta. His friend Conte Albert Panov may be just the person Marko was looking for.

"Will Conte Panov offer his protection to those pirate women?" Worry laced Rocco's voice as the black double door blocking the archway came in sight.

Marko drew a long breath. He and Conte had parted ways over a year ago and were not on best of the terms, but it was such a minor disagreement. "We shall see." He had been regarded as one of the duke's favorites for a few years. Hopefully he had not fallen from grace.

"We made it, Cap'n." Rocco swiped his free arm over his sweaty brow.

"We didn't *make it* until I hold Sirena in my arms, alive." Marko had to hold on to his hope and not think of her as dead. "Let's see if anyone's home."

He clenched his teeth and pushed through the last few long steps to close the distance to the gate. Deep burning pain multiplied in Marko's hip with each step he took.

Rocco rapped three times with a heavy brass knocker. There was no answer nor any sounds on the other side. Damn, either Conte Panov was out or he enjoyed the company of a lady or, most likely, more than one.

Marko tweaked his head toward the door. "Knock again. Harder this time."

Rocco wrapped his bony fingers around the hinged knob and rapped again. Still no one answered. Double damn.

"Again?" Rocco asked.

Marko nodded. Sweat permeated his clothes and glued his shirt to his torso, intensifying his discomfort and pain.

Before Rocco reached for the knocker the third time, the door swung opened. A man in a nightshirt and cap stood on the other side. The flame of a candle in his hand cast shadows in his sunken cheeks.

"Good evening, Otto." Marko said in a kindly tone, in spite of gritting his teeth in pain from his aching wound.

With his spectacles askew, the sleepy man leaned forward to inspect Marko's face. "Young Nobile Lucin, is that you?" he finally croaked with wonder in his voice.

Marko breathed in relief when the servant recognized him. "It is me, indeed. Otto, I need an audience with His Lordship."

"He is being...um...entertained, but I'm sure he would like to see you." Stepping aside, Otto opened the door fully. "Come in. I'll tell him you are here."

"Thank you," Marko said through an involuntary groan as he raised his foot over the high marble doorsill.

Otto led the three men through the flagstone-paved inner courtyard. The scent of lemon and mandarin wafted from the trees encircling the rim of the water cistern. It reminded Marko of the careless days he had spent here perched on the highest branches, daydreaming of grand adventures at seas. Well no one could say his dreams didn't come true.

One hand on the knob of the heavy door at the far end of the yard, Otto ushered them inside a long hallway then into the Conte's study. The two men lowered Marko to a wide leather chair. With great difficulty, he stretched his left leg and let out a long sigh as the constant pain in his hip eased once his weight wasn't pressing down on it. Rocco took a seat facing him.

Otto's blinking eyes traveled from man to man. "By God's grace, what happened to you?"

"We were attacked," Marko murmured as his eyes tracked the other sailor leaving the room. His men never lost their place or sense of duty. Marko raised his head at Otto. "Would you offer a goblet of vine to him? It took great effort for them to get me here."

"Gladly, Nobile Lucin," Otto said, stressing his title and family name. "The bad news about the sinking of the *Levant* reached us, but that was weeks ago. You look like you've been in battle not forty-eight hours ago. Rumor has it there was a fight near Vis." The old man gave Marko a dubious look. "You haven't been there by any chance? I've heard they captured the notorious pirate Sirena. Can you believe it? She is real." He shook his head with wonder. "I mean, *really* real. And there—"

"Otto!" Marko shifted in discomfort. "Would you just go and get His Lordship, please? And don't forget about the sailor."

"Of course, young Master." Otto's footsteps dragged on the tiles then up the creaking stairs. Muffled voices drifted to Marko before footsteps came downstairs again.

A tall, strong man entered the library after Otto. Tightening the waistband of his velvet house coat, Albert's eyes scanned the room. His dark eyebrows arched and after a short pause, he let out a loud aristocrat's laugh. "By all that's holy, Marko, you are alive!"

Pleased by his friend's honest welcome, Marko attempted to stand, but the pain pulled him down. "I'm not a ghost yet, but I don't feel far from it either."

"Pardon my appearance. I'm afraid you pulled me out of a warm bed." Albert ran his fingers through his thick chestnut hair and stroked his beard. He stepped up to Marko and squeezed his shoulder. "I shall dispatch a messenger to your house. Oh, your poor father has been grief stricken."

Marko pushed against the armrests and got on his feet, despite the pain, then gave his friend a proper greeting, by looking him in the eye and giving him a firm handshake. "My apologies for interrupting and pulling you away from whatever lady you might have been enjoying. But the matter is pressing. Please don't send your dispatcher. It is essential that my father doesn't know of my fate yet. If he sees me unable to stand on my two feet with this hip sliced, he'd take it harder than if I'm truly dead."

Albert turned to Otto, standing at the doorway. "Otto, bring a bottle of the best Malvasija. These men need something strong." Turning, his intelligent eyes on Marko, he added, "And judging from the sorry state of you, I'll need it too." He gestured with his broad hand toward the chair. "Take a seat. That leg doesn't look good. So, what is this pressing matter of yours?"

Lowering himself to the chair, Marko examined the Conte's face. Could he trust his friend? He had not seen him in some time and people tended to change. Hell, even he had changed. A year ago he'd never have dreamed of settling down with one woman for life. But had he met Sirena then, he would have been a married man by now and none of this would have happened.

A familiar, curious smile crept to Albert's face. "The unexpected visit in the middle of the night and your poor condition tells me you're in deep trouble and need my help. I'm willing to bet all my wealth a woman is behind this."

Instilled with encouragement by Conte's words, Marko spoke. "I'm sure you have heard of the battle two nights ago."

A deep scowl replaced Albert's smile. His eyes scanned the two men seated in his library and stopped on Marko. "Tell me you have nothing to do with it."

"I—I have everything to do with it."

After a hard stare, Albert burst into laughter. His gales of amusement quickly ceased when no one joined in. He whirled to Rocco. "Rocco, you've always been a man of reason. What kind of prank is your captain trying to pull on me?"

"It is not a prank, Your Lordship."

As Albert's eyes widened, he slowly raised his arm and pointed at Marko. "Didn't I tell you, you have the strange ability to make your life difficult?"

Marko opened his mouth in protest but shut it fast as Otto re-appeared, carrying a tray with an uncorked bottle of wine and three crystal goblets. All conversation ceased while the servant poured the bronze liquid of the *prosecco* wine into the glasses and handed them to the men. He stood by the door waiting on further orders.

"Thank you, Otto," Albert said, his tone somber, not taking his eyes off Marko. "That will be all."

"Very well, Sir." Otto bowed slowly and left the room, closing the door behind him.

"Tell me all you've heard of Sirena's capture." Marko spoke first, not giving Albert a chance to bombard him with questions. The time to tell tales would come. Saving Sirena was of most importance.

Albert took a long sip of his finest wine and smacked his lips. "I hear they arrested that swine of Gaspar on the insurance scam. He'll be sent to serve on the slave galleon for the rest of his miserable life."

"The Devil comes to claim his own." Marko spun the long stem of his glass in between his fingers and watched the liquid swirl. At least something good had come out of this. "What of the two women captives?"

After a long and foreboding silence, Albert answered, "They'll bear the worst of it, I'm afraid. My contact informed me, they are held in the dungeons in the port of Ploče. That is where the trial and execution will take place."

Rocco sprang to his feet. "Forgive my impertinence. They'll be given a trial?" A hint of hope trembled in his voice.

Turning to him, Albert placed a hand on his arm. "The trial is just a formality. They'll be hanged all the same. It is the proper end of all those rogues and ruffians who dare to practice the villainous business of piracy."

The light went out in Rocco's eyes and he returned to his seat, letting out an exasperated sigh. "The two women are nothing of that sort."

A fist squeezed Marko's heart. He placed the glass on the side table, fearing it would crush in his grip. "They are corsairs, not pirates. Once a noble profession, they attacked the enemy's ships and paid the duke's quint."

Albert wobbled his head. "Those are the ancient times. When corsairs were granted patent and were ruled by certain laws agreed by nations. Then the duke turned against them and they pocketed their profits." After a loud sigh, he continued. "I cannot intervene in the affairs of the duke's navy. No one can." He gestured with his strong hands. "This is not something we can bother His Excellency with." Bringing the glass to his lips, he studied Marko with his eyes narrowed. "I'd ask why you have such interest in the women, but I can see it all over your face. You are in love with one of them."

Marko closed his eyes and nodded.

The mere thought of Sirena locked up in the dungeons, in the hands of men who'd resort to torture to extract information from her, filled Marko with dread. Rocco's face showed equal despair when Marko cut him a glance. The urge to act pressed hard on Marko's mind. "We'll have to do it then. The execution, when will it take place?"

"In a week's time, but you are in no condition to fight." Albert scurried out of the room and called Otto, then returned. "My physician should have a look at your hip."

Scratching his chin, Albert's glance moved from Marko to Rocco. A slow smile crept on his lips. "I'll take a ship with no coat-of-arms, no insignia, and a few men from my personal guard."

Puzzled, Marko furrowed his brow, but quickly realized that without the distinguishing marks of honor, the Conte couldn't be implicated in this rescue. "I'm not expecting you to come along."

"Well, I have to." Albert said, tilting his head. "Not completely out of unselfishness, I must admit. A heroic act like that will help the people here to eventually forget about my scandalous affair involving a certain actress."

"The lady you left in your bed, I presume."

"Yes. And no." Albert sighed. "But the affair is winding down. She overstepped my hospitality. Come morning, she'll be instructed to pack her belongings and leave." Albert placed the empty glass on the table and spun on his heel, his hands poised at his sides. "Cruel of me, you may think, but the word matrimony crossed her lips more times than I like to hear."

Marko let out a short chuckle. He was right, his friend hadn't changed one bit. Always in the company of ladies and a bottle of fine wine. "May true love find you one day."

Helping himself to more wine, Albert shot Marko a glance. "Curses of such nature are wasted on me, Nobile Lucin. And had you not set sail you too would be immune to such useless emotion."

The door opened and Otto stepped in. "You called, Sir."

"Ah, yes." Flicking his head at Marko, Albert said, "Do fetch the physician. He has a patient to see."

"Right away, Sir. It may take a few minutes. His quarters are on the far side." Otto nodded and scurried from the room.

Shifting his feet, Albert faced his visitors. "Otto is getting old, I'm afraid. He can't take a single order without complaining. Anyways, it will take us two days to sail to our destination. I suggest you all get plenty of rest. You'll need it."

"You have been very generous with your time." Rocco spoke, graveness lacing his voice. "All of our surviving men took a wife from the *Strega*. However, a few are still hiding. Will Your Lordship help them too?"

Arms wide open, Albert raised his palms toward the stucco ceiling. "They have my pardon and can come freely to the village."

"We are deeply grateful and indebted to Your Lordship." Rocco stood and bowed.

"I appreciate you honoring me, Rocco. However, save it for later, when all of this is over."

"This," Marko said loudly, stopping Albert on his way out of the room, "is not one of our childhood games." Shaking his head, Marko cast his friend a side glance. "This is real and you can lose your influence at the court, or worse, get killed."

With one hand behind his back, Albert strutted toward Marko. "It is about time I too get a taste of a real fight. And my influence has been on decline for a long time. The duke is both ungrateful and forgetful."

Marko caught a glimpse of bitterness and disappointment in Albert's eyes. Younger flamboyant people replaced the aged ones in the duke's court, just as his friend here once had taken someone else's position. Albert had known his time too would come and judging by his face, he wasn't prepared to live without certain privileges that came with the title of The Duke's Favorite.

"Will you extend that pardon to me and my men? We were pirates, too."

Cocking his thick eyebrow, Albert regarded him. "For how long?"

Marko pulled a wry grin. "For a day."

"Ah!" Albert expressed his annoyance with a wave of his hand and a click of his tongue. "You are pardoned."

"The physician, Sir."

Otto's droning, coming through the closed door, stopped Marko's chuckling. He leaned closer to Albert. "Before you ask him in, I should show you something."

Curiosity flashed in the Conte's eyes and he pulled the door open. "One moment." Closing the door, he whirled to face Marko. "Let me see."

Marko nodded at Rocco and grabbed the bottle from the table. "Go sit with the other sailor. You two can finish this."

"Aye, Cap'n." Taking the wine in his hand, Rocco left.

"What I'm about to show you must not leave this room." At his devoted friend's nod, Marko pulled a thin scroll from inside his shirt. "This was tucked in my waistband. It slowed Gaspar's blade and saved my life."

Unrolling the aged and slit paper, Albert brought it into the light of a candle. His dark eyes traveled across the page as he read. For minutes, he stood motionless, then he straightened, drawing a long breath. "You are the Young Marquis."

"So it seems." Marko took the scroll from Albert's hand and rolled the paper back into its casing. "It is my understanding that my title has been forfeited."

"I'm afraid so. The title of Marquis is gone from these parts." After another deep breath, Albert continued. "Keep this to yourself and never show it to anyone. Don't even mention it. The proof you hold in your hands now could very well bring an end to you, your family, and your friends."

"I had to die to get rid of Contessa de Montagne. If she finds out about this, I'm sure she'd come back to claim me again."

"What makes you think you got rid of her?" Albert chuckled. "She is here and rumor has it with your child."

A sharp pain shot through Marko's leg and up his spine when he sprang to his feet. "Dios Santos, she is what?"

Albert's lips curled. "I knew the girl was lying. Don't fall for a well-known woman's trick. Otherwise I'd have to ask you how drunk you had been that night."

"Impudent woman. I was never that drunk," Marko sneered, his fingers curled into tight fists.

Chapter 15

Hot wax splattered in the pool of the melted candle and the blue flame slowly died. Through the stale air of the cell, the smell of a burnt out wick drifted to Sirena. The bleak light of a new day chased away the darkness from the corners. The pain in her arms and shoulders should have eased since the guards unchained her. Instead, her entire body burned.

She found a little comfort in the belief that she would be seeing Marko soon, but her throat closed with the thought of never again smiling down on Nikola or hugging her brothers.

Eyelids partly opened, she scanned the interior of the prison one last time, before the guards took them to the gallows. On the stone walls, countless blood stains, some almost invisible, stood as witnesses of torture. The rat Marta had killed by stomping on its head with her bare foot lay in the musty straw with its legs up in the air.

The priest's monotonous voice and Marta's pious mumbling had calmed Sirena's racing mind. But now she needed her head clear, so she focused on the preacher who still knelt in the middle of the cell and spoke his words of absolution. Soon she too found herself repeating prayer after prayer. Asking God for forgiveness and confessing her sins. The one night of passion she had spent in Marko's strong arms, she kept to herself. She could never think of their love making as a sin.

The cold dirt floor pressed against Sirena's knees. Her captors had not taken her for another rough interrogation for two days. The number of beatings they'd given her had declined when they realized their efforts were of no use. She would be sent to the rope all the same. If she had not squealed under their blows and lashes by then, she wouldn't at all. With an ironic laugh, Sirena thought they must be ill in their minds, if they believed for one second that she would give them any information about her son or her good friend Antun.

She wished the preacher would stop his charade of holiness and her life would end so she could close her eyes one last time and never wake again.

The sound of keys clinking drifted to her. Sirena held her breath. The door opened and two soldiers stepped in. "It is time."

She exhaled. Soon all her pain would be gone.

The priest got to his feet and retrieved two tiny biscuits from his deep pockets. Holding one in front of Sirena's face, he said, "Body of Christ."

"Amen." Her whisper was scarcely audible. She opened her mouth and the priest slid the dry, round wafer inside then moved to Marta.

With their last rites given, the man of cloth strutted out of their cell.

One of the soldiers stepped behind her and mercilessly chopped her hair with his dagger, ensuring her neck would be exposed to the rope. Tears burned her battered face as they slid down her cheeks. With every strand cut off, her humiliation mounted. A moment later, Marta's gray frizzes dropped to the floor, too. Sirena cringed at the sight of the old woman's red-rimmed eyes sunken in dark circles. Lowering her gaze, Sirena focused on her bruised arms. She imagined she must look the same as Marta, if not worse.

"On your feet," the soldier ordered.

The slightest movement caused great pain in her crippled joints, but she stood straight and proud. Manacles and fetters once again cut into her already swollen and bruised wrists and ankles.

"Move." The constable shoved her toward the door. She stumbled, but steadied her footing. Her fetters clunked along the stones on the floor.

Climbing the narrow stairs presented a challenge and at times she doubted she'd make it to the top, but the lash on her exposed calves urged her to push forward. Her foot slipped on a step. Unbalanced, she fell. The cold stones scraped her knees. Fresh blood stains didn't escape her eyes when Marta attempted to hide them with her wide feet.

Sirena blinked against the bleak sun trying to burn through an early morning fog. The two gallows ensured her that the trial would be swift and unjust. They also eased her fear of more captured crewmembers. At least only she and Marta would hang today. Gaspar must not have found the dinghy full of survivors, or he would have delivered them and claimed his prize. And every killed member dragged at least a hundred Sequins with them to the bottom of the sea. Had he captured the entire crew alive it wouldn't have been enough to pay off the debt to the navy for the scam he had run. A slow smile crept to her lips. She'd die content the pig got what he deserved.

Dazed by the meager sunlight, Sirena stopped in front of the long table. Men in uniforms of all ranks sat on the other side. She focused on the gathered crowd behind. The peasants, fishermen, common folk she and her crew had helped, now came to see her beaten and broken body and spirit and witness the spectacle of her demise.

"Carmen Ventura of Sylba," the Admiral said. "Or better known as Sirena of the Adriatic. You and your crew have caused the duke's navy and Venetian merchants a tremendous loss, in men, ships and cargo. Anything you have to say now will not suffice to save you."

She hung her head in shame. No, there was nothing she wanted to say. Her only regret was that she got captured, instead of dying alongside Marko.

The plums on the Admiral's hat swayed as he turned his head toward the scribe. The balding man, who had ordered her beatings, unrolled the scroll and read the list of her and Marta's crimes, all punishable by death. The audience cried in distress when Marta was handed down the highest penalty.

The drum roll filled the air announcing Sirena's verdict was about to be read. The scribe unrolled another scroll. "Sirena of the Adriatic, by the decree of his Excellency Duke Ludovico Manin, you are sentenced to death by hanging until you are dead!"

The crowd's booing and throwing of rotten eggs muffled his words. The scribe took cover under the very scroll he' read and scurried back to the table.

A smile of relief spread over Sirena's face. Another minute was all she'd have to endure and the relentless pain in her burning body would end. With a hard pull, two executioners dragged Sirena and Marta under the nooses. A soldier beat his drum with their every step until they reached the esplanade in front of the outer defensive walls. As the drumroll ceased, the clinking of the chains filled the eerie silence while the two women climbed the six steps to the top of the platform. The noose dangled in front of Sirena's face. She turned her head to the top of the wall.

From there the vast Adriatic spread in front of her. Soon, she'd meet her fallen sisters and all her family on the other side, in the afterlife.

"No, stop!" Carlo's desperate voice threw the crowd into a new disorder. He freed himself from the hold of two soldiers. Loose strands of his captain's doublet showed torn epaulettes and buttons and confirmed Sirena's suspicion. Her brothers had been stripped of their ranks. He stepped in front of the gallows. Dirt had settled in the lines around his wide eyes highlighting his fear.

Fighting tears, she shook her head. "Don't..."

He turned to the tribunal and addressed the Admiral. "With all due respect, Your Mercies, you've got the wrong woman. This cannot be Sirena. She's my sister." Whirling around, he faced her again. "For God's sake, tell them you are not Sirena, Carmen. Beg for justice."

Desperate and ashamed, she feared her legs would fail her. A look of astonishment replaced his disbelief. Through no fault of their own her brothers' military careers were over with dishonorable discharges. She pressed her lips tight and strangled a cry in her throat. What could she tell him, standing in front of the platform where she'd hang in a minute? Her fate was sealed. She'd brought shame on her family and uncertainty to her brothers' futures. But he was expecting an answer and no right words came to her.

One of the uniformed men stood. "She is a bloody pirate and now she'll get what she deserves. Step back, Captain. Or should I say ex-captain?"

At the man's sharp tone, Carlo spun to face the Commodore.

A row of soldiers, with muskets pointed toward his heart, formed in front of Carlo. He gasped, stretching his arms out, standing protectively between his sister and firing squad. "No."

"Don't be daft. There is nothing you can say or do to change her verdict. She must hang." The Commodore jerked his head at the armed soldiers.

The metallic sounds, of muskets packing powder into pans, set Sirena's spine on a shiver. These men swore their obedience to the duke's navy and given the order, they would pull those triggers and kill her brother. Too much blood had been spilled already, she couldn't allow this.

Carlo turned to her with horror in his eyes. "What can I do, Carmen? How can I save you?"

She inclined her head toward her brother and forced words out through her tight throat. "There is nothing you can do. I am what they say. I'm so sorry I failed you, Carlo." She swallowed against a dry throat. "I am not afraid of dying. Mama and Papa will await me, I know. Take care of the family."

Carlo gulped, but he didn't reply. His silent gaze was excruciating. The tenderness of his rough palm as he touched her bare foot filled her with warmth. He understood her words and he'd find Nikola and raise him as his own. The fact her son would know the truth was a balm on her battered mind.

Through the haze of her tears, she watched his back as he dragged his feet toward the main gate. It was for the best. He had given her his blessing and forgiveness, and she was glad he didn't stay to see the final act. The executioner stepping to her with a black sack in his hand spoiled her short moment of relief.

"No!" She jerked her head at the executioner's attempt to pull the sack over her head. She had faced death before, the only difference—today there was no chance of escaping the Grim Reaper.

The bell in the church steeple rang its sepulchral tone. The sun peeked out from behind the clouds, washing the crowd in the morning light. Two monks with wide hoods hiding their faces stood in the front row. One leaned heavily on his cane. Were they here to make sure her soul ascended to heaven? Hadn't a priest already given them absolution? Sirena shook her head at her silliness to ponder over such insignificant things when her end was imminent.

The sun's sudden arrival raised the heat to an unbearable level. Or could it be her fever? Her vision blurred the courtyard with its audience and tribunal. Everything began to spin. Weak knees grew unstable. She had to maintain dignity and not allow them to see her fall. She struggled to keep her eyes open, but failed, collapsing on the wooden planks of the podium before the executioner pulled the noose over her head. The man leaned over her. His eyes widened through the slits of his black hood. Straightening, he whirled and faced the crowd. "Plague! She's plagued!"

For a few long moments stunned silence gripped the people in the courtyard, then a collective gasp pierced the air. The metallic clicking of spurs on an officer's boots approached. A man in a navy uniform leaned over her, examining her face without touching her. He stepped a couple of feet away and spoke to another uniformed guard. "Clear the courtyard, her body has to be burned to prevent spreading the disease."

They would burn her alive. Had she had any strength left in her battered body, she'd protest. But it didn't matter as long as she died today.

"Everyone out." The executioner's voice thundered, but the people had already panicked and pushed toward the narrow gateway. Muskets fired in the air, most likely to bring the crowd under control, but the shots only seemed to bring more disorder in the courtyard.

A wooden cross dangling in front of a monk's brown habit came into her view through the haze and her own fast blinking. Deep blue eyes shone from under the hood.

Chapter 16

Marko had kept the entire spectacle of Sirena and Marta's trail under his attentive view, waiting for the opportune moment to save the woman he loved and her quartermaster. When Sirena collapsed before the rope had been placed around her neck, he didn't know whether to curse or thank God.

"Control that unruly crowd," the Commodore barked at the two guards in front of the gallows platform. They joined their comrades in pushing the people toward the gate as they rushed for the exit.

The commotion caused by the executioner's warning that Sirena was plagued had presented an opportunity to get her out of this courtyard to safety. But Marko couldn't save her from the disease. Could he bring the epidemic to his island?

Rooted, he stood while his mind screamed at him to go to her. Why this reluctance? This woman had saved him. His life and heart belonged to her. Under no condition would he leave her here at the mercy of the duke's navy. She had suffered enough.

In four long strides, he reached the platform. Crouched next to Sirena, he glanced toward the sky. The two empty nooses dangling above him. Another gray cloud covered the sun and the coolness of the early morning resumed. He exhaled and looked down on her swollen, bruised, and bloodied face. He wanted to get hold of the bastards who'd been this unbelievably cruel and show them the same mercy as they'd shown to her. None.

A deep groan caused him to cast a glance over his shoulder. He caught a glimpse of Conte Albert thrusting his sword into the executioner. Armed soldiers used their spent muskets to shove and push the screaming crowd toward the gates. He and his friends must hurry, the reinforcements would be sent to control the masses tethering on the verge of unruliness. Marko stroked Sirena's burning forehead. Next to him Rocco hastened to remove Marta's shackles.

Wiggling her battered feet out of her fetters, Marta scooped Rocco in a bear hug. "I never lost my faith in you."

"*Cara mia,*" Rocco cried and kissed her cheek. "I would die without you."

Marko urged him to unshackle Sirena. "Hurry."

Marta let go of Rocco and he kneeled next to Sirena. His skinny fingers slid the knife inside the lock and the rusty mechanism clicked, opening the rings around Sirena's wrists and ankles.

Marko whistled low. "Impressive. No one can remove these irons faster than you." He yanked the chains off and hung them over the rear wall. "There, this will send the soldiers in the wrong direction."

Albert jumped onto the podium and squeezed Marko's shoulder. "If she is plagued, you'd bring the disease to the entire island."

Marko's stomach plummeted at his friends words. "If she is, as least I'll give her a decent burial." A cold steel blade of sorrow pierced his heart at the sight of her battered face and shorn hair. He'd never forget the boils on a man dying of the black plague. The blistering on Sirena's lips appeared less deadly.

Albert tightened his hold on Marko's shoulder. "If she dies, it is God's will."

"No." Marko scanned the swaying nooses. "This is not God's doing." He looked down on Sirena's barely recognizable face. If it wasn't for her feverish forehead, he'd fear she was dead. "One way or the other the physician will know. Your fast thinking proved right when you brought him along."

Shifting his cane into his right hand, Marko got to his feet and clenched his teeth. His wound had been properly tended to and bandaged, but still caused him great pain, the kind he would feel for years. The restless nights he had paced across the floor and pondered how to get her out of prison had not aided in his healing. Neither were the two damp and cold nights he had spent on the ship the prescription for a cure.

As much as he didn't want anyone to carry Sirena but him, he wouldn't get far on his lame leg with her in his arms.

Rocco had already clad Marta in a brown monk's frock when he handed another one to Marko. "Make it fast."

After wrapping the cloth around Sirena's feverish body, he pulled a deep hood over her head and turned to Albert. "You'll have to carry her out."

Albert grimaced as if he swallowed a gag. "No offense, but the odor emanating from her is putrid."

Taken aback by his friend's words, Marko scowled at him. "You made me a captain of your ship. Do as I tell you, Conte."

Darting his glance left and right, Albert wobbled his head, frowned, and finally hissed, "I meant we'd fight our way out."

"Didn't you have enough fighting for one day?"

"I've barely tasted it." Albert sheathed his sword and exhaled. "A man could fry in this robe on a hot day. I guess that is why they are called friars."

"You may get the opportunity for more fight if we don't get out of here. For now, just carry her." Ignoring the stench radiating from her, Marko placed a soft kiss on Sirena's temple. God she burned. "It'll be all right. We have a doctor on the ship. He'll heal you."

Albert draped the unconscious body over his shoulder and headed toward the gate. The crowd pressed against it, trying to get through, clogging it like a cork sealing a bottle.

Encouraged by Albert's and Rocco's nods, Marko stepped forward. "People, please give way."

Those near him turned their displeased faces at him, but no one moved out of their way until Marko swayed his cane. "I'm asking you to let us pass."

He elbowed through and halted at the entrance facing two armed guards. With a hard swallow, he wet his throat. "For God's sake, bring these people in order. This unruly crowd caused one of our brothers to faint. We must get out and tend to him."

"By all means, friars," said the taller of the guards and leaned toward Marko as if to get a closer look.

"Wait!" The other guard stepped closer. "There were only two friars entering the courtyard."

Marko shoved his hand inside the wide sleeve of his habit and squeezed the pommel of his short sword. "Four of us brothers came to witness this...spectacle." He turned to the courtyard then back at the guard. "And quite a spectacle it is."

The guard scanned him with twitching eyes. "I only saw two come through."

His counterpart nodded. "So did I."

"Well then. That makes four, right?" Marko struggled to keep his voice steady. "We must return to our monastery, and the road is long. Please, let us tend to our brother."

Pressured by the crowd eager to get out, the two guards exchanged confused glances. The taller one shrugged and jerked his head toward the exit. Marko relaxed his hand on the sword's handle then led his small group out the fort.

"Quick," he said, ushering Albert in front. "Keep your heads down and plow onward." He raised his hand to Sirena's hood to pull it up and give her some air, but quickly lowered his arm. In this noisy disturbance, he couldn't risk anyone seeing who was under the habit.

Albert halted. "She is trying to say something."

Marko leaned his ear over her cracked lips and waited. A very faint whisper came from her. She called a man's name.

Pulling back, he cut Marta a puzzled look. "Nikola?"

For a few seconds, Marta pursed her lips. Her silence ensured Marko she knew who this man was.

"He's her son," she finally said after a long sigh. "Antun, our connection, is raising him. He most likely took his family into hiding after our capture."

Her son. Marko's stomach knotted. Sirena was a mother, but then why was he surprised? She was a widow. Therefore, she'd been married and could have a child. She'd recognized the contents of the hidden chest as a mother's trove. Only a mother would cherish a blanket, music box, and a lock of hair. He'd fallen in love with her and no circumstances would change how he felt about her.

He flinched when a dirty hand wrapped around his arm. He shot a glance at Carlo's desperate eyes.

"Who are you?" Carlo whispered. His voice trembled. "Are you planning to get yourself killed?"

Marko tapped Carlo's forearm. As it seemed the *dishonored* captain had stuck around after all and had seen the events unfold. "Killed? Not if I can help it. Find your nephew and come to the island of Vis. Ask for Marko Lucin. There you'll find a protection and new life."

He jerked his head at Rocco and Marta. They resumed their fast pace, pulling Albert along. Marko hesitated and made a sign of cross in front of Carlo, pretending to give him his blessing. After all, he was still disguised as a friar.

Stepping back, Carlo nodded once. "I think I know where Nikola is. Aye, Marko, we're in your debt."

"We must hurry. I hope to see you again, soon." Marko turned and continued down the rocky path toward the shore.

As they boarded the rowboat tied to the very end of the long pier jutting out into the bay, Marko stowed Sirena and Marta under the prow. He shed his monk's habit and rolled the robe into a ball, then slid it under her head. The sight of her crudely shorn hair squeezed his heart. How he'd loved playing with her curls. Wrapping them around his fingers when he kissed her. He adored the shine of the morning sun in her wavy hair. His throat closed as he stroked her head. It was a small consolation, but he'd gotten to hold her in his arms once more.

"Grab you oars, men."

Albert's muffled voice and sound of the oars being fitted into the rowlocks drifted to Marko. The boat rocked on the steady swells. Guilt stung him as men grunted, rowing against the waves. No matter how insignificant his help would be, his men needed him. But how could he leave her, knowing these could be her last moments.

"The men can use all the help they can get," Marta rasped, interrupting his thoughts. "You know I'll keep a watchful eye on Sirena, Cap'n."

By now the navy would realize their prisoners had been snatched from justice and they'd send every available guard to search. They needed to get far away from this deep harbor and onto the safety of their ship, anchored out on the open sea. He gave Marta a nod.

On all fours, he crawled out from under the prow and drew a long breath of fresh salt air. Albert had shed his brown friar's frock and clutched the rudder, but struggled to keep the boat on course as a strong current kept pushing them toward the shore. The four men, who had remained with the boat instead of going to the hanging, rowed fast, leaning back as they pulled on the oars.

Dressed in the ordinary garb of black vests and breeches and white shirts with red cravats around their necks, they blended in with the fishermen, olive growers, mariners, and peasants.

Stepping over wooden benches, Marko crossed the small craft and relieved Albert of steering duty. With one hard pull of the rudder, he slanted the boat and corrected the course for the bay's wide mouth. The wind had picked up and blown away the clouds, leaving the hot sun beating down on their heads.

A sharp whistle pierced the air. Marko glanced over his shoulder at the fast-approaching, long navy skiff with five oars and two men on each side. His four rowers were no match for their twenty. If he attempted to outrun them, they'd know their boat carried the prisoners. His best option was to halt and pretend he knew nothing.

"Oars up." At his order, the rowers boated their oars simultaneously.

Albert reached under the bench where he'd stowed his sword wrapped in rags.

"Woe will betide us if you pull your weapon. Just act normal and we'll be fine." Marko stood as the skiff neared.

The officer raised his hand to signal to his men to keep the boat steady. He looked at Marko with indifferent eyes. "We are searching for renegades disguised as monks."

Marko frowned then shook his head. "Sorry, haven't seen any friars."

Resting his hand on the pommel of his sword, the navy officer scanned the men in Marko's boat, stopping briefly to stare at Albert. "Where are you men headed?"

Marko barely heard the officer's question over the mad pounding of his heart. Would Albert's aristocrat appearance fool the navy man? He jerked his head toward the prow. "To cast our nets, if there's anything to be caught this late in a day."

"Ah, a company of fishermen." The officer nodded as he spotted heaped fishing nets. "As you were." He let go of the sword's handle and with two fingers touched the brim of his round hat, then turned to his men. "Onward."

The skiff moved off. Marko exhaled then ordered to the rowers to carry on. Despite the men's best effort, the trip against the current to the anchored ship was time consuming. The swells had risen on the open sea, each sending the spray over the prow and dumping water into the bottom of the boat. The sight of three masts with furled sails coaxed a sigh of relief from him. In a short while, a physician would examine Sirena. God willing, he'd have a cure for her illness. Marko didn't dare to think of the possibility that she might indeed die.

The small craft approached the bulk of the large vessel. Albert got to his feet and grabbed onto rope ladder while two men bailed the water out with buckets. He then turned to Marko with arched eyebrow.

"I don't need you to carry her onboard. It is best if the two women stay in the boat until we hoist it." Marko rushed to open the prow's hatch. He crouched and stuck his head inside the small compartment. "How's she doing?"

Marta held onto Sirena's sweat drenched shoulders while her body shook like a twig. "She had another one of her coughing fits. Must be the heat in here. She needs fresh air."

Sirena attempted to open her eyes, but they rolled back in her head. Did she see him for that brief moment? How much was she aware of things happening around her? "Soon you'll come out."

When the last of the men climbed the rope ladder onto the deck of Albert's polacca, Marko waved to the sailors to raise the boat. Once the dinghy was safely secured on the deck, he slid to the floorboards and shook his legs loose. "You two." He pointed his cane at the two mariners swabbing the deck. "Help the women out."

"Aye, Cap'n."

"The physician is waiting in the infirmary." Albert pulled his shirt over his head then hurled a bucket overboard, yanking the rope. "For me, a wash is in order. We'll set sail at sundown. What do you say?"

"I say now is the best time to set sail, or we'll lose the easterly wind." At the sound of ropes flapping against the mast, Marko gazed toward the horizon. The ship's wide berth swayed on the waves. "Pass the helm to Marta. She'll know what to do." He followed the sailors carrying Sirena into the infirmary. His poor friend knew nothing of sailing.

Despite the many ships he'd inherited, he was still a land lubber.

An elderly man was leaning over Sirena's bed by the time Marko stepped over the doorsill into the infirmary. "Out please," he said without looking at Marko. "I need to examine her."

Marko's eyes widened and rage filled him at the sight of her body covered in welts and opened wounds—a result of flogging. "Is there anything I can do?"

The physician looked over his shoulder. "It was my understanding there were two women."

Leaning on his cane, Marko nodded. "There are."

"Where is the other one?"

Marta's barking overpowered other voices on deck, drifting to Marko. "A quarter to port, damn it, now to starboard, slacken the rope, tighten that halyard!"

"She is in better shape and I put her on the helm. We are setting sail."

The doctor returned to shedding Sirena's torn shirt. "That is something you can do, take over and send her in. She needs to be examined, too."

Marko couldn't tear his eyes away from Sirena's bruised body, but the doctor was right. He must not forget he was still the captain of the ship. "Aye."

He left the infirmary and headed for helm to relieve Marta. Her face, although bruised and swollen, appeared less severe than Sirena's.

"Don't you be looking at me like I don't know what I'm talking 'bout, boys," she yelled at the sailors from Albert's crew as they stared at her with smirks on their faces.

"Get back to your duties and do what she told you." Marko propped his hands on his hips and watched the men reluctantly return to their posts.

Rocco laughed and continued to wind a halyard. "I told you so."

Marko placed his hand on the helm. "The physician wants to examine you."

With a frown and a look of disbelief, she stared at him. The knuckles on her hand holding the wheel whitened. "I don't need no examining."

"Yes, you do."

"I've never been examined in my life. Not intending to start now." She faced the deck. The full sails flapped in the wind as the anchor was heaved away.

Marko's hold on the helm tightened. He knew Marta's stubborn kind and how firmly they could dig in their heels. "Just indulge the doctor this one time."

To his relief, she let go of the wheel. "Aye, Cap'n. If it'll make you feel better."

He smiled at the old quartermaster. "It will. Thank you. For everything you've done for Sirena. I'm sure her imprisonment would have been harder if she didn't have you at her side."

Sadness flashed in Marta's eyes. "I wish I could've done more for her."

"We all do, Marta." Marko patted her shoulder. "Go see the doctor now."

"Aye." Marta left for the infirmary.

Leaning against the large wheel, Marko stared at the sea water spraying over the prow and washing the planks, then draining from the scuppers. The strong wind pushed the ship away from the mainland and the bay where Sirena and Marta had come so close to death.

Albert approached, wiping his hair. "What will you do with the Contessa?"

Marko shifted his feet, easing the pain in his hip. "What can I do? Expose her infidelity."

Wrapping the towel around his shoulders, Albert scratched his sideburn with his thumb. "Let's hope you are not too late, and she suffered a mysterious still birth. You'll never prove whether she was even with a child."

"Don't worry." Marko smiled. Doctor Breda wouldn't let her get away with such a lie. "It is never too late to do the right thing."

Torches cast bright lights over the waters of the harbor of Vis. People danced on the narrow streets. Wine poured freely from demijohns. Sailors docked Albert's ship. Marko leaned over the port railing. "What is this festivity for? It's not the day of our Patron Saint."

"No, Cap'n." A mariner wrapping the line around the peg doffed his cap. "They are celebrating our return."

Marko scanned the houses closest to the harbor. Every window of this place was lit. This meant the news had reached his father and the old man must be waiting on him with anticipation. What would he think of Sirena?

The two mariners brought her out on a stretcher. In two days the swelling had gone down but her cuts and bruises had darkened, turning the color of plum. However, her fever and coughing had worsened. Perhaps Marko should have listened to reason and allowed the doctor to administer some of his brutal cures. He just couldn't see how the solution of powdered cantharides beetles called Spanish Fly would aid in drawing out foul humors. The preparation was known to raise large, painful blisters once applied to the skin. Doctor Breda would surely find a less invasive cure for Sirena's pneumonia. Her prognoses was optimistic, still she faced a long illness and recovery. Marko thanked God every day that she wasn't dying of a contagious disease.

Once on land, Marko covered Sirena's head. Her poor state could bring the celebration to a quick end. He led the way to his house at the top of the hill. People shoved their bottles in his way, but he refused them all with a polite smile and shake of his head. Music from accordions, laughter, and loud singing surrounded him, while the smell of grilled sardines wafted on the summer air, reminding him of his hunger. However, more important issues pressed on his mind.

The opened gates to his place welcomed him home. His father shuffled his feet as he scurried to greet him. He clapped his hands together. "Thank God, it is true. You are alive."

Marko wrapped his arms around his father's frail shoulders. "Papa."

Stepping back, his father scanned him from head down, his glance stopped at the cane. "You're wounded?"

Marko shifted his weight to his good leg. "It's all right, Papa. I'll be fine."

The old man tilted his head and peered behind Marko. "You brought a guest?"

Turning to the men behind him, Marko ordered, "Take her upstairs. First room on the left."

"Aye, Cap'n." The sailors carried the stretcher with Sirena inside the large, stone house.

"She is not a guest, Papa." Marko drew a long breath. He should have accepted all those offered drinks. "The woman is very ill and needs our help. She saved my life a few times."

His father's mouth dropped open and he stared at Marko. "Well then, her good deeds will not go unrewarded.

She deserves our help." He turned to the man standing behind him. "Send for Doctor Breda."

The servant nodded and left to dispatch a messenger boy.

For a moment Marko pondered the idea of revealing who the woman was, but decided against it. His father had aged since he'd last seen him. One small detail at a time would be best.

"Why are we standing out here? Come inside. I have food and wine and all of the noble people here. Mirela, oh she couldn't sit still since the day she heard you were alive."

Marko forced a smile. "I hear she has good news. Is it true?"

"See for yourself. It's a miracle. She was bed ridden until today." His father pointed to the Contessa marching toward them. Her belly jiggled unnaturally in front of her large body.

"How dare you?" Stiff sugar coiled curls sat on her shoulders as she halted in front of Marko. "I waited all these months for you and you insult me by bringing that...that...woman here."

"I see you fooled everyone with your lie, Madam." Marko walked around her and continued up the stairs. He was in no mood to face her or the nobles waiting in the tea parlor.

The Contessa's heeled slippers clicked on ceramic tiles of the long hallway as she scurried after him. "What lie? This is scandalous. She'll just have to go elsewhere."

He placed his foot firmly on the stair and turned to her. "She's going nowhere."

Pressing her lips together, the Contessa's face turned deep red. She puffed air through her nose then slapped his cheek. "You bastard. You are to wed *me*. I'm with your child."

When she raised her hand to slap him again, he grabbed her wrist. "Calm down, Madam. It is impossible for you to be with my child."

She yanked her arm from his hold and lost her balance, skittering down the stairs on her meaty behind like a sack of turnips. Her *belly* dropped onto the floor from under her skirts. Her scream drew their guests out from the parlor. The nobles froze at the sight of the Contessa sprawled on the floor. Women covered their opened mouths with their fans.

His father pushed through the gathered group, crouched next to Mirela and shot Marko a surprised look. "You must be gentle with her. She is in a delicate condition."

Descending the few steps to the Contessa still seated on the cold tiles, Marko lifted the hems of her skirts. "I would not abandon a woman if she bore me a child, but none ever came after me, claiming so. Neither will I tolerate a lie. I might have sown my wild oats in the past." He picked the round bundle up in his hand and raised it for everyone to see. "But never before have I fathered—a cushion."

Chapter 17

At the top of the first step, Marko eyed every noble guest who ogled the disgraced Contessa. He saw no bewilderment as he'd expected, only amusement. Seemed her deceit came as no surprise to anyone, except to him and his father. The voluminous skirts of her deep red dress had sprawled around her plump body when she landed at the foot of the stairs.

Her gasps cut the unnerving silence. She pressed her hand over her mouth and whimpered. Tears welled in her droopy brown eyes while deep lines creased her prominent forehead as she looked at him.

Remorse raked through him. He couldn't stand to see a woman cry, no matter how guilty she was, and especially if he'd caused her tears. An involuntary sigh loosened the knot in his chest. The cushion she had kept hidden under her skirts plopped on the tiles as he tossed the round bundle from his hand.

"It's all right, Papa. I've got her." He wrapped an arm around her and helped her to her feet. Everyone's eyes followed his movements as he led her to his father's study.

"*La commedia è finita.*" He slammed the double door shut, expressing his contempt of the guests' smirks.

Silver moonlight glinted through the large window, washed the spacious library in soft luminescence. The citrus smell of wood polish lingered in the air. Without a word, he lowered her to a chair then sat facing her. Muffled voices in the hallway receded toward the parlor.

The Contessa sniffed, pulled the handkerchief from under the lacy frill of her sleeve, and dabbed at the corners of her eyes. She patted her curls. "Is my hair in place?"

Pain shot through his hip as he shifted, but it was her question that jolted him. Appearances meant more to her than the scandal she'd caused? Marko shook his head and dismissed her question with a wave of his hand. "Your hair is fine I suppose, but I didn't come here to—"

She sprang to her feet and smoothed her dress. "Good. Then I shall return to our guests."

Not believing her actions, he stood, too. "Contessa, you don't understand the gravity of your situation."

"I understand all too well." Her voluminous dress swished across the parquet. She stopped at the door and turned to him. "I disgraced myself and will be a topic of gossip for quite some time, and you'll no doubt send me back to my father."

Her casual tone and demeanor baffled and intrigued him. "Indeed I will. But you are acting as if you planned on this outcome."

Her soft smile and nod confirmed his words.

The nerve of the woman! She'd used him and now was acting as if the whole scene she'd caused had worked to her advantage. His stomach flipped. "Then why all this...sham pregnancy, the jealousy displays?"

One hand on the door handle, she scrutinized him.

He quirked his eyebrow when she didn't answer. "I believe you owe me an explanation."

She puffed air through her nose and relaxed her shoulders. "Now that I've brought shame on our family's name again, my father would have no choice but to grant me my wish." Leveling her eyes with his, her thin lips became invisible as she stretched them in a smile. "There is but one man I love. He calls to me and I will spend the rest of my life in devout prayers."

Marko exhaled in relief, then stiffened his back as her words sunk in. "You wish to be a nun?"

She took two slow steps toward him. Dreaminess filled her expression. "Since I was a nine-year-old, I wanted nothing more than to serve my God."

Utterly confused, he scowled. "Why in heaven's name did you not tell me? You'd have spared us both a shipload of grief."

"How could I? You never said more than two words when we met and you immediately pursued my servant girl." Scorn flashed in the Contessa's eyes as she proceeded. "I'll have you know, she ran off with a sailor a few weeks after you left."

Guilt stung Marko. He shouldn't have been so blatant about his displeasure in the Contessa to the point he had not cared whether he had hurt her with his actions. In his own defense, he reminded himself that she had spent most of her time confined to her chambers and had come out only to attend church.

"Besides," she went on. "My father would only try to wed me off to another man. The one holding the biggest purse to cover his debts." A laugh shook her. "I doubt that any decent man would want me after this scandal. I'm free. I'm finally free to do with my life as I wish. No more putting on the appearances so my old aunts could examine me through their theatrical monocles and whisper how displeased they were. But that was to be expected. You see,

I grew up hearing all about my ridiculous face and plump body. I am well aware I do not possess any great beauty." She drew a long breath. "No, Marko. You are not the first man I was betrothed to. I found a way to sabotage all three before you. Any man that would have married me would have eventually come to regret it and cast me away. My actions might not have been pure, but my thoughts are and I know God loves me."

Shame had him lowering his gaze to his boots. He had acted toward her as many others must have. She was right to turn her love and devotion to God. When his embarrassment passed, he raised his head. "What about your father's gambling debts?"

Twisting her handkerchief around her finger, she sauntered toward the round table. "He squandered all his inheritance on race horses, cards, and dice. I was his ticket out, but for how long, before he's neck deep in debts again? I will no longer play his games."

Marko scanned over her maternity dress that now hung loose around her wide hips and released a long sigh. She had never expected him to fulfill his husbandly duties with her. "When do you want to leave?"

"I'm hoping to get an answer from Mother Superior soon, I wrote to her over a month ago." The silk of her dress rustled as she spun. "Another week or two, would that be soon enough for you?"

"You can take all the time you need."

"That is very generous of you, Marko." She paused by the door, turning to him. "Is it proper if I address you by your given name?"

He nodded. Given his Marquis title had been forfeited, she was above him. "I believe we can leave the formalities out."

"I must go straight to the convent. Before my father finds a bigger fool. There are always men desperate enough to buy a title."

"As you wish, Contessa." Marko bowed and she left the room.

Seated in a deep chair, the tension that had been building in him for months slowly eased. The Contessa had wanted out of the arranged marriage as much as he, and now they were both free to love whomever they wanted. She'd give her love to God. Her excessive piety had struck him as her means to avoid him. He should have guessed her devotion was sincere.

A quiet chuckle shook him. There would be no more leaving home to get away from a woman. He'd stick to land and to Sirena. Sadness gripped him at the memories of the *Strega* and all its fallen pirates. A truly fine ship she'd been. As soon as his lame leg allowed him, he'd set out to build a bigger and stronger vessel. He could already see the day when Sirena christened her maiden voyage by breaking a bottle of his best wine against the prow. Yes, the *Strega* would sail these seas once again.

A rap on the door snapped him out of his mulling and he straightened. "Come in."

Doctor Theodor Breda stepped in, unrolling the sleeves of his white shirt. Marko's stomach knotted at the man's stern face.

"Your guest is resting. One very strong woman she is." The doctor lowered himself into the chair opposite Marko. "But she has a long way to recovery."

"Thank you." The knots in Marko's gut loosened. "Conte Panov's physician wanted to treat her with Spanish Fly. I wouldn't allow it."

Theodor peered at him over his round spectacles and ceased buttoning his cuffs. "Barbaric. Drawing foul humors into the blister fluids can't provide a cure." Stretching his lips, he shook his head. "The humoral theory has proven ineffective." While the Doctor's nasal voice usually irritated Marko, it now appealed to him as he delivered good news. "No, we'll treat her with natural remedies. It is essential she doesn't eat meats. The proteins move slowly through the weak system. When she is strong enough, she can start on a diet of vegetable juices and fruit compote. In the meantime syrup of garlic, onion, and fish oil can do wonders."

Marko couldn't dispute that Theodor's infamous concoction had cured many ailments. Nonetheless, as the taste surfaced to his mind, he gulped and his eyes teared up. "Your smile tells me you already administered the first dose."

"And she took it very well." The doctor's smile widened. "Not like small children —and one of a larger variety—who must force it down."

Marko chuckled. "Its taste is not something I will ever get used to." Relief flooded him at the optimistic prognosis, but he had one more question for the doctor. Reaching into his shirt, he slowly pulled out the scroll. "I believe you recognize this."

The thin man's eyes widened and his mouth dropped open, but he didn't reach for the document. "I never thought I'd see it again."

"This letter states that you have proof of my parentage."

"I do." Theodor snapped his glance from the scroll to Marko. "Do not pursue this any further. The slain Marquis and Marchioness' enemies are still out there and are more powerful than ever. They will without doubt attempt to kill you and your poor father." He shifted. "And me, too, for saving the couple when I've learned of the conspiracy. Who else knows of this?"

"The woman upstairs and Conte Panov." Marko stretched his stiff leg out and groaned in pain. Sitting for too long didn't agree with his hip. He said through his clenched teeth, "No worries. Neither will talk."

Theodor examined Marko's injured leg. "Let me guess, my colleague treated your wound simply by bandaging it. When did he last change the dressings?"

Marko winced as the doctor's cold hands pressed on his hip. "He never changed them and the pain is relentless."

"I'm going to fetch my bag. Lower your breeches," the doctor ordered. "I need to clean and stitch your wound. You'll be as good as new."

Marko shuddered at the doctor's order. The memory of his needlework on his skin was forever etched in his mind. "It would heal without stitching."

The doctor regarded him with a scowl. "Who graduated from medical school in Padova? You or me?"

"You of course." Marko reached for his belt buckle. The good doctor never failed to remind him of his credentials.

Mediating over how to question his father about his mother and what kind of connection she had with the Marchioness, Marko unbuckled his belt and removed the pistols from his waistband. He unfastened the buttons on his breeches and slid the rough fabric to his knees. Theodor re-entered with a lit candle in one hand and his black doctor's bag in the other. A freshly polished leathery smell wafted from the case.

"How much does my father know of this?"

Theodor placed his bag onto the side table next to the chair. "Only that you are his loving son."

Could Mother have hidden her pregnancy from her husband? Not impossible, he could have been at sea for long months and arrive home to find *his* child.

Glass bottles clinked as the doctor rummaged through his bag. "Here it is." He pulled a stubby container filled with yellowish liquid. The parquet creaked when the doctor lowered to his knees. "The woman in the guest room has been badly beaten. The news reached us that the pirate captain Sirena escaped hanging."

Marko's heart stopped. News traveled damn fast. A deep breath failed to boost him with courage, but he'd have to come out with truth. "If it wasn't for her, the trunk with the scroll would still be hidden."

Theodor's hand ceased on Marko's hip as he raised his head. "I urged the Marchioness not to leave so soon after she gave birth, but she wanted to join her husband. The woman upstairs is Sirena?"

"She is," Marko answered in a stern tone, hoping the doctor would take it as a sign and refrain from talking. The man's nasal voice annoyed him again.

"I shouldn't be surprised by any of this." The doctor snapped opened a bottle and poured the liquid onto the gauze. The smell of rubbing alcohol permeated the air.

Marko sucked in a breath as the doctor pressed the cool cloth to his burning flesh. He clenched his jaw when the stinging became too intense.

"After all," the doctor continued. "Had the Marchioness stayed, she would have endangered you. Her enemies discovered the bodies found in bed were the two servants and they searched for them. They sent men to this house, too. Thankfully, they found nothing."

For the first time, Marko understood. Her action had not been done with a selfish desire to rush to her husband's side. The Marchioness abandoned her child to save him from certain death.

The strong smell of the mint balm the doctor lathered on Marko's hip made him pinch his nose. With threaded needle, Theodor sutured the wound. "You're lucky I got to this," he murmured immersed in his work. "The skin around the stab is very red. Another day and you'd be running a fever, and this would fester."

Clutching the back of the chair, Marko endured as the needle punctured his flesh with every stitch.

"There," the doctor said and cut the end of the thread. "All done. I'll have to change the dressing at least twice each day."

Marko pulled his breeches to his waist. "Can you send my father in?"

"Of course, but I'd urge you not to reveal any of this to him. The news would break his heart. He loves you. He is old and deserves to die a happy man." The doctor replaced his instruments to his bag.

Marko crossed his wrists behind his back. "You have nothing to worry about, Doctor Breda."

The doctor nodded and left.

Marko stroked his beard. Bless his soul, he'd gone without a drink far too long. He stepped to the liquor cabinet, feeling the pull of the stitches with each step. After pouring two glasses of brandy from the ornamental bottle, he gulped the golden liquid and welcomed the warmth sliding through his chest.

The door opened again and his father came in. "I take it you sorted everything with Mirela?"

Pouring another glass, Marko nodded. He handed his father the drink with one hand, then pointed to a chair with the glass in his other, and sat facing the old man. "Mirela and I..." He shifted to find a comfortable position. "Well, Papa, we have different priorities, and I cannot wed her."

"Of course not." His father placed the glass onto the side table. "Not after the way she tried to deceive us. Do not worry, we'll find you anther wife."

Marko drained his brandy and smacked his lips. "Papa, I found the woman I'll marry, and no other will do."

Placing his laced fingers around his knee, his father cast him a puzzled look. "Your guest?"

Nodding, Marko pursed his lips. Would his father accept his decision?

The old man's shoulders dropped as he exhaled. "I should've guessed." He circled his thumbs. "You have my blessing, son. My dream of becoming a Conte will go unfulfilled, but I realize I was selfish. After all, I've risen from a common merchant to a Nobile through my marriage."

His father's words came as a surprise to Marko. He leaned forward, resting his chin on his knuckles. "You weren't nobility before you wed Mother?"

"No, it was the late Marquis who granted me the title so I could wed her." The old man's wrinkled forehead creased. "Why this sudden interest in the family affairs?"

Marko cast a glance at the brandy on the cabinet. Damn, he should have taken the bottle with him. He looked at his father. "The day I was born, were you here?"

"I wish I was. The good news reached me five weeks later, off the coast of Sicily. I was delivering wax and sacks of lentils, but I've set sail for home right away. It took me another two weeks to reach Vis."

"So you weren't here during Mother's pregnancy?" Getting to his feet, Marko took a hold of his empty glass and limped to the bottle perched on the top of the cabinet.

"The later part of her pregnancy, no I was not." His father's frail voice reached him as he poured his third glass. "She had complications and I didn't want to set my hopes too high. We've had too many disappointments over the years. Marchioness sent us Doctor Breda and he put her on a strict bed rest."

"Why would the Marquis and Marchioness go to these lengths?" Damn the brandy went down Marko's throat smoothly tonight.

"Well, your mother and the late Marchioness were twin sisters. Never before have I seen the two women so alike. It was hard to tell them apart."

Stunned, Marko coughed and spun on his heel. "But you could tell them apart?"

"Of course I could. Your mother had a small mole behind her left ear, her sister did not. That was the only difference I knew of."

An image of his mother place in the casket surfaced as he ran his finger over the cuts in the crystal chalice. The mentioned mole stuck in his mind. The right woman lay in the grave.

"Ah, son." His father sighed. "If only youth could return."

A sympathetic smile stretched Marko's lips. He studied his father with raised eyebrows. "But then you wouldn't have known Mother and neither would you have me."

"You are right, son. But—" His father stood, supporting his frail body by the armrests. "Where are my manners? You must be tired. I shall excuse you from the company of our guests."

"Thank you, Papa," Marko said and placed the glass on the cabinet. "I'll check on Sirena then retire."

Surprise and fear flashed across his father's face. "The woman upstairs is the pirate captain?"

Chapter 18

Sun specks glistened on the water. The lazy waves brushed the long stone pier. Southerly winds sent the brine of the sea into the balmy air. The dark umbrella cast a shade over Mirela's sizable figure and shielded her from the searing heat. The two mariners disembarked from the ship tied at the quay, approached her piled trunks, and grunted under the weight as they lifted the two top boxes.

She winced when they dropped them. "Do be careful."

"What the hell's in here? Rocks?" The taller sailor spat while the other one sneered, swiping his forearm over his forehead.

"Books, if you must know," she answered with a stern face.

Anger spiraled in Marko. The story of the Contessa's disgrace had spread over the entire island like a bush fire, but she did not deserve these men's insolent treatment. The clacking of his cane followed him in step as he hurried to the pier. "I demand you show respect for the Contessa and her belongings."

"Aye, Cap'n." The two sullen sailors picked up the trunks and carried them onboard.

Mirela had spun toward him at his grumble. She flipped her fan open. "Have you come to see me off, young Nobile Lucin?"

Surprised by her formalities, he examined her round face. "Yes, I have."

"Sweet, however, unnecessary." She returned her glance to the men who'd disembarked to get the rest of her boxes, one bigger than the other.

Guilt stung Marko. This wasn't how he imagined they'd part. "What shall I tell your father?"

"I explained everything to him in my letter." The fan in her hand flapped fast, sending the loose wisps of her hair to whirl. "Your father is entrusted with mailing the correspondence, along with my gowns I will not need."

"He'll see to it, rest assured." Marko nodded, leaned on his cane, and pondered how to ease the tension. Perhaps expressing how the whole situation left him with a very bitter taste would explain his actions. "Contessa, I am truly sorry—"

"I am not." She shifted her weight to one foot. "If you expect to hear me say how sorry I am our courtship didn't take, I must disappoint you. Had we fulfilled our fathers' wishes, we'd both be stuck in a marriage neither of us wanted."

She was right, of course. Marko eyed the last piece of her luggage on the pier, glad he didn't have to grunt under the weight of the trunk. "And you are sure you don't want to serve God in the Benedictine monastery of St. Nicholas right here on the island?"

"My father would find me. No one must know where I am going." She closed the fan and cast him a fleeting look. "Your guest's cough kept us all at night. Is her health improving?"

Worry filled Marko with the mention of Sirena. Though Theodor had said the road to her recovery would be a long one, concern pressed on Marko's mind. For the past two weeks, she seemed confused between her delusional fever and reality. "Her constant fever and coughing fits disquiet me. I don't know how much more she can take."

"I'll pray for her and you have some faith. She'll pull through, you'll see." Mirela's eyes traveled from his head to his boots. "How does your hip feel?"

A morsel of his worry chipped away with her kind words about Sirena. "Thank you, my wound is getting better under Doctor Breda's care."

A soft smile stretched her lips while her cheeks reddened. "Do send my apologies to the good doctor. He was right to call me a stubborn mule. Now he knows why I refused to be examined during my so called *delicate condition*."

Marko flicked his eyebrows, understanding the doctor's need to avoid the Contessa. Her pretentious pregnancy had fooled him, too, and knowing Theodor, he would stay miffed at her for some time.

An older man disembarked and approached them. "Contessa De Montagne, it is time to board." He turned to Marko and saluted by touching his fingers to his graying hair. "Cap'n."

"Ah, yes. Ships make me queasy." She gathered her skirts in her hand and exhaled, staring at her ride. "Thank you for providing such a fine vessel and personnel to escort me to my destination."

"Do not fear. The captain I employed for the journey is an old sea dog. He knows how to handle her. Fare well."

"Thank you for everything, Nobile Lucin. I apologize for the grief I caused you." Gravel crunched under her feet as she approached the boarding scale.

Marko hurried after her, untying the large purse from his waistband. "Contessa," he called as she stepped onto the deck.

Her puzzled expression settled on him. "Yes?"

Approaching the port railing, he squeezed the sack, causing the ducats to crunch. "I hope this will help your father out of his debts."

"Very admirable of you." Her chuckle ended in an exasperated sigh. "A coffer full of these would not help him. No, Nobile Lucin, his debt is much larger than one cash purse."

The cussing sailor untied the ship and threw the line on the prow. The captain took hold of her arm and the Contessa disappeared behind a cabin door. Marko stood on the tip of the pier, watching the ship drifting away until he no longer sighted the sails in the wide bay. Well, the Contessa certainly had taught him a lesson. There was more to a woman than her appearance.

"Cap'n."

Rocco's joyous call yanked Marko from his morose thoughts. He scanned the shore. Among the piles of driftwood he spotted Rocco.

Marko waved to him. "A bit early to gather wood for the winter."

"This isn't kindling." Rocco motioned for Marko to come closer. "You may want to see this."

Pain shot through Marko's leg as he forced his lame limb over the uneven stone path. If the stitches popped, he'd get the scolding of his life from Doctor Breda for not following his orders. He slowed the pace when Rocco approached him.

"Careful over the rocks. They are slippery with moss." He reached out his skinny hand to Marko.

His slow progress to the shore annoyed Marko, but determination pushed him onward and he approached the woodpile. "What have we got here?"

"People have been bringing these for days." Rocco pointed to the blackened, soaked heap. "Some of the pieces washed ashore and some drifted in the sea. It's obvious this is debris of a sunken ship, but this morning a company of fishermen found *this*."

Marko recognized the pieces in his friend's hands as partial letters from the *Strega*'s name on the stern. A wave of nostalgia swept over him. The *Strega* would forever hold a special place in his heart.

"Can we rebuild her, Cap'n?"

"We can and will. Is any of that wood usable?"

"Hardly." Rocco tossed the pieces to the pile.

Marko stared at the scorched wood, allowing memories of an old xebec to wash over him. "I'll commission the best shipbuilders and have them lay the keel as soon as possible. Put aside any pieces that can be used. I want to keep the spirit of the old *Strega* alive."

"Aye." Rocco smiled. "Marta wants her Cap'n to be at our wedding this Sunday. Do you think Sirena will be out of bed by then?"

Marko patted his quartermaster's bony shoulder and a thought occurred to him. "Well, today is Monday. Let's hope. We should call her by her Christian name. She was Carmen before she became Sirena."

Rocco's eyes lit. "By all that's holy, we should."

On the land, a man in a light suit and matching wide brimmed hat caught Marko's attention. A boy's hand held on to his and in the other he carried a large suitcase. The man spoke to the wife of the village baker. The woman in black peasant's dress, pointed in Marko's direction.

Marko shielded his eyes against the mid-day sun and approached the stranger.

"So now you're a captain?" The man spoke, but Marko didn't recognize his voice. "Last time we met you were dressed in a monk's robe and blessed me. I believe the robe was stolen. Tell me, how is Carmen?"

"Carlo, right?" Marko exhaled. For a moment he feared the duke's men had sent someone to spy on him and discovered that he was harboring the fugitive. "You found me. Your sister is not plagued. High fever caused her blistering. Nonetheless, she is sick with a serious bout of pneumonia."

Carlo's shoulders relaxed. He removed his hat and pressed it to his chest. "All these years, I thought she was raising her child. Can you imagine my shock when I found out she was an infamous pirate captain?"

Marko switched his glance to the boy in a starched shirt and brown breeches. Under the circumstances, it was understandable her brother would be baffled. "Carmen did the best she could to save him."

The boy snapped his hand out of Carlo's and ran away.

"Nikola!" Carlo took a step after the boy, but the lad carried on, raising dust on the dirt path. He turned to Marko. "I apologize. He is not taking this well at all."

Marko's heart clenched. Uprooted from the only family he'd known, the poor youngster must be horrified. "That is to be expected. He won't get far on the island. I'll try to talk to him once he's settled and we get used to each other. First, come to the house."

Carlo nodded and switched his luggage to his other hand. "What are your plans for my nephew, and most importantly, my sister?"

Marko continued down the path. Carlo would take the answer easier if he heard the plans for him first. "I always need sea captains in my merchant flotilla, and while I understand it is not the same as commanding a man-of-war, I hope you'll consider joining me."

Children's laughter bounced off the stone walls of the house surrounding the village square. Marko stopped by the small fountain and watched the barefoot boys chase a tattered ball.

Carlo almost bumped into him as he halted. "Y—you'll reinstate my captain's rank?"

Marko tilted his head at Nikola sitting on a low wall at the entrance to the village. "Of course. Carmen's past bares no consequence." He examined Carlo's face. The man was still stunned by his last words so perhaps now would be the right moment to answer his important question. "My plan is to wed her and raise Nikola as my own."

"Noble intentions." Carlo coughed in his fist. "But, you cannot. She is a widow. The Holy Church frowns upon a widow re-marrying."

"As I said, I have a plan." The ratty ball rolled to Marko's feet. He picked it up. "Let's hope it will work."

A bunch of sweaty and bare-chested boys approached him. "Kick it high, Marko."

"See who can catch this." Marko dribbled the ball in his hands. Had his leg allowed him, he'd have sent the ball flying across the square. Instead, he threw it hard and the boys chased after it. He turned to Nikola. The boy's shoulders jerked with sobs, and tears rolled down his cheeks as he had his eyes fixed on the ball in the air. "Soon we'll both play with these boys and the sorrow you feel inside today will melt away. I promise."

"Why did my papa leave me?" Nikola wiped at the tears with his dirty hands. "And Mama? Why did all my sisters and brothers have to go without me?"

"Nikola," Carlo let out an exasperated breath. "I already explained. They took you into their family, but I'm your real uncle and you have a mother and two other uncles who love you. The people you lived with had to leave you behind for your own safety."

Marko shot a surprised look at Carlo, but couldn't blame him for not having any tact with the child. He must have spent half of his life in the military.

Marko smiled at Nikola. "How about we go to my house first? It's up those steps." Pointing his cane at the narrow stone stairs, he gestured for Nikola to get on his feet.

Nikola frowned and turned his head away.

Marko took his small hand. "Come child, you will like it here, you'll see."

Nikola reluctantly got to his feet and walked with them to the house, clutching to Marko's hand. Inside the stone paved courtyard, Marko raised his hand, pointing at the white shutters covering the window above the main door. "Carmen is in the room on the upper level. I suggest you take the chamber across the hallway. It has two beds." He leaned on his cane, leveled his face with Nikola. "Unless you would like a room of your own."

Fear flashed in the boy's eyes. Snapping his hand out of Marko's, Nikola shook his head.

Carlo's suitcase thudded as he lowered the trunk next to his feet. "He is not used to sleeping alone. In fact, I'm not sure he ever slept in a bed of his own, let alone a room."

Unsure how to take Carlo's remark Marko straightened. Carlo shrugged.

"You have to understand he had many siblings until last week, and now he is alone." Marko ruffled Nikola's dark hair. The boy must've taken after his father. The round face and soft brown eyes bore no resemblance to his beautiful mother. "You can stay in the same room with your uncle, if it will make you feel safer. Would you like to see your mama?"

Nikola raised his chin. "You mean pirate Carmen. My mama is gone."

"Nikola!" Carlo scolded. "Apologize."

Marko raised his hand, palm facing Carlo. "It is quite all right. This will take some time."

"It is not all right." Carlo huffed. "The young ones should be thought some respect for the elders. Else wise what will become of this world?"

Marko stepped to Carlo and placed a hand on his shoulder. "He needs time to adjust to this life."

Nikola grabbed Marko's free hand and cast him a pleading look. "Will I have to call her Mama?"

Letting go of Carlo's shoulder, Marko lowered to the low wall behind him. Searing pain in his hip warned him he should rest. "I hope someday you will, as she would like it. Now go and change."

Nikola's face lit up with a grin and he unbuttoned the starched collar. "I can't wait to get out of these clothes."

A servant girl entered the courtyard, carrying a basket propped on her hip. Marko tried to remember her name, but several new domestic helpers had found employment in his household in the months he'd been at sea. Instead, he gestured at the girl to approach.

"Yes, Master." A few apples rolled out of her woven bushel as she placed it next to her feet.

Marko picked an apple off the floor and handed the fruit to Nikola who eyed it with hunger. "Take this boy to the second guest room and help him change from his travelling attire."

Wrapping her arm around Nikola, the young servant nudged him toward the front door. "Come child."

"I can change myself." In spite of his protest, Nikola followed the girl, biting into the apple.

"That is right." Carlo picked up his trunk. "The boy is not used to being tended to." He cast Marko a puzzling glance. "You are a Master, too?"

"Our family holds the title of Nobile."

"You truly are full of surprises." A smile crept over Carlo's face. He followed the girl and his nephew inside the house.

Marko limped to the marble bench and lowered himself to the cool seat. Twirling his cane between his palms, he eyed the straight trunk of a palm tree his father had brought from far lands as a seedling and had planted the same day he had seen *his son* for the first time.

Minutes later Nikola came running out through the front door. The boy grabbed his hand, as if intending to pull him to his feet. "Wow, your house is huge. Can I look around?"

The servant girl came after him. "The boy's uncle says their journey was long and tiring. He also wanted to see his sister, but Doctor Breda is with her."

Anxiety filled Marko at the girl's words. He couldn't bear to watch Carmen suffer with spasms raking her body while she fought to draw in a breath. At least her illness seemed to give her longer periods of rest in between her coughing attacks. "Did she have another fit?"

The girl nodded. "I think so."

"So can I?" Nikola's enthusiasm snapped Marko out his gloom.

"Yes, you can, but don't touch anything." Marko scanned over Nikola. Changed to his linen shirt and pair of worn but clean breeches, he seemed more comfortable skipping around bare-footed than in leather shoes. Unrestrained and free, he resembled his mother.

Nikola nudged Marko's hand. "Is it true what people say?"

Marko sucked in his breath anticipating a hard question. "People like to talk. What did you hear?"

"That my mother killed many men when she was a pirate."

"She did." Clamping his teeth, Marko searched for proper words to give to the boy, as it seemed he was accepting that she was his mother. Though she had said she longed for the life on the terra firma, he could only hope Carmen would not want to return to her former lifestyle. "She'll be a pirate no more. I won't let her."

"Me neither," Nikola announced. "I can't lose another mama."

Marko squeezed the boy's hand. "You will not lose this one. I promise."

Wide branches of a familiar oak at the top of the hill drew his attention. The tree house had lost its roof. The floor planks must be rotten, too. He'd have to have the whole thing replaced before this curious boy discovered the undependable structure. A thought had him chuckling, and until today it wouldn't have crossed his mind. Marko scooted to the end of the bench and patted the gray marble. "Sit with me."

The boy obeyed, not dropping his eyes from Marko's.

"I understand you are sad. Not long ago I too found out the people who raised me are not my birth parents."

Nikola shot him a surprised glance. "Really? You are not sad?"

"In a way I am." Marko shifted, trying to find a comfortable position on the hard seat. "But I'm grown up and my birth parents died long ago. Had I known about this at your age, I don't know what I would have done. You are one very bright boy and taking all of this quite well."

Nikola shrugged. "Sometimes I'm so sad I have to cry."

Marko switched his cane to his other hand and clapped the boy's shoulder. "Does it make you feel a bit better once you stop crying?"

"It does." Nikola turned his head away. "I just wish..."

"I understand." Marko pulled the boy closer, his heart breaking to see Nikola on the verge of tears. "Whenever I feel sad, I...well I...er." He'd reach for the wine demijohn, but he couldn't say that to a child. What could he say to make him feel better? A childhood memory sprang to his mind. "I know. The cook is preparing some sweets." Marko nudged him. "Let's see if she'll let us lick the bowls."

A grin lit Nikola's face as he sprang to his feet. "Will you always walk with the cane?" he asked when Marko stood, pushing on the walking staff.

"No, I should start getting used to walking without the help of my cane, but I might need to lean onto something."

Nikola stepped closer to him. "You can lean on me."

"When you get bigger and stronger." Marko took him by the hand, leading the way to the kitchen.

"Master." At the call, Marko halted with his hand flat on the kitchen's door. He turned to the stout servant woman. "Father Ignacio is seeking audience with you."

"Me?" Stunned, Marko scowled. "Not my father?"

"Yes, he asked for you. He's waiting in the study."

"Fine." Marko exhaled loudly. "See if Keka has some sweets for this boy."

The woman nodded and opened the door to a busy kitchen, allowing the fragrance of sweet and pungent onion meat out into the hallway.

With a pout, Marko gaped at Nikola. "I have to take care of man's business. Our cook's name is Keka. If you are nice to her, she'll always have sweets for you."

A mischievous smile lit the boy's face and he disappeared behind the kitchen door.

Thumb rubbing his eyebrow, Marko headed for the study. There was but one topic the reverend would want to discuss with him. The word of a sick woman in Marko's care had reached him.

"Good day, Father," Marko said, closing the door.

"Hmmm?" The plump father scrutinized him from the chair next to the round table. "Strange arrangement you have here with that woman. The island has an infirmary."

Marko balled his hands and reminded himself he must keep his temper under control. "The hospital is for the men, and the orderlies there cannot provide adequate care for her."

Monocle pressed to his eye, Father Ignacio examined the books on the shelves. "What do you want to do when the woman recovers?"

Marko dreaded this question from the father. He hadn't planned to bring the delicate issue up, but damn them all, now was as good a time as any. "Tell me, Father, how many years have you begged for someone to commission the reconstruction of the chapel's ruins? How many doors have you knocked on?"

Father sighed. "Countless years. This is my legacy and I'm afraid to die without fulfilling it."

It was the answer Marko had expected. Now he could lay the trap. "I can fund the reconstruction."

The priest cast him a wary glance. "Under what condition?"

"Two conditions, to be exact." Marko looked down on the bottle of wine on the table. "I think you can guess the first one."

The priest licked his lips as Marko slowly poured the red liquid in two goblets. He handed him one.

"You want to wed the woman in your care." Father Ignacio's double chin shook as he hissed at Marko, taking the drink in his hand. "Have I guessed right?"

"You have." Marko whispered, urging the priest to keep his voice down. One never knew who could be listening.

The father craned his neck at the ceiling "She has a child?"

Marko nodded, cursing the speed of news travelling across the island and dreading the priest's next question.

"She'd been married before?"

"Yes," Marko said, barely lowering the goblet from his lips.

Father drained his cup and smacked his lips. "What God has joined together, let no man separate."

Marko's gorge rose at Father's scornful reply. "Death separated them years ago."

"But in the eye of the church, she is married for life."

"Can anything be done?"

"Annulment," the priest said, nudging his empty goblet at Marko. "Meaning her previous marriage will be void, nulled from the moment she exchanged her vows with that boy's father."

Anger flared in Marko. Carmen might not want to agree to this solution, but he was yet to ask for her hand. "Can't it be done from the moment that man died protecting his wife's honor and his child's life from the duke's men?"

Father's heaving chest rose with a long inhale. "This is the only way, I'm afraid, and since she'd be divorced from a deceased man, she'd still be able to receive a holy Eucharist. You do know the holy matrimony means *forsaking all the others*?"

Hands poised at his sides, Marko squared his shoulders. "Of course I do, Don."

Nodding, Don Ignacio regarded him with his beady eyes. "What is your second condition?"

"I want the new chapel to be consecrated to Lady of Pirates."

The father's chocking cough and appalled expression indicated Marko's request to wed a widowed woman had been easier for the priest to digest.

"Sacrilege," the father gasped, tugging on his white collar tight around his thick neck. "How do you propose I justify this before Vatican?"

Marko poured him another cup to the brim. "Not to worry, Father, if anyone can come up with a great story it's you."

The priest wobbled his head, raised his finger, and gulped, then slammed the empty cup on the tabletop. "If the raiding pirates would return the stolen painting of the Virgin Mary, maybe I could."

"A pirate's ship was wrecked close to our island not so long ago" Marko flicked his eyebrows, swaying his hands in front. "Maybe the painting miraculously floated to the shore."

Father Ignacio poked his meaty finger in Marko's shoulder. "I knew the day I baptized you, you'd put some grays in my hair. Little did I know then that you'd be the sole cause of all of them."

"How did you know?" Though this comment enraged Marko, it provoked his curiosity. He had been told very little of his early days.

"No other infant, before or after you, desecrated the holy baptismal bath by urinating in it," Father wheezed as his face reddened.

"My belated apologizes." Marko topped Father's cup with the last of the wine. If there was any justice, maybe his innocent act in infancy had put the priest off full emersion.

Raising the goblet to his mouth, the priest said, "Apology accepted."

Marko slapped his hand flat against the tabletop. "That being settled, I shall leave you to your drink."

Nikola sprung to his feet and wiped his face smeared in almond crème as Marko opened the door. "Do I have to call you Papa?"

Marko let out a short chuckle. "It's not polite to eavesdrop."

"I didn't want to but, I heard you talking." He wrapped his little arm around Marko's waist. "So do I?"

"I'd like it if you do, but only if you want to." Marko pulled the boy closer. His small beaming face washed away any doubts of becoming an instant father. "Whatever you call me, I'll call you my son. Shall we go see your mama now?"

Nikola's smile warmed Marko's heart. He led him up the stairs and paused by Carmen's door. Not wanting the boy to see his mother during her coughing spell, he listened. No sound came from the bedroom.

The double doors made a loud thud as he pushed them opened. The heavy smell of medicinal herbs hung in the air. His hand on Nikola's shoulder, Marko led him toward a bed with a white canopy positioned against the outer wall. Color seemed to have returned to Carmen's face, but illness had taken a toll on her body. She had thinned and lost her muscle tone. Her sunken chest rose and fell with her even breaths.

Nikola glanced at him. "When will she wake?"

"Soon." Marko lowered himself to a chamber chair and pulled Nikola onto his knee. Perhaps today his angel would wake healthy. "She'd like some company. Let's sit with her."

"Do we have to sit in silence?" Nikola squirmed as if trying to get comfortable. "When one of my brothers or sisters was sick we had to be quiet."

"It's polite not to make noise around sick people." Marko dropped his voice to a whisper. "So we need to be silent."

Nikola played with his fingers, his glances switched between his mother and the window next to the bed.

Carmen drew in a long breath. She pressed her hand on her forehead and moaned.

Marko nudged Nikola and the boy got off his knee. Rising on his good leg, Marko moved to the bed. "Carmen." He squeezed her hand, afraid she would want him to call her by her pirate name. "Can you hear me?"

She opened her eyes to thin slits. Her cracked lips moved, but no sound came out. He glanced at the pitcher on the night stand. "Nikola, can you fill the glass?"

The crisp water splashed and soaked into the lace doily on the dark wood, but the boy managed to fill the cup with his shaky hands.

Marko propped Carmen up on his arm and brought the cup to her mouth. "Drink some."

Liquid trickled as she gulped. Swiping her hand under her chin, she shot him a confused glance. "Marko?" Her whisper was barely audible.

His heart soared. She was healed. "It's me, love." He pointed to Nikola sitting transfixed in the big chair next to the bed. "And your son is here, too."

Her head snapped toward the boy. Terror filled her eyes as she returned her glance to Marko. "Why is he here?"

Chapter 19

There was not a joint, muscle, or tendon in Sirena's body that didn't scream in pain. She gripped the linen gown, pulling the soft fabric away from the comfortable mattress she'd awakened on. The pounding headache was the worst by far. Perhaps she was alive. *You are dead, Sirena,* she mused and scolded herself for allowing the absurd thought. No, not Sirena damn it. If she couldn't be her Christian self in death, where could she? She was Carmen.

The image of Marko and Nikola inside this bedchamber had to be the Devil's temptation and she must not believe it a truth. Propping her elbows against the firm mattress, she stared at Nikola seated on a wide side chair.

Marko brought the glass to her lips. "Take another sip."

Cool water wetting her mouth, Marko's arm around her, Nikola in her bed chamber—could it be real? Despite the fog lifting off her mind, still she refused to believe.

Marko handed the empty cup to Nikola, tilted his head toward the pitcher on the stand, then turned to her as the boy poured another glass. "You are looking much better today."

Marko's words struck her as odd. How could she *look* better today or any other day? She'd been hanged. No, the executioner had wanted to place the noose around her neck when she...had fainted. And the Commodore had ordered for her to be burned. Had they thrown her body on the fire? It made no difference how she died. Her soul would forever burn in Hell. Antun must have not hidden his family in time and the duke's men had found them. Grabbing Marko's arm, she forced the words through her tight throat. "My son is innocent. He shouldn't be here." Panicked, she searched for some explanation in Marko's narrowing gaze. "Neither should you."

Concern flashed in Marko's eyes. "You don't recall me sitting here for days? Last night you smiled at me. It was the best present I've ever received."

She sat up straight, ignoring the dizziness and cradled his cheeks in her hands. "No. It was a dream. This is an illusion. None of this is real. I must go. Don't follow me."

His strong arms wrapped around her. "You are not going anywhere. I won't let you."

She dared not say the words, but Marko had to know. "He'll come for me and take me to the place reserved for heretics and criminals. An abode I knew my soul would go straight to the day I killed the first man."

A frown appeared on Marko's lips. He shot a surprised glance at Nikola then back at her. "Who will take you, love?"

She cupped his cheeks tighter as she pushed the words out before the Devil returned. "The man with the god-awful voice the one who sounds like he speaks with a pig's snout. Did you not see him? He forced me to swallow vile drinks."

"Doctor Breda?" A smile replaced Marko's frown. "He's harmless, but his concoctions are powerful medicine."

"You work with him?" She jerked from his hold as her heart wedged in her throat. This was the Devil's deception after all. The real Marko wouldn't be here with her and neither would her son. But this man's appearance, his sea scent, even the soft creases around his narrowed eyes, confirmed he was Marko. There was but one way to test it. "Shouldn't you be in Heaven?"

His face beamed. "I am," he said, reaching for her hand. "Seeing you here alive and healthy in my home is heaven to me."

"Alive?" She attempted to pull her arm away, but he tightened his hold around her wrist. "Marko is dead. And so am I."

Sorrow flashed in his eyes and his shoulders slumped. "No, love, we are not dead, but we came close. The wound I received will keep me up on damp, cold nights. But with you by my side, I can take anything."

"Alive," she whispered still afraid to believe it. The soft bristles of his beard tickled her palm as she caressed his cheek. None of this was Satan's trickery? "I'm in your home, alive, with you and Nikola."

"You are having hard time believing it, but you've been very ill, Carmen." Marko brushed a strand of her hair away from her face. "I feared the disease would take you from me. Thank God you came through."

Tears of joy clouded her vision. Damn, other than the death of the old Sirena, in almost a decade she hadn't shed a tear—though not for the lack of opportunity—and here Marko's words turned her into such a wimp. "The last thing I remember was...blue eyes looking at me deep within the hood of a monk's habit. I never imagined it could be you. I saw Gaspar kill you."

"Shhhh, let's not mention him. I should have come to your rescue sooner. I thought I'd lose mine mind with worry." He his knuckles down brushed her cheek. "These are happy tears, right? The only kind I'll have you crying from now on."

She sucked in a breath. With a heavy exhale, she leaned into him. He pressed her to his chest and kissed the top of her head.

"What was I thinking? You are yet to gain your strength," he said as he stroked her back. "And as much as it pains me to tear myself away from you, I shall send a servant girl to tend to you. If you chose to get out of the bed, she'll help you get ready."

"I've been through a lot worse than a bit of a fever." Carmen's attempt to get out of bed was met by Marko's firm hands on her shoulders, but it was dizziness that convinced her to give up the fight.

Marko fluffed the pillows. "I'm sure you have. You sure are strong, but you also need to take it easy for a day or so. Your illness wasn't just a little fever."

She studied him in disbelief. It had taken her eight years to toughen up against the world and in a few weeks all her hard work had come undone under Marko's love and caring.

After replacing the cover over her, Marko got to his feet and ruffled Nikola's hair. "Would you like to sit with your mama on her bed?" The boy nodded but stood up slowly. Marko gave him an encouraging nod. "Go on. She'd be very proud of you for talking me into casting away the cane as Doctor Breda has urged me for days." He then limped to the chamber's window where a gray tabby eyed a sparrow perched on the branch of a pomegranate tree. "This fellow kept me company every day."

An indistinct sound resonated in her memory, something close to a cat's purring. It might have been the tabby lying next to her that she had confused as the Hell's gate keeper. She turned to Nikola and patted the mattress. He granted her a quick smile and sat on the edge of the bed. His gaze was fixed on her, but he remained silent.

Soon, she reminded herself, soon she'd make up for all the missed hugs and kisses she had not had a chance to give him all these years. Grownups most likely told him about her, but she'd still be a stranger to him. Right now, she must not overwhelm him. She gripped the linen to restrain from wrapping him in her arms.

The silence grew excruciating. Nikola reached out to her, but pulled his hand back when she touched him. She smiled and wiped at her tears. Her mind raced for proper words a child his age would understand. A shaky breath escaped her. He nibbled on his lower lip, switching his glance between her and Marko.

Lips stretched in a gentle smile, Marko quirked his eyebrows in his usual adorable way. Nikola faced her with a grin and threw his arms around her neck. Her arms closed around him and she pressed him to her. "Nikola, I'm sorry. I never should have left you behind. We should have stayed together and..."

Tears choked her words. Nikola pulled away, sitting on his haunches on her bed. "Marko said you wanted to come and get me."

"I—" She brushed his dark hair off his forehead. "Yes, that is what I wanted more than anything, but I couldn't."

"That is why you always gave me money and were so nice to me? Because you are my real mama."

Mama, the sweet name her son called her set her heart on a soar. She gazed into his amber eyes that held the wisdom beyond his age. "Yes, my sweet little..."

She'd always think of him as her little periwinkle, but she couldn't call him by his baby nickname anymore and she clamped her mouth shut before she said it out loud. But the memory of his innocent days would stay etched in her heart forever.

A knock broke the tense moment. Silver buckled shoes clicked on the parquet, thick calves clad in white hose flexed under the golden trim of Marko's royal blue doublet as he opened the door. Handsome as a devil in his aristocrat's outfit, he still kept a bit of his rebellious appearance. No wonder her heart had raced the moment she'd seen him on the beach of the desolate islet, and it still refused to slow down.

With a hand gesture, he ushered someone inside the room.

The sight of Carlo made her wince. Unrestrained tears rushed to her eyes and trailed down her cheeks. The wide smile on her brother's face eased her heart.

"I'm sure you and Carlo have lots to talk about." Marko took Nikola's hand. "And Nikola wants to kick ball with the village boys. We'll be back for lunch."

"Lunch?" The surprise worked to her advantage and gave her an opportunity to gain her composure. "Have I slept the morning away?"

Marko chuckled. "Love, you slept away the last two weeks."

"In that case hurry back, I don't want to miss another minute with any of you." Gathering her strength, she got on her knees in the bed, and opened her arms to him and Nikola. She placed a kiss on their cheeks. A grin she couldn't contain spread her lips at the sight of Marko's hand on Nikola's shoulder. Marko's wink sent sparkling tingles rushing through her.

Carlo tilted his head in their direction as Marko led Nikola out the door. His warm eyes turned to his sister. "My nephew is very adaptable and I should say one chatty little boy. We only arrived today, and he took to Marko in an instant."

She smiled, despite a lump forming in her throat. Her brother's expression told her he had come to terms with the truth about her, but no doubt he'd have questions which would require difficult answers. "How did you find Nikola?"

Carlo drew a sharp breath. "The day we parted in Ragusa, I returned to my ship and found a stack of letters on my desk. Among them an envelope from Veronica marked urgent. She wrote of a man, Antun, who came to see her and brought a boy with him. The man pressed upon her to write to me and to relay a message to you that he'd been wrong about someone named Angelia. With regret, he left Nikola behind."

Carlo paced the room, stopped in front of the window. Crossing his wrists behind his back, he continued. "I knew then something had gone terribly wrong. For hours I searched the streets of Ragusa but couldn't find you."

The sadness in her brother's voice made Carmen yelp. "Where is Veronica?"

He turned to her and looked at her as if he was seeing her for the first time, then he gazed out the window again with a long sigh. "Her father sent her away and doesn't want to tell me where."

Guilt washed over Carmen. Her actions would forever affect her family. "Oh, Carlo, I'm so sorry. None of this would have happened if I..."

"Do not blame yourself, sister." He approached and lowered himself onto the edge of her bed. "Marko has reinstated my captain's rank. I am sure her father will approve of me as his future son-in-law once again."

Knowing how timid Carlo could get around ladies, Carmen squeezed his arm to boost him with encouragement. "Don't give up. Fight for her, I know she loves you."

Soft lines formed around his eyes as he smiled. "Thank you, sister. I needed to hear it."

With fear gripping her mind, she contemplated her next question. "What became of our brothers?"

"The two are sitting at home, drowning their sorrows in wine." Anger laced Carlo's voice, and he inhaled deeply. "Fools, what is done, is done, and nothing will change it. Fear not, they will come around, I am sure. Marko kept his offer open. I will urge them in my letters to consider it, but they would rather command the navy ships. With the duke's flotilla shrinking, we would have lost our posts sooner or later."

She turned her head to the wall so Carlo wouldn't see the guilt on her face. But she couldn't hide her trembling voice. "At least neither of you will be dishonored."

He squeezed her shoulder and she faced him. "You should have told me what was going on with you."

Her stomach knotted. Searching his eyes, she tried to speak but couldn't find the proper words. Her brother had every right to be furious with her. "I wanted to, but your look of disgust the day I left our home with my husband is forever etched in my memory. I thought you'd never forgive me for breaking my promise to Papa on his deathbed."

His expression mellowed and he eased his grip on her shoulders. "I was angry then, I do admit. Long months at sea had me thinking and I realized I had no right to be. But by that time, it was too late. Your husband died. I didn't know how or why until a few days ago."

Carlo's words lessened the tightness in her chest. She cupped his cheek and smiled. "Your forgiveness meant a lot. When I was a pirate, I couldn't bring myself to talk about it, even to you."

A loud knock made her snap her head toward the door. "Come in."

An aproned servant girl stepped through, a basin of steamy water in her hands. The pleaded skirt of her *fustanella* work-peasant dress bobbed as she bowed. "My Master summoned me to tend to the Mistress."

Doctor Breda stormed into the chamber after her. "I see the patient is awake and sitting up," he announced with his irritating voice. He proceeded toward the night table and unbuckled his leather bag. "First, I need to examine you, then if I say it is safe for you to get out of the bed, you can."

"It's a nice day." Carlo cast the Doctor a pleading look. "Some fresh air will do her good."

"I am the one to determine that." The doctor rolled back his sleeves. "Please leave the room." He wiggled his finger for the servant girl standing at the door to come closer.

Carlo squeezed Carmen's shoulder. "He means well."

Carmen dismissed her brother with a smile and a single nod. The doctor wasn't the Devil's advocate, as her delusional fever had her believing. She no longer feared him and he was about to find out just how tough pirates were.

"Let's see." The Doctor's parched palm scratched her forehead. "Good, no fever. Are you experiencing any discomfort?" She shook her head. He pressed the wide end

of a long cone to her back and the narrow one to his ear.
"Long inhale."

She drew air in and exhaled at his order.

"Lungs sound clear." He took her hand and removed
the dried bandage, then examined her skin. "Poultice
worked. Your wrappings can be removed. The lesions are
healing nicely though you may have some minor scarring.
Can I have you lie on your back?"

What were a few scars to add to the many on her
body? The pillows wrapped around her as she sank into
them and slid flat on her back.

The doctor pushed on her stomach. "Does this hurt?"

"No." She pressed her chin to her chest and stared as
the physician paid special attention to her lower abdomen.
"Is there something wrong?"

Worry filled her at his concerned expression as he
peered over his round spectacles. He cleared his throat.
"Everything seems fine." He turned to the servant girl.
"Tend to the Mistress and help her dress." Facing Carmen,
he unrolled his sleeves. "You recovered nicely as I
predicted. Still, do not over exert yourself. Should you feel
tired or experience any shortness of breath, you must return
to bed. Do I make myself clear?"

"Yes, Doctor." Her initial anxiety eased with his
approval. Her strength was returning at the thought of
spending the rest of the day with her family.

Free from her bandages, bathed in lavender scented
water, and dressed in a gown the servant had found for her,
Carmen descended the flight of curving stairs. Thank the
angels, her dizziness and spinning head had cleared, but her

knees had not yet steadied. She couldn't recall such a bad case of wobbly legs even after months at sea.

The silk of her powder blue gown swished with her movements. One hand propped on the banister and a grin lighting his face, Marko waited at the foot of the stairs.

Awareness of her crudely cropped hair struck her all of a sudden. She patted her curls. The servant girl had done a good job of weaving the longer strands into a single braid and leaving shorter tresses lose around her face. Still, the coiffure threatened to come undone with every turn of her head.

"I must look awful," she croaked, feeling the heat of shame in her cheeks. The bottom step caught her by surprise, and she lost her balance.

Marko caught her in his arms. "You look ravishing. This brings back some very fond memories."

Regaining her composure, she said, "Gowns make me awkward. At least this one doesn't require a tight corset."

"I'm glad you don't want your pirate's attire back."

His kiss on her knuckles and his eyes fixed at the chemise peeking above the décolleté of her dress sent a sensuous shiver up her spine. He wrapped her hand around his elbow.

"Come meet my papa in the dining room. In a day or two we can stroll to the shipyard. The new keel for the *Strega* has been laid."

She winced and her mouth dropped open. Another boost of energy ran through her. "You are not intending to go on another pirate's adventure. For that, I'll have to steal a pair of your breeches and a shirt."

Chuckles shook his shoulders. He paused by a pair of double doors with frosty glass panes. Longing reflected in his eyes as he gazed at her. "No, love. No more pirate's business. She'll be a merchant ship."

"The age of piracy is coming to an end, and while it shortened lives of a few and made some rich, it did not change history," said a man's deep voice from the dining parlor.

One hand on the door knob, Marko exhaled. "Papa is having another one of his conversations with the staff. They'll agree to anything he says. Or else he is reading the gazette out loud."

Cold shivers shook her. Marko's father must have known who she was. "In either case, your father is right."

A soft smile lit Marko's face and he kissed her brow. He opened the doors. Her mouth watered at the sight of platters of prosciutto and cheese on a long table set with fine china. The scent of freshly baked bread wafted in the air. Nikola circled the table, piling his plate with sweet pastries. A servant woman entered through the kitchen side doors, a steaming tureen in her hands. She placed the large dish on the cabinet then stepped to an older man. "The lunch is ready, Master."

"You can dish up the soup," the man said and turned to Carmen. "Pardon my impertinence. My late wife was the one who handled the everyday domestic affairs." Golden buttons on his black velvet vest shimmered in the beam of sunlight coming in through the window. He raised his hands, causing the sleeves of his crisp linen shirt to bunch. "I think this is what she would have ordered of the servants. How are you feeling, dear?"

Granting the man a polite smile, Carmen tightened her hold on Marko's elbow. "I was sore when I woke this morning, but my strength is returning rather fast, and now I'm famished."

The old man patted her forearm. "Then you've come to the right place."

Marko leaned toward her and smirked. "Papa was quite scared of you when he first found out you were commanding a ship of pirates, but I assured him there was no reason for fear."

Though there was no physical resemblance between the old Master and his son, their similar demeanor, and way they gestured with their hands, implied the two were of the same gentry.

"I was merely concerned the soldiers would come search our house." His wintery blue eyes, appearing larger behind his spectacles, switched to Carmen. "Thank God, no one came."

"I thank you for your hospitality and care, Master Lucin." Carmen expressed her gratitude with a slight bow of her head.

His parched hand took hold of hers. "It's the least I could do to repay you for saving my son. You are not a servant here, please call me Fillip."

"Ah, the guest of honor is finally out of bed." A man's smooth voice, laced with amusement, caused her and everyone else in the room to whirl around. A tall man stood by the door and passed his intricate walking staff to the servant. Silver buttons on his deep red doublet and the expensive outfit he wore suggested another aristocrat. A young lady on his arm drew Carmen's attention. Every curl in its place and dressed in a sunflower-yellow silk frock, the girl scanned the dining room with interest.

"My God, aren't you from the *Strega*?" Carmen examined her closely. Could she be the one with the smooth singing voice?

The young woman ceased twirling her purse around her finger and shot Carmen a sharp glance as if she was afraid. Then she huffed and a grin replaced her worried expression. "Captain?"

"I am Carmen again." In two steps, she closed the distance between them and hugged the girl. "I am afraid I only know you by—"

"Andrea De Nassis," she blurted, pulling away.

Carmen leaned toward Andrea. "You are a Contessa?"

"Yes, my mother is Conte De Nassis's fourth wife." Andrea exchanged glances with Albert and squeezed his hand. "I never thought I'd miss this life, but I did. I must admit."

Confusion spun Carmen's mind. "What were you doing on the *Strega*?"

Andrea sighed. "Hiding from getting wed to a man old enough to be my grandfather."

A cold realization washed over Carmen. Her ship had been a sanctuary for women from all walks of life, and she had steered them all straight into a trap.

Fillip stepped forward and took Andrea's hand in his. "Welcome back to the gentry, then."

Marko gestured toward the tall man filling the threshold. "Carmen, meet Conte Albert Panov. Your rescuer is fashionably late, as always."

Baffled, she angled her head. "My rescuer?"

"Yes." Marko patted his hip. "My lame leg wouldn't allow me to carry you out of the courtyard. So he did it."

She bowed. "I am deeply grateful, your Lordship."

Conte Albert took her hand. "As I said the first time I saw you, it is no wonder my friend lost his head to you. You are a rare flower whose beauty will only increase with age."

Heat seared her cheeks. She thought Marko to be a great charmer, but Conte Albert was ten times worse. She huffed in surprise, not knowing how to respond, and turned to Marko. His mocking grin directed at Conte Albert had her creasing her forehead.

"Well." Albert released her hand and coughed. "Perhaps, I should not have phrased it in those exact words."

"I doubt my appearance then or now is worthy of your flattery."

His warm brown eyes scanned her. "Ah, but my dear. You are mistaken. My words of admiration are the simple truth."

"The meal is served, let's eat," Fillip announced with his old weak voice.

Marko held the chair out for her. "You'll sit next to me."

She lowered herself into a firm seat with high backrest. The bowl of steamy chicken soup made her mouth water all over, but she had to recall her table manners and not slurp. Following Marko's example, she placed the napkin on her lap. The sight of Nikola, on the other side of her, using the silverware like a real young Master, coaxed a smile.

"No one will be happier to hear of your recovery than poor Rocco," Conte Albert said, tucking the napkin inside the frilly collar of his shirt with classy elegance.

"Oh yes." Spoon poised in midair, Marko shifted. "Marta postponed their wedding twice, if I'm not mistaken." He leaned toward her. "She's determined to have you as her Matron of honor."

Joy surged through Carmen and for a moment she allowed her pirate-self out. She pounded her fist on the table, sending the silverware and fine china to clink. "Blistering barnacles, the bilge rat made it. Did any more of my wenches survive?"

Marko exchanged glances with Conte Albert. Seeing both barely able to keep their faces straight made her clench the napkin. Nikola's giggled with his mouthful. Carlo, Doctor Breda, and Fillip's frozen and appalled expressions made her realize her slip. Only the young Contessa remained unmoved by her words. Carmen slapped her hand over her mouth.

Then Conte Albert exploded in gales of amusement, as did the rest of the party. He stroked Andrea's cheek. "My butterfly here speaks like you sometimes. God help me, she can also swing her sword better than any man, but I find it irresistible. Keeps my skills honed."

Marko cocked an eyebrow. "Didn't I tell you as much?"

His hand wrapped around the stem of his glass, Albert nodded. "And for once, you were right."

Fillip raised his glass, encouraging the others to join him in a toast. Flutes in their hands, everyone stood. "To laughter, a table surrounded by my family and friends, alas, life is back among these walls, and to the priest who will stay busy with weddings and, soon, baptizing."

"I'll drink to that." Marko tapped his glass with Fillip's.

Conte Albert followed suit. "And so will I."

Carmen wrapped her fingers around the glass of Doctor Breda's honey sweetened blend of herbal tea. Could she salute with a non-alcoholic beverage? Instead, she opted to raise her drink half way. Marko helped Nikola, holding a glass of watered down wine in his hand, stretch his arm up and tap it with Fillip's.

The silver spoon clinked against the crystal stem as Marko placed his empty glass on the table then lowered himself into his chair. "Fifteen of your women escaped and I lost one man."

Tightness closed her chest. Her hot head and hunger for the treasure had brought nothing but death to so many. "Less than half survived?"

"We'll remember them." His big hand squeezed hers. "Be happy for those who lived, not so long ago they were fierce pirates and now all of them are blushing brides."

She leveled her eyes with his. "I should thank you for ordering the retreat when you did or there would be no survivors at all."

Sadness flashed in his eyes. Letting go of her hand, he picked up the spoon. "Let's enjoy our lunch."

Fillip's eyes traveled around the table. He took a sip of his red wine and lowered the glass. "So, I hear Bonaparte's army is advancing on Serenisima. The duke may have to surrender. Napoleon's military machine will sweep through our defenseless lands."

"Father," Marko scolded. "Must we talk about it now?"

Carmen glanced at Carlo as fear of war pressed on everyone's shoulders. He lowered his spoon and leaned over his plate to look at Marko's father sitting at the head of the table. "The Republic of Venice can no longer defend itself. Four galleys and seven galliots are all that's left of its war fleet."

"Carlo," she hissed, scowling. Her brother had left the military, but the army would never leave him. "You are a merchant captain now."

Albert stroked his beard. "The duke will not surrender that easily."

Doctor Breda pushed his spectacles up his nose. "What is to become of Istria and Dalmatia, I fear?"

"The provinces will be given to Austria, most likely. Makes no difference under whose rule we are." Fillip shoved another spoonful of soup in his mouth then smacked his lips.

Carmen placed her silver utensil in her empty soup bowl. Though this seemed to be the hot topic on everyone's lips, she preferred not to join in the conversation. The politics, she could do without. Yes, these were the changing times, but the future of common folk appeared just as grim. Perhaps the transition for the better the old captain had tried to implement would not happen overnight. Years might pass, decades, centuries even before the living and working conditions of the peasants and laborers advanced.

"Your healthy pirate's appetite is back. Or could it be you haven't eaten a decent meal in a while?" Marko winked, placed his napkin on the table and stood, taking her hand in his. "Please excuse Lady Carmen and me."

Lady Carmen? Puzzled, she shot Marko a glance. She'd never claimed to be a member of the gentry. What was he up to?

"May I be excused, too?" Nikola cast Marko a pleading look. Through the ordeal of uprooting and placing him among total strangers, the boy had kept his sense of propriety and recognized Marko as the head of the household.

"Of course, son, you may." Marko dismissed him with a smile and a pat on his head.

Nikola gave Carmen a peck on her cheek and scooted out of the room.

Andrea and the Conte seemed lost in their own game of spoon-feeding each other a slice of cake. Marko shook his head at the heated discussion among Fillip, the Doctor, and Carlo. "No one cares if we are here or not."

Her hand in his, Marko led Carmen out of the parlor through the patio doors and into the garden. Fallen leaves crunched under her feet. Most of the blossoms had dried out in the early autumn's sun and the foliage on a climbing wine had turned yellow.

A cool breeze played with the frills of the swing-for-two.

"Marko," she said, lowering herself to soft cushions. "I don't know how to thank you for everything you've done for me and my family."

At his longing look, her heart squeezed. "There is one thing I want from you," he replied.

They'd been down this road before, and he still didn't seem to understand. "As much as I'd love to be yours, I do hope you realize that I'm a widow and therefore married for life."

Warmth seeped over her skin when he tucked a strand of her hair behind her ear. The brush of his hand against her cheek sent goose bumps racing over her. "I spoke with the priest, there is a way. If you'll agree to it."

She gazed at the distance. Red roofed houses spread toward the shore. Blue sea with no end encircled the island. The peaceful scenery did little to ease her tension. "An annulment?"

Love reflecting on his face, Marko nodded.

A deep sigh failed to loosen the knot in her chest. "I cannot dishonor the memory of my husband like that."

"I am not asking you to forget him or to stop loving him." Marko squeezed her shoulder and pulled her to him. "I know he'll be in your heart forever. Your place is with me now."

Tears stung her eyes. "He made me promise I would not remain alone if death separated us. But back then I never believed this a possibility, so I swore."

Marko pulled back and locked his piercing eyes with hers. "Then honor him by fulfilling it. Don't let your pledge be an empty one."

A tear slid down her cheek. She laced her fingers with his and nodded slowly. Marko was right. Her departed husband would be happy she listened to the voice of reason for once. "I will do it."

A grin replaced Marko's stern expression. He kneeled in front of her. "I should do this the proper way." Keeping his glance joined with hers, he licked his lips. "Carmen Ventura, will you marry me?"

She smiled through her tears. How could she not wed this good man who loved her so much? The truth was, she stood defenseless against the power of his love. He'd opened heaven's gates for her when the whole world seemed against her. God help her, she loved him. "I will."

He pulled her up with him as he sprang to his feet and wrapped her in his arms. "You made me the happiest man alive. Let's go inside and tell everyone. My father will be ecstatic."

A thought occurred to her and she halted. "What about your Marquis status?"

"Conte Albert made some inquiries without revealing the identity of the Marquis. The best I could hope for is maybe honorary status. But my poor father doesn't know I am not his son. The news would kill him and, most importantly, I wouldn't be able to marry you." He shrugged. "No, I'm willing to forgo the possibility of some mediocre life for the fabulous existence with you and Nikola."

"There you are." Gesturing at the swing, Doctor Breda strolled toward them. "Sit. I need to talk to you."

Marko frowned then shrugged and led her back to the seat. The doctor leaned against the low garden wall. "I want both of you here. Knowing your reputation, Marko I suspect you have everything to do with it."

He shot him a glance of surprise. "With what?"

Breda scratched his neck. "Time will confirm, of course. I suspected it, but now I am certain Lady Carmen is with child."

Carmen stared at the Doctor as his words seeped in her mind. Her mouth slowly opened and she gulped air. "I dreamt of a child, but I thought it was Nikola when he was a baby."

"The fact this child survived your torture and illness is nothing short of a miracle." The doctor's nasal voice snapped her back into the moment. "I recon you conceived around mid-August."

Happiness surged through her. She turned to Marko's beaming face. "The Blue Cave," they said in unison.

Doctor Breda quirked his eyebrows. "I was right then when I suspected you." He extended his hand to Marko. "I'll leave you to your happy moment."

Marko stood and shook hands with the doctor. "Thank you."

Carmen laced her fingers with Marko's and stared at the doctor's back as he strode out of the garden. "Does this change anything?"

"I'll have to press on Don Ignacio to speed up the annulment." Marko leaned close to her and nudged her. "And the re-construction of the chapel. I think it's only fitting that we wed in this new little chapel. I hear it will be named after a very brave and special woman who fought hard out at sea, *Lady of Pirates*."

His blue crescents misted as he locked his gaze with hers. Wrapping his arm around her, he pulled her to his chest.

She inhaled his fresh scent. "You gave me a whole new life. I wish there was something I could give you in return."

Nikola ran by on the path below the garden, followed by a small but loud group of boys, flying a kite. A soft smile lit Marko's face. "How about a little girl."

Smiling, she tilted her chin and gazed into those eyes she had mistaken for a merman's the first time she had seen him. The strong beat of his heart drummed in rhythm with hers and spoke to her of the future she'd longed for. She caressed his face as his mouth covered hers, setting her skin on fire. The kiss went on and on, escalating the heat between them.

Carmen pulled away and stared at his handsome face. "I feel a need to lie down all of a sudden," she said, when her breathing caught up with her heart.

Marko jumped to his feet. "Are you unwell?"

She bit her lower lip and flashed him a shy smile. "I'm fine, but the doctor said I shouldn't over do it today. Care to join me?"

He let out a smirk, released his breath, then wrapped one arm around her. "Don't ever scare me like that again." He led her toward the back entrance, concern filling his features. "Are you sure you can do this?"

She cast him a wary glance. What must she do so everyone would stop treating her as an invalid? The torture during her imprisonment and her illness were just minor setbacks for a pirate. But she no longer belonged on a ship's deck among fierce pirates skilled with blades. This was what she'd wanted all along, and she would not allow her nostalgic feelings to stand in her way.

"A little bit of gentle passion won't hurt me, or the baby. Though I'm sure if the doctor knows what we are about to do, he'd stop us." Surprised by her own words, she halted. Her delicate condition had been a blessed excuse she'd used to keep her late husband away. But here and now she was luring her next husband to her bed with it. "Besides, you promised me in the cave that not a day must pass you by where you wouldn't show me how much you loved me. I hold you to it."

Giving her a wink, he chucked her chin. "What are we waiting for?"

Suddenly aware of her half-starved body with faded bruises and crudely shorn hair, she paused at the foot of the servants' stairs in the narrow foyer. "What if our absence is noted by our guests?"

"Keka," Marko said, turning to the woman who had dished out soup at lunch and now carried a stack of dirty dishes to the kitchen. "If anyone should ask for me or Lady Carmen, I'm helping my fiancé back to her chamber."

Pushing the swivel doors with her wide hip, the cook arched her eyebrows, but surprise quickly left her round face, replaced by eagerness to spread the news. She nodded before disappearing inside the kitchen.

Marko stroked Carmen's back. "There, the news of you as my future wife has been unleashed. It will confirm what islanders suspected all along, so it shouldn't come as much of a surprise to anyone. At least no one will dare to disturb us during our afternoon..." He cleared his throat. "*Rest.*" Then he gestured toward the stairs. "Shall we?"

"By all means." She placed her foot on the first step, winced as he scooped her in his arms.

"You didn't think I'd let you climb these wobbly steps in your condition." The kiss he pressed on her neck ignited a raging inferno in her.

Tilting her head to his ear, she whispered, "Get me to the chamber and fast."

"That is why we are taking the servants' stairs. Remind me to have these steps fixed," he said as he took them by twos. Out of breath, he paused at the top and gazed in her eyes. "For when I'm with you I forget everything. Even my bad hip."

She shared his smile, which reminded her of their night alone under the prow of her old dinghy, inside the Blue Cave. Astounded by a rip of anticipation, she felt her limbs shiver, her breasts tighten, and her womb throb as he lowered her to the bed. She ached for fulfillment of the ecstasy only Marko could give her.

Raw need surged through her with every clasp of her dress he unfastened—deliberately slowly.

"Blasted buttons," he murmured against her lips, spreading the bodice open. A sharp pain of desire shot to her center when he teased her nipples through her thin linen chemise.

She yelped at his pinch.

Marko jerked back and stood. "Did I hurt you?"

"No, you can never hurt me." Her husky whisper revealed her need for him.

"Now that I'm up," he said, reaching for the buttons on his breeches. "I may as well undress."

He held her gaze as he unfastened the clasps and slipped his drawers down his legs, standing naked in unrestrained glory before her. The deep red scar on his hip added to his masculinity. She reached for him and he lowered himself to the bed then proceeded to remove the last of her clothing until she, too, lay nude underneath him.

His head braced on his hand, he rubbed her stomach, lowered his face, and kissed the sensitive skin around her belly button. "You hang in there, little one. Do you hear me?"

She chuckled at the tickle of his soft whiskers. If he only knew how big and heavy she'd get toward the end, he might want the baby to come sooner rather than later. He covered her body in kisses, starting at her throat and working his way down to her breasts. Nibbling, teasing them with his tongue and fingers until they ached. Wrapping her legs around his hips, she pulled him to her. Grunts escaped him as he braced his weight on his elbows.

She brushed a lose strand of his hair aside. "It's fine. You won't hurt me or the baby."

He kissed her hand. "Are you sure?"

Placing her hands to his sides, she wiggled in anticipation as his hardness teased her. "I am."

Moisture flooded her when he spread her legs and eased inside. Her every nerve clamored and pulsed as his warm body settled over hers.

His slow, sensual thrusts rocked her. Face buried in the crook on her neck, he licked and kissed her hot skin, bringing more heat to the surface.

Deepening his thrusts, his hot breath brushed her ear. "Carmen, my love, my wife."

With each push, Marko created an escalating wonder inside her, bringing her to climax. She clasped the bedding, her body arched, and she screamed her release. Then she tightened her hold on him when his body stiffened against hers. The pleasurable tingling in her body slowly dissipated but she still floated while he kissed her all over. Their hearts beat in unison when he pressed her to his chest and at this remarkable moment she knew her hunger for her skilled husband could never be satiated.

Epilogue

The smell of fresh timber thrilled Carmen. She squinted against the early February sun as she scanned the deck of the new *Strega*. Sliding her palm on the smooth wood of the helm, she couldn't help but moan in sorrow at the memory of her old vessel. No doubt this ship was bigger and better, but it could never measure up to the old one. It needed to be put in use so that the mighty planks could get weathered and the ropes greased.

"So?" Marko strutted to her, one arm wrapped around their baby clad in woolens. "What do you say?"

A long sigh escaped her. She shrugged.

"You are speechless." Amusement laced his voice. "I thought I'd never live to see the day. Ha!" He turned to the baby. "Luigi *mio bambino*, in your ten months of life, did you ever see Mama as stunned as now?"

The four small teeth exposed by his grin, his soft cooing, and the wind playing with the baby's soft blond curls brought a smile to Carmen's lips. Her boys were irresistible.

"My words, exactly." Marko placed a kiss on Luigi's forehead then leaned toward Carmen. "The new *Strega* is quite something, isn't she?"

"She sure is. How many hands will she need to handle her?"

"Minimum of twenty five, but over a hundred sailors can be accommodated on board easily." He covered her hand with his. "Shall we set sail?"

Confused, Carmen turned to him. "We don't have twenty five pairs of hands."

Marko stuck two fingers in his mouth and let out a loud whistle. Men and women climbed on board. She recognized her old crew, or what was left of it, gathered around Marta.

One arm wrapped around her waist, Marko nodded toward crowd. "I think we have more than enough." He nudged her. "Do we have a heading, Captain?"

"No..." She winced in surprise. "I don't have one."

"Still deprived of speech, I see." He shifted Luigi to his other arm. "The helm of the *Strega* is yours." A smile stretched his lips as he regarded her. "For an hour. Then we switch. You take Luigi and I take over the command."

She lowered her chin and her voice. "The crew is waiting on my orders, and I have no idea where we are going."

With two fingers, he stroked his beard and scanned the deck. "I think this ship is worthy of presenting in the Ragusa's harbor. Let's show those rich merchants we are still standing."

Holding his gaze for an immeasurable moment, she beamed. "Certainly." She turned to the awaiting crew. She had vowed she'd never return to the sea, but standing here on the gallery deck, a realization struck her—she could have best of both worlds. "All hands to braces!"

"Aye, Cap'n!" they replied and set to work.

"Step lively, you mangy cockroaches." Marta gave them an encouraging boost and soon the sails were unfurled.

"Can you really command this large ship, Mama?"

At Nikola's excited voice, Carmen whirled around and faced her grinning first-born. "When did you get on board?"

His eyes lit up. "Aunty Marta brought me along with Daro and Kris."

She ruffled his hair and glanced at Marta's adopted boys who stood a couple of steps behind him. "You three are inseparable."

"So can you steer this ship?"

"Of course, she can." Marko wrapped his arm around Nikola's shoulders and handed Luigi to his nurse. "Better than anyone else. Come here, I'll show you."

Nikola and his two friends stepped closer to the helm at Marko's urging.

"If you want the ship to go straight, keep the helm like this." He clasped the top handle on the big wheel. "When you want to turn the ship left or right, all you have to do is tilt the wheel slightly in the direction you want to go." Turning to the boys, he cocked an eyebrow. "Who wants to try?"

"Later," said Nikola. "Can we explore this ship first, Papa?"

Daro nodded, his brother joined him. "Can we, Marko?"

Hands braced on his knees, Marko leveled his gaze on the three wide-eyed boys. "I see how boys like you can be attracted to explore every nook and cranny on this ship, but don't go below on your own." He straightened. "Now, I trust you'll obey or you will not see the inside of a ship for a very long time."

Three heads nodded and the boys scurried down the stairs to the deck. The wind filled the sails and propelled the ship faster. Carmen returned her attention to the steering.

One arm behind his back, Marko studied her. "Handles nicely?"

She nodded. Unlike the old *Strega*, turning the helm of this ship took no effort. And while this was a good thing, it reminded her of her dear old friend blown to smithereens. It would take some time getting used to this ship. But this was Marko's present to her, and she'd love it just the same. Someday. Just as she'd gotten used to him massaging her lower back each night when she'd hurt under the weight of his baby. Though she missed those days, she was sure they'd return. After all, Marko had kept the promise he'd given her in the Blue Cave.

Rocco approached the gallery deck. "It took less people and time to have her ready for the voyage than I thought. I must admit, the shipbuilders outdid themselves. No wonder this ship has been a topic of conversation for weeks, months even."

Carmen exhaled in relief. People had found something else to talk about. "At least the islanders stopped laughing about our wedding."

"Everyone knows Don Ignacio wanted the roof completed before the winter and wouldn't stop the construction. Not even for the wedding ceremony." Laughter shook Marko. "Oh, he thought I was bluffing when I demanded that he wed us then and there. I thought he'd die before he pronounced us man and wife."

Rocco strained to keep from bursting into laughter. "The stone masons barely stopped chiseling long enough for the two of you to exchange your vows."

"The villagers have no reason to complain. They celebrated and feasted till dawn." Marko gripped the bulwark of the gallery deck. "Neither does Don Ignacio. He would have drained my wine cellar had I not locked the door in time."

Arms folded over his bent leg, Rocco leaned forward. "Never before have we known of a better festivity."

Carmen cast a glance at the narrow land passage where people gathered at the point. "Wave to the folks, we are leaving the bay."

Marta scurried toward them, the three boys in front of her. Their faces a bit on the pale side. "Let these three sit on the stern where the roll of the waves is felt the least. The sea is very choppy out of the bay, and they cannot stomach the movement of the ship. We'll have to toughen them up."

"They'll grow their sea legs soon enough. For now, I'll take them," Rocco said, chuckling.

"Brace yourself." Marta turned toward the deck. "In a minute we'll have clean full and will be rolling on high waves."

Excitement filled Carmen. She had not felt the spray of the sea on her face since the day she'd lost the old *Strega*, over twenty months ago. "Take the helm, Marta."

"Where are you going?" Marko's puzzled voice reached her at the bottom of the stairs.

She whirled around to face him. "To the prow."

"You are mad. You'll get soaked to the bone."

"That is the idea." Carmen resumed her pace then halted and faced him with a grin. "Are you afraid I'll get your shirtsleeves and breeches wet?"

"No," Marko bellowed, but a smile replaced his baffled expression. "Who knew you'd fill my rompers so nicely?"

Cocking her head, she studied her husband. "Last time you wore these, you couldn't have been more than...what? Twelve?"

His boots thumped on the planks as he followed her. "About that."

"Don't be scared of a sea spray. We've endured worse."

He raised his voice over the high wind. "Me? Scared? Never."

She took his hand and pulled him with her to the very tip of the *Strega*. Her long hair whipping her face, she shouted into the wind. "Look at that. Beautiful!"

He pulled her into his arms. "Not as beautiful as you are."

The gray and choppy waters of the Adriatic rocked the ship from side to side. High winds howled around her, flapping the wide sleeves of Marko's shirt, which she was wearing. Waves pulled the *Strega*'s prow toward the surface and broke against the ship's hull.

Carmen sucked in a breath as the icy spray soaked into her back and sent freezing shivers up her spine. "You are right, it is cold."

Marko tightened his embrace. "What did I tell you?" He grimaced as another wave sent its crest spraying on his back. "The memory of you in my soaked-through clothes will never leave me. I won't be able to dress in the mornings without getting aroused."

Wet strands clung to his skin. She brushed them away, revealing his handsome face. "Didn't I tell you, you won't regret getting wet?"

"Aye, Captain." His lips seized hers. Her hand slid to his chest. The steady beat of his heart reminded her of a poem in the departed captain's journal. And suddenly Carmen understood—the treasured chest that had inspired people's wild imagination was nothing else than this very man's chest which she had placed her hands on now.

> *There is no trove*
> *I would protect more*
> *But a treasured chest*
> *Holding the heart that beats*
> *And makes me complete.*

About the Author

Zrinka Jelic lives in Ontario, Canada, with her husband and two children. A member of the Romance Writers of America and its chapter Fantasy Futuristic &Paranormal, as well as Savvy Authors, she writes contemporary fiction—which leans toward the paranormal—and adds a pinch of history. Her characters come from all walks of life, and although she prefers red, romance comes in many colors. Given Jelic's love for her native Croatia and the Adriatic Sea, her characters usually find themselves dealing with a fair amount of sunshine, but that's about the only break they get. "Alas," Jelic says, with a grin. "Some rain must fall in everyone's life."